CANDLELIGHT REGENCY SPECIAL

CANDLELIGHT REGENCIES

A COMPANION IN JOY

Dorothy Mack

A CANDLELIGHT REGENCY SPECIAL

Published by
Dell Publishing Co., Inc.
1 Dag Hammarskjold Plaza
New York, New York 10017

Dell ® TM 681510, Dell Publishing Co., Inc.

ISBN 0-440-11263-X

Printed in the United States of America
First printing—September 1980

To Marcia,
the First Reader

Chapter One

The young man slowly ascending the steps to the entrance door of an imposing stone mansion on Brook Street would have rated a second glance from almost any passerby. To the masculine eye his impressive height and breadth of shoulders, combined with a fluid economy of movement, would unerringly bespeak the natural athlete. An assured, not to say arrogant, carriage of the dark head, allied with an elusive refinement of facial planes and features, betokened good breeding, while a certain something in the challenging glance of those dark eyes would be sure to quicken the interest of the majority of females meeting that glance. To the discriminating observer the superb cut and faultless set of the blue morning coat across the wide shoulders proclaimed that the wearer patronized no less noteworthy a tailor than the great Weston himself. A perfectly brushed beaver was set at a precise angle atop crisp waving hair and a snowy expanse of neatly tied cravat showed beneath moderately starched shirt points. Mirror-polished Hessians with gold tassels and a well-kept hand holding gloves and walking stick con-

7

tributed their share to the *point de vice* appearance of the caller, who, on attaining the top step, put up his free hand to give an unnecessary regulatory tug to his neckcloth before taking a deep breath as he rapped smartly with the huge brass knocker. These small actions, accompanied by a lowering, black-browed stare bent on the inoffensive oak-paneled door, might be construed to reveal a certain reluctance to carry out whatever errand had brought him to this particular door at the moment in question. However, the spontaneous smile bestowed on the still powerful appearing but rather elderly butler who opened the door presently held nothing save affectionate raillery.

"Hallo, Marsden. Are you ready to go ten rounds with me as we were used to?"

The portly individual thus addressed returned the smile with interest while declining the invitation. "Not ten rounds, Mister Nicholas. I'm afraid I'm past that feat nowadays, being slightly touched in the wind, as they say." He accepted hat, cane, and gloves, then brushed an imaginary speck of dust from the shoulders of the caller before adding formally, "I trust I find you well, Mister Nicholas?"

"Of course, Marsden, and how do you go on these days?"

"The same as usual, Mister Nicholas," was the imperturbable reply. "His lordship is expecting you. He has been in his book room all morning."

At this intelligence the younger man's lips twisted in a somewhat wry expression, and he had difficulty in restraining an urge to square his shoulders like a condemned soldier on his way to face the firing squad.

"Perhaps we'd best settle for five rounds after I've seen my father," he suggested, half jokingly.

The butler's brief smile acknowledging this pleasantry was immediately succeeded by an expression

8

compounded of sympathy and complete understanding, and the young viscount grimaced anew at the sudden reflection that in all probability every old retainer in his parental home was cognizant of the fact that the earl had summoned his heir for the purpose of reading him one of his patented lectures on the irresponsibility of today's youth with special emphasis on his son's propensity for living beyond his means. He schooled his mobile features to polite blankness and followed the butler into the square apartment that had been his father's sanctum for as long as he could remember.

"The Viscount Torvil," intoned Marsden sonorously.

Nicholas barely repressed a grin at the affectionate pride underlying his former mentor's formal tones, but he need not have been concerned about displaying untimely merriment, for the figure behind the enormous mahogany desk did not immediately pause in his perusal of a sheet of paper held in one thin, elegant hand. Nor, for a full ninety seconds, did he betray by so much as the flicker of an eyelid the slightest awareness of another presence than his own in the book-lined room. It did not require a gigantic intellect to predict that the ensuing interview would be more than ordinarily difficult, Nicholas mused, resisting anew a double compulsion to tug at his suddenly tight neckcloth and square his shoulders. With an effort of will he remained standing motionless in an easy stance. There had been no invitation to be seated, and he wondered grimly if some of his more pressing creditors had dared approach his father for payment. They'd catch cold at that ploy, of course.

After an uncomfortable interval the earl lowered the paper that had been occupying his attention and raised a comprehensive gray glance to his heir's rigid countenance. One hand gestured languidly toward a winged green chair.

"Well, Torvil, I am honored that you were able to fit me into your busy schedule, and so quickly too. I believe it to be no more than four days since I sent a message to your lodgings desiring you to wait upon me at your earliest convenience."

Only by a slight twitching of a muscle in his cheek did the viscount reveal his annoyance at his father's heavy irony.

"My apologies, sir, for keeping you waiting, but I did not return from Newmarket until last night." Which was a superfluous piece of information, to be sure, for there existed no doubt in his mind that his father had been well posted on his heir's whereabouts. No one had ever accused the earl of being a *doting* parent, but that he was an observant one was a fact that had been uncomfortably borne in upon his sons on several occasions in the past. The consequences of their occasional scrapes at Eton and, later, at Oxford had been rendered even more hideous by the inevitability of a subsequent dressing down from their parent in that indifferent, sarcastic style they had early come to dread. He schooled himself to remain still under his father's thoughtful gaze, refusing to add to his explanation, though the silence became definitely uneasy before the earl spoke again in a pensive fashion.

"I must confess myself at a loss whether to applaud the audacity or deplore the temerity of a man in your, shall we say, *precarious* financial position who undertakes to attend a race meeting."

"I didn't lose any blunt at Newmarket; in fact, I won," his son replied evenly.

"How gratifying for you. Am I to understand that you are now in a position to cancel your other gaming debts and pay all your duns?"

A dull red crept over the young man's cheekbones at this polite inquiry, but he replied quietly, "I regret that

10

I am unable to confirm your assumption at this moment."

"Ah! Well, you will forgive me for pointing out that the ability to judge horseflesh does not invariably march with good fortune at the tables."

His son inclined his head slightly but made no rejoinder.

Suddenly the earl abandoned his pointed suavity and decisively pushed his chair back from the desk.

"I did not command your presence here today to discuss your debts, at least not directly."

Nicholas raised an inquiring eyebrow.

"You will remember six months ago during our last conversation on the subject of your failure to live within the very generous allowance I make you, I gave you notice that I had settled your debts for the last time. I also expressed the opinion that it was more than time that you settled down and found yourself a wife. A wife is a very stabilizing influence on a man. I further stated my strong desire to see you married before your twenty-ninth birthday. Does your recollection of the conversation tally with mine?"

Apart from a slight affirming nod Nicholas was very still in his chair, his eyes dark and intent on the older man and his jaw rigid while a nasty premonition scuttled up his spine.

"Your birthday is in less than a fortnight. Not unnaturally I have been existing in a state of eager anticipation of a happy announcement for some time now. You must excuse an old man's impatience if I request the name of your intended bride before the betrothal notice appears in the papers."

"Naturally you shall be first to learn of any nuptial intentions on my part, but I must disappoint you that as of this date I have formed no such intention."

A tense silence followed this admission while two

identical gray glances clashed in a wordless struggle for mastery. Father and son were very alike as to facial configuration and coloring, and even seated it could be seen that the earl was still a large, powerful man. His iron gray hair had the same crisp vitality as his son's dark locks and both stared from under winged brows whose rising angle gave a slightly Mephistophelian cast to the haughty features.

The older man spoke with a sinister gentleness. "Does that remark signify that you have as yet selected no candidate for the position?"

"You speak as though it were a case of interviewing applicants for a housekeeper's job. One does not select a wife on the basis of needing a stabilizing influence," Nicholas protested with pardonable impatience.

"You have had ample time this past half dozen years or more to select one on some other basis. Lord knows you've had enough high flyers and game pullets living under your protection from time to time and caused enough clacking of tongues by your indiscretions with women who should know better to prove you're not indifferent to the sex. Well, that is neither here nor there. No one expected you to be a monk." His lordship paused and cleared his tones of irascibility. He resumed the purring irony so much disliked by his sons.

"Since, despite your more than adequate experience of the fair sex, you seem disinclined or unable to make a selection, I have done the job for you." The corners of the earl's mouth pulled in while he studied the effect of this bald pronouncement on his heir.

Nicholas sat up straighter and those black brows flew up, enhancing the devil image. He spoke each word slowly and distinctly. "Do you mean to tell me you have arranged a marriage for me?"

"Allow me to commend you on your quickness of understanding."

"Without even consulting me?"

"A time-honored custom." The earl nodded calmly and watched unmoved while the viscount launched himself out of his chair and strode over to the fireplace where he kicked violently at a half-burned log. Not until the dozens of sparks thus born had faded away did Nicholas turn back to his father, his lamentable temper (also inherited from his sire) once again firmly on leash.

"You cannot compel me to marry," he said quietly.

"Very true. I can, however, refuse to rescue you from this latest bit of financial idiocy. You'll find it difficult to pursue your *affaire* with that flashy redhead from a cell in the Fleet."

His son's face suffused with angry color once again. "The lady in question," he began, with emphasis on the noun, "is perfectly respectable and has the *entrée* everywhere."

"She's every day of thirty, and *entrée* or not, it's still a case of mutton dressed as lamb. She may have captured a senile peer old enough to be her grandfather and been clever enough to keep her *affaires* under cover until he died, but that doesn't alter the fact that she's no better than a whore. If you were thinking I'd stand still for that type being brought into the family, you'll find you're sadly mistaken."

"I thought I had expressed myself with admirable clarity when I stated that I had no intentions of marrying at present. My *affaires* are no one's business but my own."

"They are when you conduct them full in the public eye," returned his father icily. Then, abandoning the topic, he launched an attack from another direction.

"You have two notes totaling just over seven thousand pounds coming due within the week," he observed with that uncanny omniscience that was the bane of his sons' lives. "How do you propose to meet them?"

"That also is my business," grated Nicholas, preparing to take his leave. "I shall come about."

"Accept my best wishes for your success. But, in the event you do not succeed, you now know my price for settling your debts. Are you not even interested in discovering the name of your prospective bride?"

On the threshold the viscount flung a disclaimer over his shoulder and strode out, carefully closing the door behind him. His aspect was so forbidding that Marsden silently handed him his belongings without venturing the least remark, and so absorbed was he in his furious inner ragings, that Nicholas failed to note this event which was quite unique in the long history of cordial relations existing between the two.

14

Chapter Two

The next few days had a nightmare quality about them as the young viscount threw himself into a frenzy of gaming activities designed to recoup his former losses and reestablish his credit. Flush from his recent victories at the races and enriched by a modest stake totaling something over six hundred pounds, he visited all his usual clubs in the daytime and broke new ground by seeking admission on several evenings to certain establishments whose respectability might be in question but where the play was deep enough to be inviting to someone bent on amassing a fortune in the shortest possible time span. That some of these dens were frequented by a set of persons known as Greek banditti, whose custom it was to pluck unwary pigeons and separate them from their money by a variety of sharp practices, was not allowed to weigh against his urgent need for quick results. He was driven by an all-consuming desire to thwart his parent's cold-blooded design to arrange his future for his own convenience. All consideration of caution and good sense faded before this primary motive.

For the first three days the issue hung in balance as the viscount won several hundred pounds in marathon whist sessions at White's by day and enjoyed an unprecedented run of luck at the Faro tables by night. At one point he had increased his stake five-fold, but never did Dame Fortune smile at him so consistently that he could add steadily to his winnings to bring the goal within reach. If his present success had occurred before he had managed to dig himself so far into dun territory, he would have considered himself one of fortune's favored few. Given the present situation, however, he had scant leisure for the enjoyment of his unusual luck. Always the necessity to continue playing was upon him. Those of his friends whom he encountered during this period were at first astonished and then alarmed at the change in one whose easygoing nature was a byword amongst his acquaintance. From the most accommodating of good fellows he turned overnight into a grimly dedicated gamester, canceling all previous engagements and refusing all invitations to join congenial parties for an hour's shooting practice at Manton's or pugilistic exercise at Jackson's. He must have eaten somewhere, but it was certainly not in the company of his friends. And not even to his most intimate crony, Mister Oliver Waksworth, did he feel able to confide the reasons behind his sudden obsession with gambling. If, God forbid, he should fail to come about and were forced to accept his father's terms, it would never do to have the story bandied about in all the clubs of London. He might harbor an unreasoning resentment against the unknown bride selected by his father, but the poor girl had done nothing to warrant such a fate. Nor did he care to make himself a laughing stock, richly though he might have deserved it.

At the outset of this hideous episode he had pushed any considerations of failure to the back of his mind.

He needed all his wits about him to counter the seething and simmering cauldron of anger directed at his father which would have boiled over and swamped his concentration had he not firmly clamped the lid on such a dangerous brew. As the days and nights passed in a frenzy of gaming activities, his expression grew grimmer as the possibility of failure emerged and attained maturity almost without his conscious awareness. After the third day there was a gradual but inexorable diminution of his winnings until on the fifth day his original stake was reduced by half. Though he still won considerable sums from time to time, these wins afforded him no pleasure. Moreover, he had made the somewhat startling discovery that he possessed neither the faith in his star nor the capacity to enjoy gambling for its own sake that characterized the true gamester, although his current behavior might with some excuse be misread as that of a chronic gambler. Inevitably, he cast all caution to the winds and punted ever deeper in increasingly desperate attempts to recoup all his losses with one big strike that continued to elude him.

Abrupt changes in his usual regime involving the curtailment of all healthy exercise and the substitution of long hours of tension-packed inactivity, allied with erratic eating habits and lack of sleep, combined to produce the image of a man thoroughly burned to the socket. It didn't need Mister Waksworth's disgusted characterization of his friend as "a death's head on a mopstick" to enlighten him as to how he was being regarded by those of his friends who had the doubtful felicity of meeting him during this bleak interlude. But perhaps his friend's outburst contributed to the long overdue stocktaking that took place on the sixth day of his grace period.

Unblinkingly, he watched his *rouleaux* being swept

17

away and with them his dying hopes of avoiding the future his father had planned for him. With his eyes fixed unseeingly on a crookedly hung landscape adorning the opposite wall, he performed rapid mental sums and, making allowances for a bit of error due to the unaccustomed great quantities of wine upon which he had been existing for several days, came up with a rough figure of five hundred pounds total assets, not counting the value of his blood stock, curricle, and phaeton. His debauched and profoundly uncomfortable week had resulted in a net loss of one hundred pounds. The strangers on either side of him started slightly at his ironic burst of laughter, each pretending a disinterest in the dark, saturnine face of the young man who rose from the table with unsteady dignity and slowly made his way to the entrance, uncaring that his place was immediately taken by another hopeful child of fortune.

Although he wouldn't have cared to wager any great sum on his ability to calculate odds at the moment, Nicholas felt himself to be sufficiently clear headed to assess his future. He had already made the momentous discovery that his was not the true gamester's nature and, though still somewhat fuzzy minded, he was arriving at a rather unpalatable picture of himself as an inveterate idler and hedonist. Small wonder his father wished to see him safely buckled before his way of life became too firmly ingrained to change. Not that an arranged marriage looked any less undesirable one week after the ultimatum, but, he asked himself, what would he do with his life if he were free to choose? The main thing, of course, was that he would choose to remain unwed until a woman succeeded in giving him a leveller. But at nine-and-twenty, as near as made no difference, no female had had even a semipermanent effect on his sensibilities. He had enjoyed numerous flirtations with high-born beauties and fewer but more intense relationships with women of another stamp, but though he had been open handed with his various mistresses, none had inspired him with more than a fleeting devotion.

For the first time in almost a week his mind dwelt on his current mistress, Lady Montaigne, Cécile of the glorious red hair and insatiable appetites. He had begun to grow disenchanted with the sameness of the female of the species when Cécile had crossed his path. She had succeeded in reviving his flagging interest. Each of his mistresses had been beautiful, but Cécile was possessed of wit and vivacity and great eagerness to taste all of life's pleasures in addition to her more obvious charms. He had been first intrigued and then captivated by her and, six months later, was still in a state of fascination, though familiarity had not rendered him blind to her less appealing characteristics, among which must be included a childish greed and a decidedly jealous and possessive nature.

Nicholas had been furious at his father's knowledge of the *affaire* and his disparagement of Lady Montaigne, but not because the earl refused to countenance her admission into the family. At no time had he ever confused his feelings for Cécile with those for the one woman a man wished to make his wife. More than he knew was he his father's son and fully cognizant of what was due to his name.

But he was twenty-nine years old and had never experienced anything approaching a grand amour as depicted by the poets. There had never been a female whose face he could bear to contemplate meeting over the coffee cups for the rest of his life. He had often felt desire but was a stranger to love, and at his age might be safely considered to be immune from this laudatory but dangerous ailment. Except for the fact that it always went against the grain with him to fall in with his father's wishes, there was really not all that strong an argument against entering the bonds of matrimony. He would not feel himself bound emotionally in an arranged marriage, not constrained to faithfulness toward the partner he had had no part in choosing.

With amused cynicism, he knew that his father was blatantly eager to secure the succession in part because he disapproved of his younger son even more than he did of his heir. At six-and-twenty, the Honourable Robin Dunston was the complete care-for-naught with an abundance of charm and good looks but with more hair than wit. Although frequently disgusted with his heir's life-style and disinclination to become more settled, the earl grudgingly accorded him some slight respect for his academic achievements at Oxford and often consulted him about changes that became necessary from time to time in the management of his estates. Though this was usually by way of educating the heir for the position he would someday occupy, there had actually been the rare occasion when the earl had deigned to accept his son's advice in some minor matter.

Whether because the drink had made him maudlin or his feverish gambling of the past week had left him with an unaccustomed sense of the futility of his customary activities, his mood was much more promising for a change along the lines long advocated by the earl. At this point he was even willing to admit to his father that his frequent criticisms were justified. On the subject of an arranged marriage, however, his sentiments had undergone no slightest change. He still found the idea exceedingly distasteful. If there existed some vague notion in the back of his mind that a sincere expression of his willingness to alter his habits might induce the earl to rescind his demands concerning marriage, or at least extend the time period to allow his son to choose a bride for himself, the second confrontation in the book room soon put an end to such wishful thinking.

On the subject of marriage the earl was adamant. Though gratified beyond description (a phrase that caused Nicholas to flinch) to hear of his son's resolution to reform, he insisted on receiving his pound of flesh (a phrase of his son's that should have caused him severe pangs of conscience, but, unhappily, did not seem to prick him in the least). A marriage had been arranged, by God, and a marriage should take place. He remained unmoved by his son's furious declaration that he would ask the first girl to cross his path to marry him rather than submit tamely to a match made by his father. When Nicholas ceased his ranting to assess the effect of this threat, he was reminded gently of the notes still outstanding, an obligation that would now have to be assumed by the earl. This argument being unanswerable, the interview came to an abrupt conclusion with the earl carrying off all the honors.

Nicholas did not slam out of the house as on the previous occasion, but his aspect was equally forbidding as, while descending the steps, he glanced up at a hail from across the street.

"Nick!"

He made no answer but waited on the flagway for the hailer to cross the street and join him.

"Judging from your expression which is ugly as bull beef, you must be coming from a cozy chat with our esteemed parent," said the newcomer with a broad grin. He took the viscount's arm, indicating that they should proceed in the direction Nicholas had started to take.

His hand was shaken off as the latter refused to

21

budge. "Were you not about to enter the house, Robin? I'll see you later."

"Don't go, Nick, or at least let me walk along with you for a short way; I want to talk with you. I was only going to try to hit up the pater for a pony, but perhaps you can spare me the ordeal. I heard you won at Newmarket. Care to lend me a hundred?"

"Very well," was the indifferent reply.

The Honourable Robin stopped short in surprise, cheerfully cursing himself for a fool not to have asked for a monkey while he was about it.

"Which I'd have done had I guessed you'd be so accommodating," he confessed ingenuously.

His brother permitted himself a faint twist of his well-cut lips and resumed walking. Robin hastened to fall into step.

"You'd not have gotten it, however. Barring the fact you're a bad risk, my entire fortune would liquidate at about five hundred pounds."

"That's five hundred more than mine," observed Robin with unimpaired affability. "Thanks, Nick. Glad to be able to avoid the governor anyway." He shuddered theatrically. "A bit like walking into a tiger's cage before lunch—the tiger's lunch, that is. What were you doing in the ancestral hall?"

"Acquiring a bride," answered Nicholas shortly. He did not slacken his step as his brother stopped dead once again, and Robin was obliged to stretch his legs to catch him up.

"Assuming I heard you correctly," said the latter, carefully feeling his way, "do I offer felicitations or condolences? Somehow you don't have the look of a happy groom."

For a long moment Nicholas returned no answer. Robin waited patiently while the sounds of the city street provided a muted background. At length he seemed to make up his mind and bent a dead serious stare on his brother's interested face.

"The story's not for public consumption, so keep your tongue between your teeth." He frowned and continued slowly, "Father told me six months ago when he settled my debts that he wanted me married before my next birthday. He also said that it was the last time he'd bring the dibs in tune for me. Knowing Father, anyone with an ounce of sense would have realized that his continued happy existence in the single state depended on keeping out of the river Tick, but I blithely ran up more debts and, the long and short of it is, I had the choice of wedlock or a debtor's cell. I chose wedlock," he added unnecessarily.

"Good lord, how glad I am that our paths should have crossed today!" declared Robin with heartfelt gratitude. "I might have walked right smack in there as merry as a grig. He'd have made mincemeat of me. Think I'll keep away from Brook Street for a spell in the event he has plans for *my* future. Who's the bride? I can't recall hearing talk of you dangling after anyone in particular." He paused, thunderstruck. "Not the red—urrhumm," trying unsuccessfully to convert an exclamation into a cough.

"Certainly not Lady Montaigne," agreed his brother coldly. "I haven't met the girl yet. In the circumstances my father has graciously agreed to waive the marriage deadline. I merely have to become engaged by my birthday."

Robin's eyes were nearly starting out of his head at this intelligence.

"You've not even met her?" he gasped in awe.

"No, I told you I had not."

"Who is she?"

"Her name is Katherine Harmon. She is Langston's eldest sister. Are you acquainted with him?"

23

"We are on nodding terms only. He is three or four years younger than I. Father quit several years ago and left the family all to pieces. I am slightly acquainted with Miss Harmon and Miss Deborah Harmon as well."

For the first time the hard glint in the viscount's eyes gave way to some show of interest. "What is she like?"

"Kate? She's a nice enough girl, I suppose. Nothing out of the common style, but well enough looking in her way."

"How very descriptive," remarked his brother dryly. "And what is her way?"

Robin seemed slightly at a loss. "Well," he began, drawing the word out to two syllables, "she is average sized, I guess you'd say. Has sort of mouse-colored hair."

"Her eyes?" prompted Nicholas when his brother fell silent.

Robin seemed to be making an effort to conjure up a picture of his brother's intended wife, but the results were obviously less than complete. "Can't say as I've noticed. Brown maybe, or gray perhaps—don't believe they're blue."

"Knowing my father, the lineage must be impeccable, but I'm sadly disappointed he did not buy me a beauty as well."

"If you must have a beauty, you'd best take the younger one; she's a real diamond."

"How old is Miss Harmon?" asked the viscount, startled. "Has she been on the marriage mart for several years without my having met her?"

"No, if I remember correctly, they sent Kate down to take care of her grandfather after her father died. Lived with him until he died, I believe, so she's just come out this season. She's a quiet sort of girl, not one you'd be likely to notice in a crowd." Then, fearing this statement might be construed as derogatory, he added with a desire to please, "I've danced with her once or twice at Almack's. She's almost the best dancer among the season's buds. Yes," more decisively, "I distinctly remember thinking her an elegant dancer."

"One does more than dance with a wife, however," Nicholas returned with a slight edge to his tones.

"She's got a dashed good figure," offered Robin, ever helpful. "There's nothing wrong with the girl, you understand; she's just not the sort who warrants a second look. She'll probably make you a nice, comfortable wife."

Much later Nicholas was to recall this optimistic prediction.

Chapter Three

By eleven o'clock the ballroom had become absolutely stifling. The girl heading for the shelter of some potted palms in an adjacent saloon was thinking that Lady Westerwood must be deeply gratified to know her affair would earn the highest accolade the *ton* could bestow upon a social event—that it was a sad crush! It would indeed be ungenerous of a guest to begrudge her hostess this sublime satisfaction simply because over-crowded rooms and the exertion of dancing reduced one to a state of limp discomfort. And it would be excessively carping of this particular guest because for her there had been no lack of fine partners from whom to choose. In fact, she was enjoying herself immensely, but it was absolutely essential that she stop to catch her breath and smooth the wrinkle in the silk stocking that had fitted perfectly three hours before but had since, in the unaccountable way of inanimate objects, contrived to work itself into a hard ridge under the ball of her foot. Limping slightly, she slipped behind a screen of palms and spotted a small footstool the servants must have overlooked when decorating the room.

Thankfully, she subsided onto it and took a moment to relax every muscle in her body. Wonderful luxury! Welcome though the respite was, she must not linger because the next dance was promised. Sighing softly, she bent double to untie the strings of her sandal after a swift glance had reassured her that her position was well screened.

It was just as she removed the torturing object from her foot that she became aware to her intense dismay that she was no longer completely alone. Someone had elected to sit on the settee in front of the palms. Of all the mortifying circumstances! Obviously she must make her presence known or find herself trapped in this corner and compelled to play gooseberry at a private tête-à-tête. Accordingly she fumbled with suddenly clumsy fingers to smooth out the foot of the stocking.

Too late! A feminine voice floated clearly back through the greenery.

"Darling, I had to snatch a moment alone with you to find out what is causing you to resemble a bear with a sore head tonight. I've had to repeat every remark I've addressed to you at least once in order to capture your attention. What is wrong?"

"This is scarcely the place for a private discussion, *chèrie*. I'll see you home later and we'll talk then."

A delicious laugh drifted back. "Nonsense, we never do talk then. Can't I coax you into telling me now, my sweet?"

The lady's voice was attractively husky and contained an intriguing seductive note. For a breathtaking moment the gentleman remained silent, but that caressing voice exerted a powerful effect on their unknown listener. Her eyes widened and a tinge of pink crept up from her bare throat. What perfectly hideous luck to have landed herself behind two lovers! Her situation had gone from embarrassing to utterly impossible. There was now no remotest possibility of discovering herself to the couple on the settee and making good her escape. She bit her lip and scarcely dared breathe while awaiting the man's answer. Perhaps he would insist on going back to the ballroom.

"Please tell me, Nick."

"Very well." The man's voice was totally without expression. "The news will be abroad before long. I will be announcing my betrothal within the next fortnight."

The girl behind the greenery could almost sense the wave of shock that washed over the woman on the settee. She experienced some pale echo of it herself.

"You cannot be serious, Nick! You would not do that to me!"

"I was not aware that I *had* done anything to you, my dear. My marriage need not make any difference to our relationship."

"Not make any difference!" The husky tones were taking on a trace of shrillness, and the man cautioned her sharply lest they be overheard.

Behind them the eavesdropper instinctively crouched even lower over her shoe.

"Who is the girl?" the woman asked, her voice once again under control.

There was a moment of hesitation before the man answered with obvious reluctance, "I am not going to tell you her name yet, my sweet. In any case, you are unlikely to be acquainted with any of this year's crop of hopefuls, so it would mean nothing to you, and I have not yet offered for her hand. After all," he finished carelessly, "I might be refused."

A bitter note sounded in the feminine laugh that greeted this remark. "Refuse you, plus your father's title and fortune? No girl would be such a fool! Nicholas, why are you doing this?"

"Not from choice, I assure you. My expensive habits have landed me on *point non plus*. My father refuses to pay my debts unless I marry. I would not be much good to you in the Fleet, you will agree. It is the only way."

"But, if you must marry, you could marry me, Nick. I know how to please you better than some whey-faced chit of a girl. We suit exactly."

The short silence that followed this soft but impassioned plea was fraught with embarrassment, at least for the girl behind the palms. She pressed shaking hands over burning cheeks.

"Marriage was never an issue between us, my dear. Even if you were acceptable to my father, which you are not, I have no fancy to be a cuckold."

"*Nick!* How can you insult me so?"

The listener found herself so much in agreement with this tragic utterance that she sat up indignantly, completely forgetting for the moment the need for concealment. *Infamous man! Snake! Cad!* By the time she had run out of epithets to apply to the man on the settee, she had come to a belated realization of her own predicament, and hastily she bent over again, almost missing the man's level reply.

"Is it an insult to express the very natural fear that a woman who had been unfaithful to her first husband would be a rather poor matrimonial risk?"

"How can you be so cruel? The baron was old enough to be my grandfather! What was I to do, sit around and wait for him to die? I was young; I wanted to *live* my life! *Our* marriage would be vastly different. I am in *love* with *you!*"

"Until you cast those beautiful eyes at someone more exciting than a mere husband? I hesitate to call it to your mind lest I be considered unchivalrous, but I must remind you it was not *I* who made a cuckold of the baron. Come, my dear, enough! Let us return to the ballroom. Talking will change nothing. There is no need to let this upset you. I assure you my marriage need not affect our relationship in the least."

"How can you say this? Of course it will. She will take up your time. I shall see much less of you. Oh, I cannot bear it!"

"You will certainly see less of me if you intend to enact me a Cheltenham tragedy each time we meet."

The girl behind the palms clapped a hand over her mouth to prevent her tongue from giving voice to some of the chaotic thoughts chasing themselves around in her skull. What a cold, inhuman monster! Nothing the woman had said seemed to affect him in the slightest degree. She shivered slightly from reaction and put a hand to her back which was beginning to ache from her cramped position. Thank heavens, the monster had persuaded his partner to return to the ballroom. They were rising now.

The girl had been so engrossed with the drama being enacted on the other side of the greenery that she had not thought about the identity of the participants, but now she was consumed with curiosity to see them with her own eyes. Cautiously she raised her head and parted two of the boughs, but her efforts were only partially successful. She could see the back of a big, dark-haired man whose body shielded his companion from view as they strolled slowly away from the alcove, and she caught no more than a tantalizing glimpse of a green and silver gown. For an instant the man's head turned slightly toward her position, and her curiosity was rewarded by a sharp image of a haughty profile and one winged black eyebrow. Dark devil! He perfectly fitted the part she had cast him for.

The girl gave a little chuckle as she rose stiffly from her unnatural position and stretched gratefully. The drama she had witnessed would have been reduced to farce had the villain been thin and reedy with a receding chin. She sobered abruptly, knowing that she should be profoundly shocked by what she had witnessed and ashamed of her own interest, but guiltily aware that she had not been so much entertained since her return from her grandfather's house. A delicately nurtured female of her tender years should have swooned away of course upon hearing such strong stuff, or at the very least have had the propriety to cover her ears with her hands to avoid such an assault on her maidenly sensibilities. Actually, the idea of blocking her ears out of common decency to the unwary speakers had occurred to her at the outset, but aside from the practical aspect of not then knowing when it would be safe to remove her hands, in the beginning of that extraordinary scene, she had been too occupied with her troublesome stocking to be physically able to pursue this laudable course. Then had come the man's announcement of his imminent betrothal, and, she might as well admit her depravity, *nothing* would then have induced her to forgo the rest of the titillating scene.

As she wended her way back to the ballroom, the girl was so occupied in speculating upon the identity of the parties to that tête-à-tête that she almost walked past her intended partner for the dance that was already well underway. Abruptly recalled to the present, she made a graceful apology and set about soothing the young man's wounded feelings. Because she was basically a kind-hearted girl, she bent her best efforts toward concealing from him and her succeeding partners for the remainder of the evening the awful truth that not their most graceful steps or cleverest repartee had the power to anchor her mind in the present.

Surreptitiously her eyes swept over all the twirling couples on the floor and searched among the guests seated in small groups around the room, looking for the protagonists of the scene she had just witnessed. Naturally she would not be able to recognize the woman by sight, but her voice had been quite lovely and very distinctive. Once she caught sight of a green and silver gown and gently led her escort in that direction only to come smack up against a formidable matron with an enormous bosom who was definitely on the shady side of forty. She had difficulty in stifling the giggle that rose in her throat at the picture of this woman who was obviously the soul of respectability taking part in that impassioned scene. No, the heroine of that drama was undoubtedly exceedingly beautiful—anything less was impossible to contemplate. She would do better to seek out the man—she refused to refer to him any longer as a gentleman—whose satanic profile was engraved on her memory. She'd know him twenty years hence in whatever disguise he might adopt; besides, no one of such imposing stature could pass unnoticed in a crowd. *Nicholas!* She tasted the name on her tongue and tossed it around in her mind, worrying it like a dog with a ball, but positively the only connection she was able to make was the youngest stable hand at Broadwoods, a sandy-haired lad of twelve.

Though she lingered at the ball until her mother and sister declared themselves bone weary and insisted on leaving, her hopes of coming upon the couple were quite dashed. Riding home in the carriage, her relatives found her rather abstracted and agreed among themselves that it had been an exhausting evening, thanks to the oppressive heat, and that bed would be most welcome to all.

Though physically tired, the girl found sleep eluding her, so active was her brain in speculating about the two people who had monopolized the better part of her attention for hours now. Thanks to having spent the last two years of his life as nurse, friend, and principal confidante of her grandfather, she was well aware of what frequently went on behind the facade of proper social behavior demanded of all aspiring to the top level of society. He had not believed in raising girls to be ignorant about the world in which they were to function. Nor had he considered them a fragile species set apart by inherent delicacy and too exquisitely sensitive to face the ugliness that existed in society at any level.

She knew, for instance, that there were a number of women like the one with the husky voice who remained acceptable only because discretion was also a way of life with them. The only sin in Society was to cause a scandal. *That* would close doors to the sinner that would have remained open in the face of private knowledge of the offending behavior. But, morals aside, the woman was definitely in love with that monster, though *why* was a question that passed her understanding. And he had been callous and even casually cruel to one who was obviously his mistress, which argued a sad want of loyalty, though she recognized that society held that such women deserved no better. It was a moot point as to who was more deserving of sympathy, the mistress he refused to marry or the poor innocent (one assumed) who would find herself shackled to an uncaring, unfaithful husband. For the latter's sake, the eavesdropper sincerely hoped she was not some romantic child head over ears in love with that spoiled devil. Well, she herself would never know the outcome and she had wasted too much time on unpleasant strangers as it was. On the thought she fell asleep, but in her dreams she was pursued by a ghost in a green and silver dress holding a devil's mask.

The knock on her door that chased away the remnants of troublesome dreams was greeted with relief by the girl in the testor bed.

"Come in!" she called, in the expectation of seeing the maid she shared with her younger sister.

However, it was not Becky's flaxen head that peeked around the door, but her sister's lovely face with its frame of riotously curling black hair. Twin dimples appeared beside her mouth as she taunted laughingly, "Sleepyhead! Do you know it is past ten o'clock? Becky tells me you did not so much as stir when she brought warm water in a half hour ago."

The girl on the bed sat up guiltily and stretched like a cat. With head on one side she studied her sister thoroughly and found nothing to criticize. Deb was the loveliest girl! Those black curls and huge brown eyes made the creamy skin of her perfectly oval face even more dramatic. Both girls had inherited their mother's short straight little nose, but, regretted the girl in the bed, there the benefits ended as far as she herself was concerned. Deborah was the very image of Lady Langston, who had been a celebrated Beauty in her day. Her coloring was warm and vibrant, she was the happy possessor of three dimples, and her petite daintiness made the frequent appellation of Pocket Venus by members of her devoted following not altogether inappropriate. Her sister always felt her own more generously curved figure took on a vulgar voluptuousness when compared with Deb's fairylike proportions.

"Ah, well, the grass is always greener," she remarked rather cryptically, and bounced out of bed.

"Greener than what?" inquired her puzzled sister. "Sometimes I think you enjoy being mysterious, Kate." She pouted prettily, an accomplishment her more pro-

34

saic sister had never been able to acquire, partly because she felt so unutterably foolish when displaying any affectation, no matter how highly regarded the trait might be.

"Never mind, love. I was merely dithering. One must accept one's fate, after all." She proceeded to the basin and began washing her face.

"There you go again, uttering enigmatic remarks that have nothing to do with the topic of the moment," protested Deborah reasonably.

Kate laughed merrily. "I promise you, from now on I shall keep to the topic of the moment. What is it, by the way?" She rinsed her face and commenced patting it dry with a towel.

"Last night's ball," declared Deborah rapturously. "Was it not the most delightful evening you've ever spent?"

Her sister raised her face from the folds of the towel. "Aside from nearly expiring from the heat and thinking the refreshments sadly devoid of interest—did you taste those awful raspberry tarts?—at least I *think* they were intended to be raspberry tarts—I found it most diverting. The music was excellent and the company most distinguished, especially a certain Captain of the House Guards," she finished, with a teasing smile that brought a most becoming blush to her sister's cheeks.

"Well, I do think he is *most* distinguished in his regimentals, and so very handsome," insisted Deborah, somewhat pugnaciously.

"I perfectly agree, love, but I cannot resist teasing you. In the two months since you have appeared on the social scene, Captain Marlowe is the seventh beau, at least, to capture your interest. I fear you are sadly fickle, my dear one." In the act of scrambling into a pretty, white-dotted, red muslin gown, a smiling Kate

35

glanced over to her sister, inviting her to participate in the joke. What she saw caused her to drop the gown precipitously.

"Deb! What have I said to make you cry?" Hastily she stepped over the fallen dress and put an arm around her sister's shoulders.

"If *you* don't believe that what I feel for Stephan is quite, quite different from anything I've felt before, how shall I ever convince Mama that I am serious when I say I'll marry him or no one?"

Kate's expression mingled consternation and sympathy as she strove to soothe her sister and prevent her from sinking into a fit of the vapors. Truth to tell, she had rather avoided recognizing Deb's growing preference for Captain Marlowe as the lasting passion it now appeared to be, knowing his circumstances, both social and financial, rendered him quite ineligible for consideration in the marriage schemes their ambitious mother had devised for her daughters. He was a younger son of a solid but undistinguished Hampshire family and, though perfectly capable of supporting a wife in comfort, not being dependent on his army pay, he could not be compared with others of Deborah's admirers. Mama entertained high hopes of achieving a brilliant match for the lovely Deborah whose social success had brought scores of eligible suitors in her train. Kate could find it in her heart to be grateful that their parent's unexpressed but patent disappointment in her elder daughter's looks had caused her to moderate her ambitions where she was concerned. She shook her head over the folly of it all and bent her attention to the task of soothing and supporting her sister's spirits. To this end she reminded her that they would be attending the ball at Almack's this evening and basely predicted that red-rimmed eyes would drive Captain

Marlowe straight into the arms of another, more cheerful girl.

"For men dislike females who resemble watering pots, you know, and will go to any lengths to avoid them."

Deb gave a watery chuckle at this nonsense, innocently confident of her power over the haplessly smitten Captain.

Soon the sisters were discussing their wardrobes for the evening and the crisis was past—for the moment only, thought Kate soberly, as she once again stepped into the muslin gown and absently accepted her sister's assistance in doing up the buttons. She was turning the possibility of approaching their mother on Deb's behalf over in her mind when the younger girl brought her back to the present.

"Stephan told me Mister Robin Dunston would be joining him at Almack's tonight. You rather like Mister Dunston, do you not, Kate?"

Her sister was relieved that Deb, busy with the buttons down the back of her dress, could not see the blush that heated her own cheeks at the introduction of this name.

"Oh, yes," she answered with airy unconcern. "I find Mister Dunston quite conversable and a better than average dancing partner, especially in the waltz. Deb," she interpolated, hoping to change the subject, "do you recall anyone whose given name might be Nicholas—a tall man with broad shoulders and very black hair?"

After a moment's cogitation Deborah declared herself unacquainted with anyone by that name except the stableboy at Broadwoods. "Why, do you know someone of that description?"

"No, but I had the strangest experience at the Westerwood ball last night. My stocking had gotten itself into an uncomfortable ridge under my foot so I sought privacy to fix it and ended up behind some palms in that anteroom. I was well hidden when a couple came to sit—come in!"

The knocker proved to be Becky with a message that Miss Deborah was wanted in the sewing room where Miss Fiddleton, the seamstress, was ready to fit her new ball dress. The maid moved into Deborah's position to finish doing up Kate's buttons. The sisters went their separate ways, and her experience of the previous evening slipped from Kate's memory.

During the remainder of the day she found her thoughts racing forward to the evening. She could not deny she was looking forward to tonight's ball at Almack's with more than her customary anticipation, nor that the expectation of seeing and perhaps dancing with Mister Robin Dunston was the cause of her eagerness. At the same time she resented feeling this way. She had never been self-conscious in masculine company before. She and her brother, Roger, two years her senior, had been boon companions throughout their childhood.

When her father was alive, Broadwoods was often full of Roger's school friends, some of whom she was pleased to call her own friends even now. There were young men she enjoyed dancing with and men she enjoyed conversing with, and she found the fathers of some of her friends absolutely delightful creatures, but until Mister Robin Dunston had appeared on her horizon, no male had ever succeeded in bringing a blush to her cheeks. She shrewdly suspected there was not a great deal in his cock loft, to employ one of Roger's phrases, despite his agreeable party conversation, so she must suppose his attraction for her lay primarily in his undeniably handsome face, plus his talented performance on the dance floor—and more shame to her for this admission. She did not feel, as Deb apparently did about her captain, that life could contain no greater happiness than to marry Mister Dunston; in fact, she entirely distrusted the institution of marriage as productive of contentment for a woman. Her parents had dwelt together on terms of armed civility for as far back as her memories extended. As a child she had adored her father, but with maturing had come the unwelcome knowledge that his philandering had greatly contributed to turning her still beautiful mother into the near hypochondriac she was at present.

Lady Langston almost reveled in poor health. She was never without her vinaigrette, and the collection of bottles, phials, jars and containers for the medications prescribed by the physician currently enjoying her patronage would cause a stranger's eyes to start out of his head. Her daughters were well used to dosing Lady Langston and catering to her invalidish whims, but Deborah, who had a gentle, uncritical nature, was by far her preferred attendant. She had been a loving mother during Kate's childhood. The girl often wondered of late if her mother's gradual estrangement from her elder daughter had begun when Kate had urged her to make an effort to rise above her physical difficulties and try to do without some esoteric prescription of the practitioner of the moment. Of a certainty, Lady Langston's frequent animadversions on people "bursting with rude health themselves who lacked the sensitivity to appreciate that others were less fortunate" were pointedly addressed to her elder daughter. Kate had not repeated her error of casting aspersions on any of the treatments prescribed since, but she knew herself unforgiven.

Her mother had been the moving force behind Kate's long sojourn with her paternal grandfather. When Lord Langston had commanded the presence of one of his grandchildren for a short visit to ease his loneliness

39

following his son's death, Lady Langston had said quite reasonably that she could not spare her son in her bereavement, and since Kate was the child who most favored her father, she was the ideal choice.

The short visit had lasted until her grandfather's death, not that Kate had begrudged that irascible but decidedly entertaining individual one day of her company. Had her mother asked for her return before she had rendered her final tender service to her grandfather, she'd have pleaded with her to allow her to remain where she was most needed, but there had been no such request; and when she had come home after an absence of more than two years, it was to find that the gap between mother and daughter had widened insensibly. Deborah had grown from a worshipful young sister into a poised young woman. The sisters got along famously together, but the closeness that had previously existed had inevitably diminished over such a long separation. Instead of her sister, other girls had shared Deb's first experiences on being released from the schoolroom.

Deborah and her favored suitor were much in Kate's mind that afternoon as she went about some minor housekeeping tasks. She had still not decided on an approach to her mother when it became time to dress for the evening. Lady Langston was going to be severely disappointed, to put it mildly, if Deborah's preference for Captain Marlowe persisted. The quiet routine of their lives suddenly looked like it was becoming rather complicated.

Chapter Four

On learning that Robin was acquainted with his prospective bride, Nicholas had requested that his brother present him to Miss Harmon informally. The thought of being introduced to the girl one moment, and making her an offer in the next breath, made his head reel. Apart from the general awkwardness of such a situation, it was not particularly complimentary to Miss Harmon either.

Accordingly, on Wednesday evening he found himself entering the sacred portals of Almack's Assembly Rooms on King Street for the first time in at least three seasons. Year after year the newly launched buds of society made their debuts here and the matchmaking began. To be refused a voucher for Almack's meant social ostracism. The code of behavior was strict and its enforcement was assured by the six hostesses whose approval was essential if an aspirant was to obtain admission.

Glancing around for Robin on his entrance, Nicholas was immediately pinpointed by two of these social arbiters. He greeted Maria Sefton warmly, exchanged some rapid fire repartee with Lady Jersey, and successfully evaded Mrs. Drummond Burrell, who thoroughly disapproved of him. He noted with chagrin that the young ladies seemed suddenly much younger and their escorts more callow, and for the first time felt the icy breath of approaching old age. Fortunately some old friends absorbed him into a laughing group before he had become too conspicuous, because Robin was nowhere in sight at present. Obviously he would be obliged to dance sooner or later lest his presence become a subject for speculation. He was aware that Sally Jersey had him in her sights already, and that busy brain of hers never rested. Glancing around quickly, he spied one of his former flirts, now a dashing young matron, and answered the invitation in her smiling eyes.

While pleasantly engaged in conversation, his assessing look dwelt briefly on one or another of the dancers whirling by. There were one or two accredited Beauties and a number of quite attractive girls, but for once he was more intent on trying to discover a quiet, mouse-colored girl of average size, eye color uncertain, but with a good figure, he amended, trying to form a picture from Robin's disjointed description. There was a very drab little figure sitting over there amongst the dowagers, and a sense of fatality warned him that she was the one until he noted with relief that she was wearing spectacles. Robin would not have forgotten that detail.

The dance ended and he excused himself from his conversation to resume his search for his brother. He thought he spotted him on the other side of the large square room and slowly headed in that direction, stopping often to exchange greetings with friends, and on one occasion to be presented to one of the Beauties he had previously noted. Ordinarily he would have solicited her hand for the very next dance, but tonight he was too intent on his mission to do more than smile warmly and make his excuses as soon as civility allowed.

A shifting around in a group to his left suddenly revealed a charming profile that captured his attention. The light from a chandelier was bringing out red and gold lights in hair the color of a highly polished acorn. She turned her head slightly to attend to the man on her left, and the viscount had a too brief three-quarter view of the roguish smile that illuminated her quiet face before the profile was once more presented to him. The connoisseur in Nicholas desired to remain where he might eventually discover whether the full view was as enchanting as the profile, but regretfully he moved on toward the spot where he had espied Robin. True, the girl had brown hair, but "mousy" was the last appellation that could be applied to anyone with that smile.

Before reaching Robin who was holding court in an alcove, he passed two girls who might possibly have fitted Robin's description, both decidedly plain and quiet looking, but he rather doubted that either had a figure which would excite favorable comment from his brother. He was growing bored with his guessing game by the time he came up to Robin in the midst of a chattering, laughing crowd. There was no time for any private conversation because the musicians were striking up for the next dance.

"Sorry, Nick, I am engaged for this set," said Robin in an undertone. "I'll present you to the girl immediately afterward." He started to lead a pretty blonde onto the floor when his brother stopped him with a hand on his arm.

"Can you point her out to me?" he whispered.

Robin hastily scanned the room, then nodded in the

43

direction of a set forming for the dance. "The girl in the coffee-colored gown," he tossed over his shoulder as he proceeded to join another set at a distance from the musicians.

More nervous than he would have believed possible, if his rapid pulse was any indication, Nicholas allowed his glance to be directed toward the spot Robin had indicated. For an instant his breathing stopped as his startled eyes fell on a coffee-colored, lace-trimmed creation and climbed almost reluctantly to dwell with gratified surprise on the girl with the profile. A tiny, pleased smile flitted across his lips. For the first time since his father had issued his ultimatum life seemed to hold some promise for the future. The girl was lovely! He almost laughed aloud as he recalled his brother's indifferent description. Trust Robin to call a girl plain unless she was so obviously flashy that she was a born honey pot.

Yet he could see what Robin had meant. One's glance might pass over the quiet-faced, brown-haired girl initially, but a second glance was sure to linger, especially if she were smiling as she was now at her partner. From this distance the color of her eyes remained uncertain, but he could definitely corroborate his brother's judgment as to the excellence of her figure in the demure, but highly becoming gown. He had ample opportunity during the lengthy number to applaud mentally her graceful performance on the floor and also her modest behavior. Her entire attention was fixed politely on her partner though the disparity in the couple's standard of performance was enough to excuse some pettishness on the part of a highly accomplished dancer constrained to go through the paces with one who might with justification be termed a clumsy oaf. No one could have guessed from Miss Harmon's demeanor that she was less than perfectly contented with

44

her partner. Nicholas thought her a true thoroughbred and looked forward to his introduction to his future bride.

With the unexpected force of an earthquake he was rocked by a question that had not once occurred to him since his first conversation with his father. Was Miss Harmon aware of the fate that was in store for her, and if so, had she acquiesced readily or was she being coerced? He wondered if he would be able to tell from her reaction to the introduction whether or not she was aware of his identity. He had no doubts at all that the earl would have dangled a princely settlement in front of Lady Langston or her son had he been dead set on Miss Harmon, but was this indeed the case? If the Harmon family were old acquaintances of the Dunstons, it was not a relationship he had ever been aware of. Perhaps the marriage idea had originated with the girl's relatives and not with his father after all.

There was no time to ruminate on these new possibilities, however, for the dance was winding down. He saw Robin looking around for him and signaled that he was following. There were still several people between the brothers, however, as Robin approached Miss Harmon. She looked up at his greeting, and Nicholas stopped dead on observing the glow that irradiated her face and the telltale flush that sprang to her cheeks.

"Sits the wind in that quarter, then?" Abruptly he turned on his heel.

The impatient rapping at the door to the lodgings on Saint James's Street caused Perkins to glance in surprise at the clock, but one look at his master assured him that the call at this extraordinary hour was not unexpected. He had barely opened the door wide enough to admit a wraith when the Honourable Robin Dunston burst in and demanded: "What the devil were you

45

playing at tonight, Torvil, leaving me standing there looking like a fine fool in front of the girl? There I was preparing her to meet my brother and I turned around, and no brother!"

"Have a glass of brandy, Robin, and contain yourself for the moment. That will be all, Perkins. I shan't need you anymore tonight. Go to bed." He waited until the valet had handed Mister Dunston a glass and silently left the room before turning his attention from the liquid he was slowly swirling in his glass to his still fuming brother, pacing the room agitatedly.

"Well?" insisted Robin. "Why did you tell me you wanted to meet the girl if you did not want to meet her?"

"Why did *you* not tell *me* you had an interest there yourself?" retorted his brother. "And I'd prefer you not to walk a hole in my very expensive carpet. Sit down."

"What d'you mean, an interest?" Robin stopped pacing and stared at his brother, stupefied. Then, enlightened, he dropped heavily onto the chair indicated. "Have you taken leave of your senses, Nick? I told you the girl wasn't my type—not that she's not a perfectly amiable girl, as I also told you."

"Answer me truthfully, Robin," said the viscount quietly, his eyes intent on his brother's face. "Are you quite sure you do not wish to marry Miss Harmon yourself?"

"Good lord!" exclaimed Robin, aghast. "Why would I want to do a fool thing like get married? Do you feel quite the thing tonight, Nick?"

For a moment longer his brother continued to drive the point of his dagger stare into him, then he relaxed, but there was a slightly perplexed air about him.

"I saw the way Miss Harmon colored up when you spoke to her. The girl obviously has a *tendre* for you.

Naturally I would not dream of offering for her if you returned her affection, no matter what Father threatened."

"Eh, you say the girl rather fancies me?" Robin looked startled, but more gratified than disturbed at this interpretation.

His brother snorted: "I must confess it gives me a poor idea of her intelligence."

Robin grinned but did not rise to the bait, and the subject was allowed to drop for the remainder of his brief visit. Not until he was about to take his leave did he remind his brother that he had still not actually met his intended bride. His offer to perform the introduction at the earliest moment convenient to both was declined with civil thanks by the viscount who declared that he had decided to write to Lady Langston to request that she arrange a time for him to call upon Miss Harmon. His earlier objections to making the girl an offer at their initial meeting no longer seemed particularly relevant.

The morning after the ball at Almack's Kate approached her mother's boudoir in answer to a summons conveyed to her by Lady Langston's maid. She was a trifle surprised at this departure from habit. The uncertain state of Lady Langston's health precluded any rigorous morning activities, especially following a late evening. She rarely appeared in the breakfast room anyway, preferring to consume her meager morning repast of thinly sliced bread and butter in her bed before undergoing the rigors of a toilette that was never completed in less than two hours. Before tapping on the door Kate gave her curls a hurried pat and repinned the lace of her gown at the throat. Her mother always presented an exquisitely turned out appearance and deplored a tendency in her daughter to dress by guess and by golly when pressed for time.

Morrell, Lady Langston's long-time dresser, opened the door and indicated that Kate was to proceed into the bedchamber before she exited from the suite. Kate noted with some surprise that Lady Langston was already exquisitely coiffed though she was still wearing a dressing gown of some drifting gray material that emphasized her extreme slenderness. Despite her ill health, there was not a single gray hair amongst the shining black tresses that represented her most lasting claim to beauty. The lovely dark eyes, so like Deborah's, seemed huge in a face that had grown thin and sharp these last few years. The remnants of great beauty were certainly present, however, and on the rare occasions when she was moved to display some animation, youth returned to her face and one would find it difficult to credit her with three grown children. At Kate's approach she turned from contemplating her image in the mirror.

"You wished to speak to me, Mama?"

"Yes, my dear." The faint smile on Lady Langston's lips disappeared as she surveyed her daughter's appearance. She sighed. "Kate, that dress does not become you at all. Pale blue is too insipid for your coloring."

"Yes, Mama, I know. It was a mistake to buy this fabric only because it was such a bargain, but I must get some wear out of it or it would indeed be a sad waste of money."

"I suppose so. How tiresome it is always to be forced to make hateful economies." Lady Langston had sounded a trifle fretful, but now she smiled at her daughter. "Our fortunes are going to take a turn for the better, however, if you will be the sensible girl I know you are. I have some marvelous news for you, my dearest child."

"What do you mean, Mama? What news?"

"I have received a most flattering offer for your hand. I made sure you would be delighted."

"Not if it is from Sir Geoffrey Morecambe, I shan't." Kate spoke quite firmly. "He is old enough to be my father and a widower into the bargain. He simply wants a wife to manage that odious daughter of his and chaperone her to all the *ton* parties. I have been doing everything within the bounds of civility to convince him that I do not appreciate the attentions he has been showering on me this past month."

"Well, you must have succeeded," said Lady Langston dryly, "because the offer is not from Sir Geoffrey."

"Oh," said Kate faintly, the wind taken out of her sails. Her forehead creased in puzzlement. "Then who?"

"The Viscount Torvil." Lady Langston's triumphant air changed to mild annoyance at Kate's bewildered expression.

"But, Mama, I am not even acquainted with Lord Torvil—in fact, I do not know who he may be. Why should someone who doesn't know me wish to marry me?"

Her mother seemed to hesitate briefly, then she gave a little laugh that rang falsely to the girl whose senses were instantly alerted. "Well, as to that, my dear child, it is not necessary to have met you to know that you have all the qualities necessary to make a good wife for a man in Lord Torvil's position. You have the breeding and upbringing essential to someone of his rank, and you—"

"Rubbish!" stated Kate roundly, abandoning completely the dutiful manner she strove for in dealings with her mother. "Why, I might be dull witted or wildly extravagant, or a veritable shrew for all Lord Torvil knows of me personally! Why can't he court a

49

bride in the usual manner? What's wrong with him, and who is he anyway?"

"Katherine! I must insist that you moderate your language. It is most unbecoming in a delicately nurtured female," Lady Langston protested, groping for her vinaigrette. Her voice became plaintive. "I knew it was a mistake allowing your grandfather to keep an impressionable young girl chained to his side. I said at the time that no good could come from such a course. His rough ways might do well enough for a boy, but they have almost ruined my daughter."

Kate refrained from pointing out that her recollections of the events leading up to her prolonged sojourn with her grandfather differed in all essentials from her mother's. From long experience all of Lady Langston's children recognized that the introduction of her vinaigrette into a discussion boded ill for its calm continuance. She hastened to apologize for her unseemly language and brought the conversation back to its essentials.

"Mama, *who* is the Viscount Torvil?"

"He is Sedgeley's heir. I believe you are slightly acquainted with the younger son, Mister Robin Dunston."

Kate gasped in shock. "So, *that* is why Mister Dunston wished to present his brother to me last night at Almack's!" She fell silent, gnawing fiercely at her bottom lip as she digested this startling development.

"Then you *have* met Lord Torvil, Kate?"

"No, no! Mister Dunston was on the point of making the introduction when his brother disappeared." She straightened her shoulders and sought her mother's eye. "He cannot have been too eager to meet me. In fact, the whole thing sounds like a hum to me." She ignored her mother's remonstrative "Kate!" and continued relentlessly, "Did Lord Torvil wait upon you, Mama?"

Again that slight hesitation. "No, my dear. Only conceive of the honor! The earl himself paid me a visit to request that I use my influence as a parent to persuade you of the desirability of the match. And you may take that look off your face, Miss. It is in all respects a more advantageous match than I dared to dream of for you. For it cannot be denied that you have not enjoyed the signal success of your sister." Perhaps it was the hurt look that Kate could not quite conceal before her thick lashes veiled her eyes, but Lady Langston relented and added hastily: "Although you have taken well enough, I grant you, and I have had several compliments from my friends on your modest demeanor."

"I'm sure it is an honor indeed to be singled out by the Earl of Sedgeley, only you must excuse me when I say I could wish it were his son who had done me this honor. Obviously the father seeks to arrange a marriage for his son." She swallowed with difficulty and faced her parent squarely. "Do you expect me to agree to an arranged marriage, Mama?"

Lady Langston lowered her eyes and fiddled with the ties of her gray dressing gown for a moment before answering this appeal. Then, for the first time in their discussion she met her daughter's serious gaze honestly and proceeded to enlighten her about the family's financial situation. Long before she had come to an end, Kate had grown pale and had gripped her hands tightly together in her lap. She had already sunk down upon her mother's bed on learning the identity of her suitor.

Now she bowed her head in submission and tonelessly said, "Very well, Mama. If I see nothing in the viscount to disgust me, I shall accept his offer. But only," she interrupted Lady Langston's fervent expression of gratitude, "on the condition that you allow Deb to marry where her affections lead her. The Earl of Sedgeley's generosity is such that there is no need for both of us to be sacrificed to repair the family fortunes."

"Remember that you will be gaining an enviable place in Society too, Kate. It won't be all sacrifice. And I think you are not of a romantical disposition in any case. *You* would not be so foolish as to allow a handsome face to persuade you that marriage to him would insure a lifetime of bliss."

Kate averted her eyes from the bleakness in Lady Langston's face, but she could not screen out the bitterness in her voice. She sighed a little for the departure of vague, girlish dreams and rose to her feet.

"I am persuaded you are quite correct, Mama. Am I to expect a visit from Lord Torvil, or will the earl deputize for his lordship again?"

"The viscount will wait upon you this afternoon. Don't look like that, dearest," begged Lady Langston with tears in her eyes. "I understand that Lord Torvil is a very personable young man, and his father assures me he is not wanting in sense or spirit either." She essayed a smile. "A poor-spirited looby would not do for you who have so much quickness of understanding. You will probably deal wonderfully together."

Kate's attempt at a smile was no more successful than her mother's.

"Yes, Mama," she said, and quietly left the room.

Just as she was closing the door behind her, Lady Langston hastily called, "And do not neglect to change that gown, Kate."

Chapter Five

If Kate shed a few tears in private over the cards she
had been dealt by a malicious fate there were no
witnesses to affirm her weakness. Of a certainty no
mingling of tears took place during the afflicting scene
later enacted with her sister. Tender-hearted Deborah,
easily aroused to sympathy for a fellow creature's mis-
fortunes, wept a few inevitable tears over her sister's
plight, but since she was torn between sorrow that Kate
was being forced into a loveless marriage and pride
that she was to marry into one of the leading families
of the nation, and would eventually become a countess,
there was no danger that she would present the appearance of a female who had allowed herself to succumb
to an emotional frenzy when the viscount arrived for
his first meeting with his intended bride.

All three ladies had been sitting in the pink parlor
for a good hour exhibiting varying degrees of sham en-
thusiasm for their individual pieces of handwork resur-
rected for the occasion. Kate, who was rather pale,
doggedly worked at a piece of embroidery, though her
mental state was so abstracted every stitch would even-

tually have to be removed. Deborah's pretense of industry was less accomplished. She jumped up at each new sound in the street below and ran to the window, hoping for the first glimpse of the unknown viscount. Lady Langston displayed a becoming serenity that differed from her usual languid air, but from time to time she darted assessing looks at her elder daughter. Kate's absorption with her thoughts was so complete that she remained totally unaware that she was being studied somewhat anxiously.

The gown she had chosen for the occasion met with her mother's unqualified approval. It was a bronze green affair in a soft cotton, styled simply to flow from a high waistline. The tiny puffed sleeves left Kate's smooth-skinned arms bare. Her only jewelry consisted of a narrow gold bracelet on one shapely wrist and a gold locket on a chain. She looked young and sweetly serious, an expression her mother judged to be wholly appropriate to the occasion. Of course it was a pity Kate had not inherited the black hair and dark eyes that so distinguished her sister, but really her healthy brown hair was rather pretty, especially under a strong light, and it curled naturally in a style that was quite becoming, which must be counted a great asset. However, the girl was too pale. She seemed to have lost what little color she had had upon entering the room.

"Kate," she ordered abruptly, "you are appallingly pallid. Go and rub a little rouge into your cheeks. Mind you, do it lightly, though."

"Yes, Mama." Obediently the girl rose and left the room.

Deborah was once again peering eagerly out of the window.

"Do stop that continual jumping up and down, Deborah, my nerves won't stand much more. I think I am beginning to develop a headache. Where is my fan?"

54

"Right here, Mama. Shall I fan you for a bit to cool your cheeks? It will refresh you."

"Yes, thank you, my dear. Hark, do I hear a carriage stopping?"

This time it was not a false alarm. When Kate returned to the front saloon five minutes later, she could distinguish a low masculine rumble running along with Deb's infectious giggle, and she knew a moment of sheer panic.

"Don't let him be too awful," she breathed in heartfelt prayer and put a trembling hand on the knob.

For a split second following her quiet entrance she was unobserved, and the tableau in front of her was indelibly etched in her mind. Her still lovely mother and sparkling sister were bending their dark heads forward to attend to another dark head, another profile that looked distressingly familiar.

"Oh, no!"

Kate was unaware that she had given utterance to the instinctive protest that surged up in her breast at the instant of recognition, but three people turned as one and stared at her in astonishment. Initially, she was unaware of this also as her eyes were locked to the man's for a charged interval.

"Kate, what is it?"

She wrenched her glance away from his startled regard and faced her mother with a queer blind look in her eyes. Then she made a visible effort to regain command of herself. Her hands were gripping each so tightly the knuckles showed white.

"Kate, what is the matter with you?" The hint of impatience in Lady Langston's repeated question got through to her.

"Nothing! I . . . may I speak to you privately, Mama?"

Lady Langston ignored the urgency in her daughter's voice. She gestured to Lord Torvil, who had risen to his feet and was still standing, politely attentive but now carefully expressionless.

"Kate, my dear child, you are forgetting your manners. We have a guest." She laughed archly. "Lord Torvil is most anxious to be presented to you."

"Mama, *please!*" begged Kate, but her mother shot her a quelling look that did not escape the man's alert dark eyes, and commenced an introduction that was destined never to be completed, for a pale, determined Kate interrupted passionately:

"Mama, I *cannot* marry Lord Torvil. I beg your pardon, sir. Pray, forgive me, but I . . . I . . ." Her voice trailed off, she flashed her rejected suitor one beseeching look, made a small, hopeless gesture with one hand, and dashed out of the room as though pursued by furies.

Her mother was the first of the speechless trio to recover the use of her faculties. She sprang to her feet before the door had closed behind her daughter.

"Kate, come back here this instant! Oh, that wretched girl will be the death of me!" Catching the viscount's speculative eye on her, Lady Langston's angry voice sank precipitously to a faint, plaintive cry. "Oh, I feel one of my spasms coming on. Deborah! My vinaigrette!"

She accepted the aid of the viscount's arm in staggering to the sofa where she collapsed in a graceful heap with her face in her hand. Her younger daughter, who had been a stunned spectator to all that had taken place, came to life and took over her accustomed role as attendant to her mother after one quick, apologetic look at the viscount.

He, realizing he was indeed *de trop* in this scene of domestic discomfort, murmured a graceful apology and bowed himself out of the room before his stricken hostess could recover sufficient self-command to summon him back.

In the corridor he came upon the butler whose perturbed expression rather betrayed his calling.

"Lady Langston was about to desire you to show me out," the unusual guest said smoothly. "If it is not too much trouble," he added gently when the butler cast an undecided glance toward the saloon before moving to obey this request.

"Certainly, sir," assented that individual woodenly.

The viscount accepted hat, gloves, and walking stick with a faint smile of thanks upon his lips and blandly wished the butler good day.

Once out on the flagway, however, his careful blankness disappeared as he replayed that fantastic scene in his mind in an attempt to make some sense of it. One fact was glaringly clear, of course. Miss Harmon, for some reason as yet obscure, had refused him before he had even made her an offer. One part of his brain was rather interested in discovering the earl's reaction to this unexpected turn of events. He hesitated momentarily, debating whether to head for his parental home, then walked on toward his lodgings, having resolved on the wisdom of postponing yet another confrontation with his father. For one thing he had no answers for the questions the earl would inevitably fire at him. One had to assume the girl had agreed to the match originally or her mother would have denied him the interview today. But she had entered the room in great agitation and flatly refused to marry him, or indeed even to allow her mother to perform the introduction. Perhaps she was given to distempered freaks. What did he actually know of her character—nothing at all.

His steps did not falter, but here his mental process slowed to a halt and reversed itself. Actually there *were* a few things he had learned about Miss Harmon from his own observation. He knew, for instance, that she had a sense of humor as evidenced by the mischievous smile that had caught his eye originally. She was an accomplished dancer with enough kindness to overlook the inadequacies of a bad partner. Though not an obvious beauty, he considered she had a great deal of countenance, and her behavior at Almack's had indicated a natural, easy manner and considerable poise. The attitude of stunned disbelief evidenced by her relatives would tend to support his hunch that the display of temperament he had just witnessed was totally uncharacteristic of Miss Harmon, the inescapable conclusion being that she, uncharacteristically, had taken him in instant dislike.

He shrugged his shoulders slightly. Well, he should now have a bit of a respite before his future was sealed. It would take his father some time to select another suitable candidate, which was a great relief, of course. This taut, irritated sensation must be due to bruised vanity at such a decided rejection and, in the circumstances, was utter nonsense. Still, no female had looked at him with such an expression of loathing, almost of horror, since he had chased his cousin Sally with a garden snake at the age of eleven. Even a saint might find himself slightly put out at such a reception. When he thought about it dispassionately, it was actually quite amusing and he would enjoy seeing his father's reaction when he described the incident to him. This last reflection brought him to the door of his lodgings which he closed with a decided snap behind him.

A meeting of those dark brows belied any amusement as he entered, but a sudden thought did bring a smile, albeit a sour one, to his face. He would have found the scene that was doubtless taking place between mother and daughter at this very moment vastly

58

diverting. Ten years on the social scene had well equipped him to judge the vagaries of the female of the species, and he was not unacquainted with the type who used ill health or delicate nerves as a shield behind which they exercised a real tyranny over their hapless families. He had not been long in Lady Langston's company but he had seen enough to place her with fair confidence in this sisterhood, and he surmised that she would be entirely capable of making her recalcitrant daughter regret the tantrum she had enacted.

It would have soothed the viscount's wounded vanity to know that his surmise was amply confirmed. Lady Langston did indeed put her daughter through a very difficult half hour, and Kate did regret having behaved in such an unrestrained manner. She was perfectly willing to pen the most abject of apologies for any embarrassment she might have caused Lord Torvil to suffer. What she did *not* regret and what she was *not* willing to do was reconsider her decision not to marry him. It would be understating the matter to say that relations between mother and daughter were consequently somewhat strained.

They persisted thusly until the following afternoon when a wildly weeping Deborah sought her sister in the privacy of the latter's bedchamber. It took Kate a full twenty minutes to soothe Deborah sufficiently to make sense out of the jumble of pleas, self-recriminations, and heart burnings that tumbled from her lips, but at length it emerged that Mama had received a visit that morning from one of Deb's well-connected suitors requesting permission to pay his addresses. Which permission Mama had given. She had summoned her younger daughter to inform her of the happy fate in store for her and had met with (she said) rank ingratitude and flagrant disobedience for the second time in as many days. Kate was unsure just how much of Deb's misery was due to losing Captain Marlowe and how much to having fatally wounded her mother. Evidently when she had persisted in her refusal to give Mama's choice a favorable answer, Mama had made it abundantly clear that she would never receive permission to wed her captain. For the first time in her life she had abandoned her prostrated parent wholly to Morrell's care and had gone looking for her sister. As Deborah grew calmer and her statements became more coherent, the anxious look on Kate's face was replaced by one of quiet hopelessness. She dealt firmly with Deb's half-hearted threats of elopement, adjured her to bathe her face and lie down upon her bed for an hour, and made ready to reopen negotiations with her mother.

She found Lady Langston still lying on the chaise longue in her sitting room which reeked of camphorated spirits of ammonia edged a bit by lavender water. Morrell was still with her, bathing her temples with the lavender water, but she rose quickly to her feet, more in relief than deference, Kate guessed, at her entrance. At first Lady Langston was not at all inclined to dismiss her dresser, whose presence was more agreeable to her at that moment than that of either of her daughters, but Kate said pleasantly to Morrell that she wished to be private with her mother.

"Oh, very well, leave us," Lady Langston said, dismissing her dresser with a resigned wave of one white hand. The other was still clutching her vinaigrette, which she now raised to her nose, presumably as a precaution against whatever new disaster her daughter's appearance might herald. She eyed her offspring with faint hostility but remained silent, leaving it up to Kate to open the interview.

"Mama," she began without preamble, "I have come

to tell you that I have changed my mind about marrying Lord Torvil. I will accept his offer if you will allow Deb to marry Captain Marlowe." She paused, unable to interpret the quick gleam that appeared in her mother's eyes before long black lashes swept down to conceal all expression. Surprise? No, Lady Langston had not been pleased precisely to see Kate, but there had been an air of expectancy about her. Triumph then? Perhaps, but what did it signify in any event? The deed was done.

"Very pretty talking," said Lady Langston waspishly, "but what gives you to suppose Lord Torvil will still be of the same mind after the way you treated him? No man would wish to wed a female who shows herself so averse to his appearance that she cannot bear even to acknowledge an introduction."

"Most probably not, but he will do what his father tells him, just the same."

"You seem very certain of this." Lady Langston studied her daughter's wan, cold face intently.

"I am," Kate answered shortly, making no attempt to satisfy her parent's curiosity. She put a question of her own. "Was the earl very set on having *me* for his son, Mama?"

"Quite decided. It seems he knew your grandfather—old Lord Langston—in his youth, and corresponded with him before he died. The two of them hatched this little plot together."

"I . . . see." This simple statement left much that Kate was thinking unsaid. She was genuinely astonished that her grandfather had been busy matchmaking for her while she was companioning him, and without her knowledge too. She had also noted the hint of acid in Lady Langston's tone, and wondered idly if her mother had offered the earl Deborah in her stead or if she merely resented having the two men present her with a *fait accompli*.

"Well, I shall leave it up to you how you go about letting Lord Torvil know of your change of heart." Lady Langston was washing her hands of the situation, but Kate was not to be drawn on that subject.

"Shall I tell Deb you have withdrawn your objections to Captain Marlowe?"

"Kate," and now her mother's faintly petulant air had given way to a seriousness that reached her daughter, "Deborah is very young and, I think, impressionable. I know you mean your sacrifice for her sake, but there is every chance, you know, that she will have forgotten this soldier of hers within the month. Brompton is an excellent catch, and she would have a position of some consequence in society."

Kate drew in her lip and returned her mother's regard honestly. "I have thought of that, too, but she does not care for Lord Brompton, Mama. *His* suit must be rejected, but I suppose we need not rush her into a marriage with Captain Marlowe. Perhaps if you were to tell her merely that if she feels the same way about the captain six months from now, you will withdraw your objections."

"Very well." Lady Langston bowed her head in acquiescence, and Kate prepared to leave the room after thanking her mother. As her daughter's face once more acquired that desolate look, the older woman added quickly, "Kate, Deborah and I both received a most favorable impression of Torvil in the short time we were engaged in conversation, and there is no denying he is most attractive. You may find he will make an unexceptionable husband who will deal famously with you."

"He will be a *vile* husband, and for my part, I shall make him an *abominable* wife," Kate declared viciously, and went out, leaving her mother gasping at the intensity of her daughter's dislike.

None of this was permitted to show the following day, however, when the viscount was ushered into a small study where he was received privately by Miss Harmon. His ruminations on the abortive proposal had led him to postpone informing the earl of his failure to secure a favorable answer. He had done some checking on the financial status of the Harmon family, and the results of his investigations, combined with his guesses concerning Lady Langston's control over her daughter, decided him on this course. He had accepted his post each day with more interest than was customary, and his patience was rewarded on the second day after his visit to Lord Langston's townhouse when a letter directed in an unfamiliar feminine hand came to his attention. Nicholas surveyed it thoughtfully, then consigning the rest of the pile to a convenient table, he strolled toward his bedchamber with this one item. He read the text of the politely worded request that the Viscount Torvil might call on Miss Katherine Harmon at his earliest convenience, then reread it carefully, but there was nothing to be guessed at from the formal wording. Still, he *did* hazard a guess or two and he even permitted himself a tiny, smug smile.

There was no hint of a smile in the exquisitely polite countenance he presented to Miss Harmon when the butler closed the door, and his bow was a masterpiece of quiet good manners.

"Your very obedient servant, Miss Harmon."

She inclined her head and requested, with equal politeness, that he be seated. If he had expected to be received by a nervous, cowed young girl offering stumbling apologies for her conduct at their last meeting, he was doomed to disappointment. Indeed, she did proffer a quiet apology for her former rudeness but in

63

a controlled manner that belied any nervousness as she took the initiative in the interview.

"I requested this meeting, Lord Torvil, to inquire whether you still wish to make me an offer."

Her eyes matched her hair, he noted with interest, the same light brown with gold specks when the light shone on them. He noted with equal interest that their expression was a trifle inimical.

"Do you wish me to understand that you have undergone a change of heart?" he inquired conversationally.

A fleeting suggestion of a humorous quirk touched her mouth momentarily, but she answered staidly, "That is perhaps not quite the phrase I would choose, but in essence, yes." Her eyes did not shrink from his searching glance.

"Why? You don't like me; in fact, I'd venture to say you dislike me rather intensely."

"Need that signify?" There was no attempt to soften his impression.

"Perhaps I'd prefer to have a willing bride. Most men would."

"If that were the case, my lord, you'd have contrived to meet your intended bride before making her an offer," she retorted. "No, you'll do as your father wishes."

"You favor a blunt style, Miss Harmon."

"So do you, Lord Torvil." She was remembering that callous exchange with his mistress.

"Well, by all means, let us continue this admirable frankness, so refreshing in a woman." He observed the slight tightening of her mouth with satisfaction. "You have not answered my question."

"What question?"

"Why have you changed your mind? Two days ago you said you could not marry me."

She hesitated briefly. "My family is in dire financial straits. Your father has been most generous in the matter of settlements."

He was relentless in his pursuit of the reason behind her *volte face*. "This was equally true two days ago, yet you refused me."

"Two days ago I did not know that my sister would be denied permission to marry the man of her choice."

"I see." He was silent for a long moment, but the girl showed no signs of restlessness. She appeared carved from ice. He would enjoy seeing that icy facade melt into some honest emotion, he thought with surprising intensity. "You are sacrificing yourself for your sister's sake?"

"One of us must marry for money. My sister's affections are already engaged."

"And yours are not?"

"Mine are not."

And that's a damned lie, he fumed silently, but she appeared utterly cool and gave him look for look. He had never wished to shake a woman until her teeth rattled before, but his fingers itched to grab those shapely shoulders in the demure blue gown and shake this one until she told the truth.

"What was it about me that alienated you so?" he asked bluntly.

"My lord?"

"Don't prevaricate. You took one look at me the other day and cried out that you could not marry me. What was it about me that struck you so adversely?"

Thick, straight lashes the same color as her hair swept down for an instant, then those strange gold-brown eyes met his unflinchingly.

"Some things cannot be put into words, my lord."

"Which means you won't talk. Very well, my dear

Miss Harmon, you may consider yourself betrothed. Shall we seal the bargain in the usual way?"

"What . . . what do you mean?"

He was pleased to note the presence of something akin to panic which flashed across her pale countenance. "Oh, come now, Miss Harmon; you are not a child. Even Lady Langston would expect us to exchange a chaste kiss on this auspicious occasion. She has so tactfully left us alone."

She flinched at his tone and sudden color flooded her cheeks as she held out one hand against his chest to hold him off. "Please, my lord," she pleaded in a strangled voice, "this marriage is actually a bargain between your father and my mother. We are the victims, but is it necessary that we give them a total victory?"

"You'll have to clarify that statement for my benefit, Miss Harmon."

"We must stand before a minister of God and exchange marriage vows that neither of us can possibly believe in. Need we carry the farce any further?" The ice had melted. She was very lovely, he thought, pleading in earnest to remain inviolate, but his face hardened.

"You wish this to be a marriage in name only, Miss Harmon?"

"Surely it is what we both wish! I promise I'll not interfere with you in any way. Isn't that enough?"

Now it was his eyes that shifted away from the importunity in hers as he realized how strongly he resented her suggestion. But it would not do to frighten her at this stage. Her earnestness had touched some chord of sympathy in him, but his words were harsh.

"My father naturally expects an heir. I cannot make you any promises of this nature."

"For a while—for a year or two?" she begged.

"For a while," he promised grudgingly, and viewed

the easing of tension about her with very mixed emotions.

She seemed to have nothing more to say to him, and the ensuing silence showed every sign of becoming permanent. As on the night he first saw her, the delightful profile was once again presented to him, but all the life seemed to have left her; she was as remote as a statue. When he spoke again, it was obvious that her attention returned from some far place.

"My father wishes our betrothal to be announced almost immediately, but I am persuaded you would prefer that we be seen in each other's company on some few occasions before I send the notice to the *Gazette*, so if I might propose . . ."

"It is very kind of you, Lord Torvil, to seek to spare my feelings, but I promise you it does not signify," she said indifferently. "Neither your friends nor mine would be taken in by such a move, and as for the rest of society," she gave a tiny shrug of her shoulders, "the opinion of strangers is a matter of complete unconcern to me. I suggest you fall in with the earl's wishes as far as possible."

Nicholas stared in real surprise at this unreachable girl who would soon be his wife—no, he amended that, who would soon be his wife in the eyes of the world. For Miss Harmon's sake he had been quite reconciled to the need for delay in the public announcement in order that the engagement should not become any more of a matter for speculation and gossip than would be natural to a surprise betrothal following a whirlwind courtship. He had been prepared to make a stand against his father had the earl proved adamant on this point, but here was the object of his charitable impulse refusing to be done charitably by. His feelings of annoyance did not bear analyzing at the moment. She appeared to be patiently awaiting some comment. His tone was stiff.

"Very well then. I'll send in the announcement immediately. Will you and your mother and sister do me the honor of accompanying me to the Opera tonight?"

"I'm sorry, we are already promised to some friends tonight."

Nicholas gritted his teeth at her cool refusal. "Tomorrow evening, then," he persisted, and when she still hesitated, laughed shortly. "Sooner or later you will be obliged to endure my company, you know. It would be well to become slightly better acquainted before we march up the aisle together, do you not agree?"

"I . . . yes, of course. Thank you, we shall be happy to come tomorrow."

Nicholas stood up, eager to be off before he laid violent hands on this most aggravating of all females.

"I'll arrange the details with Lady Langston," he said with a blandness she found distasteful, "and we can all discuss the wedding date between the acts. It should be a delightful evening. Until tomorrow then."

He made his unsmiling bride-to-be an elaborate bow and departed.

Chapter Six

As the door closed softly behind Lord Torvil, Kate's erect and graceful posture slumped abruptly in her chair. There was no denying the interview—confrontation rather, to give it its correct name—just concluded had been intensely enervating emotionally, but on the whole she thought she had reason to be satisfied with her performance. Given the advantage of the inadvertent knowledge gained from witnessing the viscount's encounter with his mistress, she had been utterly determined to control the meeting, and except for a bad moment following her proposal that their union should be in name only, she judged she had managed the feat, surely the first time in his devastating career that a female had gotten the better of that despicable man. Her lip curled somewhat bitterly. She must not be too quick to congratulate herself, though. For a moment before promising not to claim a husband's rights, he had looked extremely dangerous, and it was no part of her plan to arouse the beast in him, or indeed to provoke the hunter in his nature. She was personally inexperienced with his type of man, but, she trusted, neither dull witted nor naive. For the sake of her survival she must seek to fade into the background of his life as quickly as possible.

Not having been prepared for other than a compliant acceptance of the arrangement negotiated by their parents, he was off balance for the moment and genuinely surprised at her revulsion from him. And small wonder, she thought, with cynical amusement. Though not quite so classically handsome as his brother, his dark good looks and rugged masculinity must have been attracting the female of the species from the time he came out of nankeens.

"Sheep!" she muttered in disgust at the common failing of womankind.

So far he had not tried to exercise any charm of manner over her; in fact, his pique at her rejection had rendered him abrupt and cold, but she would wager her eyeteeth that their very next meeting would find him following a new tack. And she would be well advised to soften her response to him also. Aside from the unwisdom of making all of Society privy to the real situation between them, she must set a course that would permit her to endure the smallest amount of attention possible from the viscount as fiancé and husband. So long as she contrived to convince him that her initial revulsion had been tempered to a cool willingness to deal politely and distantly with him, she would be safe. At least as a married woman she would enjoy much more freedom of action than a single female was permitted. She was determined to derive some benefit from this loveless match.

Deb and her mother would be avidly awaiting a detailed report of what had passed between them. She longed for privacy in which to recover from the effects of three days of unalloyed misery, but was aware that this blessing would be short-lived indeed. Too restless to sit any longer, she began a slow, thoughtful pacing of the pretty sitting room as she went back over what was surely the strangest proposal scene of this or any season. Although the interview had pretty well run along a course of her making, she had been pleasantly surprised at the viscount's offer to postpone the official announcement until they had been seen together on several occasions. Based on the feelings toward the alliance that he had revealed at the Westerwood ball, she would never have credited him with the requisite degree of sensitivity and consideration.

Then why had she refused his offer in such a deliberately offhand manner? While she wrestled with this question, her light brown gaze was directed unseeingly at the graceful little satinwood desk beside which she had paused. Her fingers traced the delicate ormolu ornamentation on the corner of the leg while she acknowledged to herself that she had deliberately left him with the mistaken impression that she was impervious to gossip. No more than any other young woman did she wish to be generally regarded as incapable of arousing the affection of the man she would marry. The silky brows drew together and the busy fingers stilled as she struggled to give substance to her instinctive reaction. It must be that she refused to be beholden to him in any way. If she were to begin thinking of him as a man capable of kindness, it would distort and blur the image of him she had received at the Westerwood ball, and it was vital for her emotional survival in this marriage that she keep this image always sharp before her mind's eye. At this point in their acquaintance it might be next to impossible to conceive of harboring even a single friendly impulse toward Lord Torvil, but if she began to doubt the validity of what he had showed himself to be, she might allow herself to form an attachment to him and *then* she would lay herself open to the wounds that only those closest to one could inflict. In this case forewarned must be forearmed.

At this point in her reflections Deb came dancing into the room, followed slowly by Lady Langston, who could not quite erase a slightly apprehensive expression. The events of the past few days had caused her to seriously question her knowledge of her elder daughter's character and she was not about to breathe a sigh of relief until she read the announcement in the *Gazette* with her own eyes. Her glance flew to Kate's face and she was slightly reassured by the serenity displayed thereon. Evidently the second meeting between the affianced pair had gone smoothly.

"Tell me everything that occurred!" Deb was being adorably imperious. "What did he say? What did you reply? Everything!"

Kate smiled at her sister's impatience but limited her comments to a vague summary of the meeting. When a disappointed Deborah demanded details she was treated to a colorful description of the viscount's sartorial appearance, and with that she had to be content, for Kate turned her attention to her mother and tendered the viscount's invitation for the following evening. It seemed that, unlike Lord Torvil, Lady Langston saw nothing to deplore in the fact that the couple's first public appearance together should follow rather than precede the announcement of their engagement, or if she did she kept her reservations to herself and began in a businesslike fashion to plan their wardrobes for the Opera.

Lady Langston had exquisite taste and was also prodigiously clever with her needle. Despite the low ebb of the family fortunes, she contrived to present herself and her daughters flawlessly gowned on all occasions. Though an experienced eye might detect the occasional refurbishing of a costume, the girls were always becomingly, if not expensively dressed, for their choice was guided by their parent's unerring ability to judge what style and color would set off each to her best advantage.

Their efforts were well rewarded the next night by the charmingly expressed compliments of Lord Torvil, himself the epitome of restrained elegance in the severe black and white evening ensemble brought into fashion by Mister Brummell some years previously. His breadth of shoulder and erect bearing would make him an outstanding figure in any clothing, but the black tail coat was particularly flattering to his lean good looks.

Lady Langston was also wearing black this evening, a flowing black velvet that made her skin appear whiter than ever. Her matching shawl, lavishly lined and fringed in white silk, could only be worn to advantage by a woman of such extreme slenderness. Her luxuriant black tresses were dressed high on her head and ornamented by white ostrich feathers held in place by diamond clips. Excitement had put a sparkle in her dark eyes and color in her cheeks, and none save the severest critic could have accused the viscount of flattery when he declared he could not accept her as the mother of two grown daughters.

The ladies received him in the main saloon so there was no opportunity for the engaged couple to be private, but with no slightest show of embarrassment, the viscount produced a small jeweler's box which he presented to his betrothed with a courtly bow. For the briefest instant Kate struggled against her reluctance to accept anything from him before coolly receiving the tiny box with murmured thanks. With fingers that were quite steady she opened it and stared speechlessly at the ring blazing away before her eyes.

"I hope you like it," Lord Torvil said with a convincing tinge of anxiety in his deep voice. "The moment I saw it I felt it was made for you. You were meant to wear topaz and diamonds." As Kate still made no move to touch the gorgeous thing, he calmly took it from the box and slipped it on her unresisting hand, kissing her fingers in a light, graceful gesture before stepping back to allow an excited Deborah to come closer to admire it.

"Oh, Kate darling, it is magnificent. Just perfect for you!"

Kate had lovely hands, long fingered and slim with smooth skin and tapering nails. The cluster of topaz stones and diamonds in an unusual spray setting of gold was indeed a perfect complement, and Lady Langston added her praises to Deborah's. The viscount had not taken his eyes from his betrothed's face, a fact of which she was highly conscious. She recovered quickly from her surprised delight at the first sight of the ring and flicked a composed look at Lord Torvil.

"Thank you, my lord; it is quite the loveliest ring I have ever seen."

Kate was a good sport and her quiet voice revealed none of the reluctance she felt in accepting and praising a gift from Lord Torvil. He might have guessed at her state of mind, however, because a slightly mocking little smile teased at the corners of his mouth.

"How clever of us to have chosen amber for you to wear tonight, my dear child."

Lady Langston's complacent voice brought her attention back. The plainly styled amber satin with only a self-trim of ruching at the hem was glamorized by the loan of her mother's colorful Norwich silk shawl which she draped gracefully about her arms. As Lady Langston had often said, "Good things pay for themselves," and Kate presented a most agreeable picture of elegant simplicity.

"I'll be the most envied man at Covent Garden tonight," the viscount assured his ladies suavely, and he grinned at Deborah's infectious giggle. Certainly no man having the honor to be seen with the dark and vivacious young girl should have any complaints about his lot. She resembled a blooming tea rose in her demure orangey-pink silk, embroidered all over with tiny white flowers. A white ribbon threaded through her bouncy black curls, and she was in sparkling spirits that enhanced her vivid prettiness. And that made two out of three ladies favorably disposed, he thought with an inward smile, as eventually he escorted the women to his father's town carriage, borrowed for the occasion, and assisted them to enter. Deborah chatted away unself-consciously, and by the time they reached the theater was already on a first-name basis with her future brother-in-law. The easy conversation between them needed only an occasional comment from Lady Langston or Kate, so the latter's unusual quietness was not noticeable. She was engrossed in her own thoughts and was rather allowing the talk to wash over her head when they entered the theater and proceeded up the long staircase toward the second tier of boxes. Lady Langston and Deborah were a few steps higher.

"Kate," began the viscount, about to address some innocuous remark to her. He noticed the slight start she gave at being roused from her self-absorption and misunderstood the reason. Just barely his lips compressed, but his voice merely held a trace of amused condescension.

"It won't do, you know, to have people hear us addressing each other as Miss Harmon and Lord Torvil. This engagement will be a nine days' wonder as it is. My name is Nicholas. My friends call me Nick."

His mistress had called him Nick with a caressing

75

note in her husky voice. "I believe I prefer Torvil," Kate murmured.

He shrugged. "Just as you like. Have you had a busy time of it today, receiving calls of congratulations?"

"Oh, yes."

He waited for a moment for any amplification she might choose to add, then continued his probing. "Was it very trying?"

"Oh, yes," she admitted with no change in the serenity of the profile that was all he could see as they continued to climb, "but I will concede that most of our callers *tried*, at least, to contain their curiosity. Very few came right out and inquired how I had managed to snare such a marriage-shy bachelor."

"And did you satisfy their curiosity?"

"I smiled a lot and agreed that it was a short courtship. After two such calls Mama allowed me to develop a sudden headache, and she and Deb handled the rest of our visitors without me."

"Well, it was inevitable, of course. You might have avoided it."

At this reference to his offer to delay the announcement, she shrugged lightly. "I'll survive the ordeal."

By now they had reached the earl's box, putting an end to their uncomfortable conversation while the business of assigning seats was accomplished. Nicholas had invited his brother and Mister Waksworth to make up the numbers, and introductions were made in a remarkably short order. He noted that Kate's smile of greeting to his brother tonight held none of the radiance he had observed at Almack's, but at least the addition of two personable males to the party had the effect of easing the strain in the few moments remaining before the curtain rose on the first act. In fact, by the time the production opened, an excellent understanding was flourishing amongst the members of the viscount's party, and he was pleased to note that his fiancée's eyes held no trace of the somberness that he had observed in his previous encounters with her.

During the first interval Nicholas leaned nearer his betrothed to quiz her reaction to the production of Mozart's *Così fan Tutte*.

Kate gave him an unclouded smile. "I am finding it quite delightful, and all the singers are marvelous, though I do not care for quite so much *vibrato* as Dorabella displays."

"Do you sing yourself?"

"Not a note," she replied firmly.

"Good."

The satisfaction in his voice prompted a gurgle of laughter from Kate, and the first duplication he had been privileged to witness of the mischievous look that had caught his attention at Almack's.

"You sound like a man who has been a captive audience at one amateur performance too many," she ventured gaily.

"Dozens too many." He grinned back with uncalculated charm, and thus it was that the first of an unending stream of visitors to their box entered to discover the newly affianced pair isolated in a strangely intimate little scene.

It was the last private moment the party was to enjoy that evening, however, for theirs was undoubtedly the most popular box in the theater, thanks to the notice that had appeared in that day's edition of the *Gazette*. For the most part the mood was gay and the felicitations pleasantly sincere. Excitement lent a particularly lovely color to Kate's normally pale, clear skin, but she responded composedly, if a bit shyly, to the unusual attention, not only from her own friends and Lord Torvil's but also from a number of persons who had known her father. Even a few people who were intimates of Lord Sedgeley came to meet the heir's bride-to-be. Lord Torvil's manner in presenting her to a number of strangers could not be faulted, and she was able to relax and enjoy herself to a degree she would not have dared to hope for even three hours previously. It was a comfort, certainly, to realize from a number of admiring glances that, with her lovely mother and vivacious sister beside her, the Harmon family made a more than creditable impression on these same strangers. Sneaking a peek at her fiancé, she was compelled to admit that he was playing his part to perfection. Anyone might have imagined, from his relaxed and faintly possessive attitude, that he had carefully chosen his bride from amongst all the most desirable girls in the kingdom, which, though ridiculous, was hardly a thing about which to complain, she reminded herself hastily.

In fact, the only uncomfortable moments of the evening were provided by her brother. Lord Langston had been spending a few days in the country with friends and Kate had not seen him since before the issue of marriage arose. On questioning her mother about the negotiations that had taken place over the arranging of the contract, she had been astonished to learn that she was not the only one who had been kept in the dark until the arrangements were concluded. Lady Langston had not thought it necessary to inform her son of her intentions with regard to her elder daughter's future. Kate knew Roger had returned to town because his valet had made his presence felt in the servants' hall, according to Becky, but Roger had not dined at home, and Kate was unsure whether he had as yet learned of her betrothal.

During the second interval she had spotted a dark curly head amongst the young bucks in the pit and wondered if it could be Roger, though she had never known him to be a patron of the Opera. Unfortunately, her attention was claimed before she could make sure of the identity of that curly head. He appeared after the next act, putting an end to her doubts. It seemed he now knew of her engagement and he was not pleased, judging from the stiffness in his manner when Lady Langston made him known to Lord Torvil. Kate eyed her brother in some perturbation. She knew that glittering look.

Roger was having difficulty in containing his ire, and she was not surprised when under his breath, he muttered, "Come down to breakfast early, Katie. I want to talk to you."

She nodded and glanced at Lord Torvil to see if he had overheard, but he was greeting more newcomers to the box and when she looked around again, Roger had departed.

The viscount had arranged for his guests to partake of a late supper at a good hotel. The repast was splendid and the party a merry one, thanks to Deborah's uninhibited high spirits and Lord Torvil's ability to keep the conversation moving over a variety of topics. Consequently, it was not until the small hours that he escorted the ladies home. They were all able to thank him quite sincerely for a most entertaining evening, though it must be added that his betrothed's gratitude was expressed in somewhat cooler terms than that of the other ladies.

As the door closed behind them, Kate was congratulating herself on the accuracy of her prediction regarding the viscount's behavior. The charm had been very much in evidence tonight, but she had been prepared for that. After all, it stood to reason that a man could scarcely acquire the reputation of being a rake without knowing how to make himself agreeable to women. Her brows drew together slightly as it struck her that the fact that he had a mistress did not necessarily brand him as a rake or libertine. Admittedly, she had jumped to this conclusion on the sole evidence of that one overheard conversation, but she had gleaned enough from the attitude of some of the people who had sought her out to offer felicitations to suggest that her guess was not far out. She had not been on the social scene long enough to have heard of him since they did not generally frequent the same places. Then, too, she had spent the previous few years away from town before her grandfather's death, and the family had been in mourning for a time afterward.

Lady Langston's satisfied voice broke into her thoughts as they attained the first-floor landing. "I must say that went extraordinarily well, a most agreeable evening."

Kate's murmur of assent was lost in Deb's huge yawn. As the tired girls headed up to their bedchambers on the second floor, Lady Langston remembered something else.

"Kate, did Lord Torvil mention anything about meeting his father?"

"Yes, Mama. Just as we entered he said he would call tomorrow—today, I mean, to discuss a wedding date. He said that I must soon meet the earl also."

"Splendid. Off to bed then, girls. It's little enough sleep we'll get as it is."

"Good night, Mama," came the sleepy chorus.

Kate's rest was to be even shorter than that of her relatives because she had promised her brother to join him for an early breakfast. True to her word, she appeared in the small dining room at eight o'clock. She had hastily donned a cool green muslin morning dress, but her hair was merely swept back from her face and secured with a ribbon. The style revealed the clear-cut oval of her face, but it also highlighted the heavy eyes and pallor after a scant five hours' sleep.

Roger took one look at her and shoved the coffee pot across the table.

"Here, get some of this inside you: You look a wreck," he commented with a brother's disregard for social niceties.

Obediently, she sipped some of the steaming brew she had poured into her cup, shuddered perceptibly at the bitter taste, and reached for the cream and sugar which she used with a lavish hand. Roger waited with a darkling look throughout this operation, then burst into speech.

"What is the story of this absurd engagement? When I left town five days ago, I'd have taken my oath you were not even acquainted with Torvil. I came back yesterday and dined at Humphrey's lodgings. He congratulated me on my sister's betrothal. You may imagine how I stared, but he had the paper and there it was in black and white. How do you think I felt, finding out that my sister was engaged from a newspaper? I came dashing home as soon as I might decently leave to find you all gone to the Opera with that fellow. I stayed just long enough to scramble into my rig and take off after you, but I apprehend I must consider myself fortunate to have gained entrance to your box for even thirty seconds."

"Roger, I'm so sorry." Looking at her brother's glowering face, Kate felt terrible. "It all happened very quickly, but I never dreamed Mother had not consulted you about the arrangement. I was so upset myself I never even thought to ask her. The announcement was wholly my fault. Lord Torvil offered to postpone it, and if I had not been so determined not to accept any favors from him, you would not have had to read about it in the newspaper." She fell silent, noting that her incoherent explanation had served merely to turn his anger into something more nearly resembling anxiety.

He said quietly, "All right, Katie, let's have the whole unvarnished tale."

She recounted everything except the conversation she had overheard at the Westerwood ball, which meant that she faltered a bit in her description of that first meeting with Lord Torvil. He interrupted her to demand incredulously, "Why should you take a man in such dislike the instant you clap eyes on him that you cannot bear to be presented to him? Come now, Kate, that won't wash. Deb might do something of the sort, she's featherbrained enough, but not you."

Kate had gotten herself backed into a corner where only the truth would suffice. As she described the scene at the Westerwood ball, Roger's face took on an alarming expression of fury. He leaned forward and grabbed the hand that had been toying incessantly with her coffee spoon and gripped it tightly.

"Damn it, Kate, you cannot marry this fellow! It isn't so much the fact that he's had his *affaires*; they don't mean much, but as I understand you, he was coerced into offering for you without ever having set eyes on you. Under the circumstances he might well feel there's no need to treat you with any consideration at all. He could make your life miserable." He dropped her hand and walked over to the window, staring out with his fists jammed into his pockets. "We're in pretty tough shape financially, and a lot of it is my fault, I know, but I'm not going to stand by and watch my sister sold to a damned, heartless rake. Somehow I'll get you out of this engagement, Katie."

Kate blinked back sudden tears at the evidence of her brother's concern for her and joined him at the window. She slipped a hand under his arm and leaned

82

her head briefly against his shoulder. "I have not yet told you about Deb and her captain," she said quietly.

As she finished her story she could feel the rigidity of his arm under her hand, and she shook it slightly. As Roger turned to scrutinize her serene countenance, she met his look steadily.

"At first I was deeply resentful about having to marry a man like Lord Torvil, but I won't see Deb sacrificed when her affections are engaged. Also, I do not think Lord Torvil is disposed to be too inconsiderate toward his wife. For my sake he offered to postpone the announcement until we had been seen together several times to curtail the gossip and speculation the betrothal would cause, and his behavior toward me last night was all that could be desired in a fiancé." She smiled a trifle ruefully and displayed her ring. "He bought me this because he said I was meant to wear topaz and diamonds."

Roger was studying her with a curious intentness. "The fellow's got charm to burn; that don't mean he'll be a good husband."

"I do not expect him to be a good husband," his sister replied coolly, "but my knowledge of him is a protection, indeed a guarantee, that he won't break my heart. He won't be allowed to. Besides," she continued with a slightly heightened color and a shifting of her gaze, "he has agreed to let the marriage remain one in name only for a year or two. So you need have no fear for me, Roger. It is necessary for one of us to marry for money, and I am better equipped than Deb to endure it."

Lord Langston stared at his sister in great perturbation. Did she actually believe such an agreement would stand in the way of a man like Torvil? He knew of his reputation, of course, although the difference in their ages was sufficient to keep them in different circles. Women represented a challenge to such a man. With a girl who looked like Kate on the other side of his bedroom door, how long would a promise keep it shut? It was madness to expect it! He opened his mouth to tell her so in no uncertain terms, but the opening of the door to the butler's pantry prevented him from speaking. By the time Emmett had departed, carrying the half-empty platter of meats from which the young baron had replenished his strength, he had thought better of his impulse. It was his experience that women believed what they wished to believe, though a man might tell them the contrary till he turned blue in the face. Kate was determined to go through with this cold-blooded marriage and nothing he could say would serve to change her mind. He had no real personal knowledge of Torvil to speak from, but nothing he'd heard or seen since last night was likely to allay the fears he felt for his sister's future. He stared gloomily at her as she sat across the table from him unconcernedly making a very good meal from the eggs and kippers Emmett had served her.

"When is this marriage to take place?"

She paused between bites. "I don't precisely know, but quite soon I expect—however long it takes to get the banns put up. We were supposed to discuss it at the Opera last night but did not get the opportunity."

"I did notice your popularity," commented Roger dryly, "but seriously, I think you'd be well advised to make it a long engagement. Take time to get to know each other."

"Frankly, I feel I know Lord Torvil better than I would wish to already. I'd liefer get married quickly so all this notoriety can fade, and we will not be obliged to be seen together constantly." At the look on her brother's face, Kate extended her hand in a gesture of comfort. "Don't look like that. I promise you I have accepted the necessity for the marriage, and I fully intend to enjoy all the advantages of the married state."

"All of them?"

"There's no call to be indelicate, Roger." Kate put up her chin.

"There's no need to behave like an ostrich, Kate," he mimicked with grim humor.

After this riposte the conversation languished. Roger was apparently sunk deep in thought. Her appetite suddenly gone, Kate pushed away her half-filled plate and took up her coffee cup in both hands. Her frowning concentration on the rapidly cooling contents did not waver until Deborah came bouncing into the room ten minutes later.

Chapter Seven

The viscount paid a morning call on his betrothed, determined to use all his powers of persuasion to press for an early wedding. Certainly his financial embarrassment dictated this course, for on his marriage his allowance would be greatly increased to support the responsibility of maintaining an establishment in the style befitting the heir to an affluent earldom. Despite his faults as a parent, Lord Sedgeley could never be accused of being niggardly. He had always made his sons a generous allowance and they would be the first to admit that he could scarcely be held accountable if the excesses of youth rendered them unable from time to time to live within their means.

Greatly though Nicholas would have preferred to arrive at a better understanding with his fiancée before taking their vows, last night's experience had amply confirmed that her initial revulsion from him would not easily be overcome. Each of his private conversational overtures had been met with a pleasant civility that was enough to chill the blood of anyone able to discern the wall of reserve behind the social manner. Thankfully, she seemed to relax her guard a bit in company, permitting a natural friendliness and interest in others to lend more spontaneity to her conversation. At these times *he* was included in the radius of her inherent warmth. He should be grateful that she contrived to conceal her true feelings in public, thus lessening the amount of gossip, but honesty compelled him to admit that gratitude was not among the feelings struggling for supremacy in his breast as he banged the knocker on the Harmon front door with more force than was strictly necessary.

An hour later he descended the same steps, a tiny line between his dark brows and their upward curve more satanic than usual as he set his curly-brimmed beaver at a precise angle. He began to stroll slowly toward White's, but his attention was upon his thoughts rather than on anything along his path. His reactions on being compelled to contract an arranged marriage had been straightforward and predictable, with anger uppermost, accompanied by a corresponding reluctance to proceed. Once acted upon, however, he would have anticipated feeling nothing save a flat boredom as he went through the motions of performing his expected part in the customary betrothal routine, with perhaps an impatience to be done with the charade. Once married, he would be able to take up his interrupted life again, though unfortunately never quite so free to order the activities of his days and nights with no reference to anything save his own interest. As matters had arranged themselves, however, boredom was the farthest thought from his mind.

If he had to describe his state of mind during the early days of his engagement, he would have to admit to feeling *baffled* rather than anything of a more positive or negative nature. His mood had swung from pleased surprise on discovering the identity of his in-

tended bride to consternation almost in the next moment when he imagined his brother might have an
interest in that direction. Once this situation had been
clarified (from Robin's angle at least) he had
proceeded to the actual proposal with an impersonal
satisfaction that the girl's looks and behavior pleased
him. And that had been the last moment when anything had gone according to his expectations. The first
interview with Kate had been productive of shock and
chagrin; his brain had been busy conjecturing during
the interval before their second meeting, and he had
come out of that one engaged but strangely dissatisfied.
Since then their two additional meetings had only
served to increase his impatience to get to the bottom
of his fiancée's inexplicable aversion to him, and, he
must acknowledge, to increase his now burning desire
to reverse her disapprobation. Kate would have been
perfectly appalled to learn just how quickly she had
succeeded in arousing the hunter in the viscount's
nature.

Nicholas paused in his ruminating to raise his hat
politely to an old friend of his mother's, and was constrained to accept the lady's gushing felicitations with a
well-concealed impatience to be gone. In reply to her
query he admitted that they had just set the date for
the wedding—four weeks hence. Once armed with
news to impart to all and sundry, she showed less inclination to dally, and Nicholas was able to extricate
himself from a conversation that had interrupted his
train of thought.

He walked on slowly, reviewing this latest session
with Kate. Again she had received him in company
with her mother and sister and again she had been politely responsive to all his suggestions. Any wedding
date he decided upon was acceptable to her and, yes,
she would have ample time to gather her bride clothes

together. At this point Lady Langston had ventured an objection but had been silenced by her daughter's calm reiteration of her willingness to accomplish what was necessary in four weeks' time. Kate would be most happy to meet her prospective father-in-law at the earliest date Torvil and the earl might find convenient, and, no, she had no objection (and no interest either, he had fumed) to taking up residence initially in his maternal grandfather's empty house on Albemarle Street. It was exceedingly kind of Lord Bartram to offer his house to his grandson and his bride, and she would look forward to making his lordship's acquaintance at the wedding.

At the time he had been too pleased to have his suggestions ratified so easily to cavil at her attitude, but the more he thought about it the more annoyed he became. She had behaved with all the insipid propriety of a Bath miss, and that she was *not*! He had been privileged to see her in a naturally mischievous mood at Almack's, in great agitation on the occasion of their first meeting, and proudly dignified at their second. For some reason she was now determined to present herself as completely cool and passionless, indeed almost without personality, but he was not deceived by her playacting, annoyingly competent though it might be. Her pretense had slipped a bit when he had tentatively suggested that she might prefer to postpone a wedding trip until the summer since the season would still be in full swing in late May. Though her voice was indifferent, her eyes had flashed defiant amber fire as she had questioned the necessity of a wedding trip at any time. This had had the unexpected effect of firing him with a determination to compel her to accede to going away the instant the vows were spoken, but common sense and sanity had prevailed, and he had made no answer except with his own eloquent eyes.

There had been one other disturbing element at the meeting—her brother. He had not failed to notice the ill-concealed grimness beneath Lord Langston's civil manner on their introduction at the Opera last night, but he had dismissed that as the natural reaction of a young man who was nominally the head of his family upon learning that his mother had arranged his sister's marriage settlement without consulting him or even advising him of the fact. Lord Sedgeley had told his son that all his dealings had been with Lady Langston, who was her daughter's guardian, though only considerations of Lord Langston's extreme youth prevented him from approaching the latter in preference to dealing with a woman. When Nicholas had noticed Kate searching the audience in the pit, she had mentioned that she had thought she had caught a glimpse of her brother, and had added that he had been away for nearly a sennight. Today, however, when presumably he had had an opportunity to discuss the matter with his mother and sister, there had been no increase in cordiality in Langston's manner when he had joined them for a few moments. The hard expression in the young man's eyes when studying himself had sat oddly upon his youthful countenance, aging it perceptibly. Obviously Roger disliked the match, though his excesses were in no slight degree responsible for the necessity for the contract. In Kate's presence he could do nothing to reassure the young chub that he would treat his sister with every consideration, but he must make an effort to see him privately in the immediate future.

As Nicholas climbed the steps to his club, he had reached the inescapable conclusion that, although far from dull, the period of his betrothal promised to be both uncomfortable and frustrating at times.

Four weeks later he could admit the rueful necessity

of congratulating himself on the unfortunate accuracy of this prediction.

Events in the interval between his betrothal and marriage had more than justified his presentiment of discomfort and frustration, and he could but be thankful that a longer engagement had not been decided upon. He had performed the task expected of him in providing an almost constant escort to the polite stranger who was his fiancée. The time had passed pleasantly enough in the main, though there had been a fair number of unavoidable engagements that had proved just as tedious as anticipated. Even if he and Kate had been rapturously in love, the necessity of being constantly on parade, as it were, could not have been less than irksome. As matters stood, however, he found himself becoming increasingly irritated at the chains that were being tightened about him, perhaps especially so when he considered that his fiancée moved imperturbably through the ordeal with a cool grace that annoyed him increasingly. Though he admired her social finesse, he would have preferred to have guided an awkward but trusting girl through the social intricacies. At least then he would have felt that he had something to contribute to the scene apart from his physical presence. Kate neither sought nor required support from him as she moved confidently through the prodigious number of social engagements and entertainments arranged in honor of the affianced pair.

Regrettably, their relationship was as impersonal at the end of the betrothal as on the day she accepted his suit. Nor, except for small gleanings from his own observation, did he know the real Kate one whit better after a dozen evenings spent in each other's company than on that, their second meeting. He knew well that this was exactly the way Kate desired matters, but hours devoted to the problem had not brought him any insight into why she preferred to keep a thick wall between them. At first he had striven earnestly to forge a better understanding, but her persistent refusal to recognize and respond to his overtures had quickly cured him of his good intentions. Though ashamed of his reactions in his better moments, he had commenced sniping at her in private, telling himself that any reaction at all was preferable to her impersonal affability. Perhaps it was fortunate that they spent almost no time in each other's exclusive company because his most provocative thrusts had met with an identical response on his fiancée's part. She blandly ignored any personal remarks and was always quite content to remain silent until he wished to discuss an impersonal topic or until he asked her something that demanded a reply. She accepted compliments unblushingly, but with an air of disinterest, and when he pointedly denied her compliments that might be expected of a suitor, she accepted this situation with equal composure, never directing at her fiancé, when complimented by a third party, a single one of those looks most females seemed unable to resist, that said plainly "others appreciate what you do not."

A case in point had been the initial meeting between the earl and his prospective daughter-in-law. Nicholas had escorted Kate to his family home for dinner one evening shortly after the official announcement of the engagement. As they ascended the outside stairs he had sought to soothe away any apprehensions or qualms she might have been suffering at the prospect of being looked over by a notoriously difficult and intimidating personage. She had turned those enormous golden brown eyes to his face in a more searching look than any she had directed at him up to then, but on her lips was a little smile that had struck him as being so condescending that it had the instant effect of causing him to abandon her to her own devices with his father. Accordingly he had escorted her to the main saloon under the benevolent eye of Marsden, then had left her in solitude while he sought out his father in his study, surprising the butler by a dismissal, but not noticeably discomposing his betrothed who was sitting on a green velvet chair taking stock of the elegant furnishings of the room. When he returned with the earl, it was to find a smiling Kate being very well entertained by his brother. She rose at the sight of his father and came forward a few steps. He knew by her quick glance from father to son that she had marked the resemblance and wondered with a wicked delight if she would freeze his sire because of the unfortunate similarity.

It seemed not.

"My dear child," said the earl at his unsuspected, courtly best, "this is indeed a pleasure. I have been eagerly looking forward to this meeting."

Kate smiled with eyes and mouth. "Your lordship is most kind. I, too, have looked forward to our meeting. I understand from my mother that you were a friend of my grandfather's."

The earl was still holding Kate's hand which he now patted with a paternal gesture that astounded his sons. "Yes, my dear, and I see that you have a very great look of him, especially about the eyes. That particular shade of brown is quite rare. Though I had not seen your grandfather for fifteen years prior to his death, I am going to claim the privilege of this old and lasting friendship to call you Kate, which I believe was his name for you."

"I shall be delighted to have you do so, sir," Kate replied simply.

Before his speechless sons knew what was happening, the earl had whisked Kate off to the library to

93

show her a chased gold inkwell that had been a gift from her grandfather thirty years before.

"Well, a conquest, by gad!" declared Robin theatrically. "Who would have thought that our little Kate was just in the pater's style?"

"I should have done, I suppose. After all she was *his* choice, albeit sight unseen." Nick's thoughtful tones became brisk as he added, "And may I correct you on one small point, brother? She is not *our* Kate, but mine, for better or worse."

Robin refused to take offense. "Well, you'll just have to lend her services when I need someone to intervene with the old man for me." At his brother's sardonic expression he explained carelessly, "At the very least, a loving sister-in-law should be good for that, and perhaps a few meals before quarter day."

It was fully ten minutes before the earl and Kate returned, obviously on the best of terms with each other, and as Marsden had appeared to announce dinner, the earl retained possession of Kate's arm to escort her into the dining room.

The talk at dinner touched lightly on many subjects and occasionally delved deeper into some literary or political criticisms. The earl dominated the conversation, addressing most of his remarks to Kate, despite a determined participation by Nicholas. Initially, Kate's sense of social duty prompted her to try to include the younger men in the discussion, but Lord Sedgeley ruthlessly overrode his heir's opinions and slew unborn any original thoughts his younger son might have expressed by forthrightly condemning him as a silly lobcock, unfit for better society than a lady's drawing room. From long habit Robin took this in good part, better in fact than did Miss Harmon, who appeared ready to bristle slightly, though whether on behalf of the Honourable Robin or in defense of the level of conversational skill

94

attained in ladies' drawing rooms, they were not to learn, for the earl immediately drew her attention back to his discourse. Soon she abandoned her efforts to promote a general discussion from the necessity to devote all her mental energies to following her host's brilliant but sometimes convoluted reasonings. To Nicholas, watching her as closely as possible while carrying on a desultory conversation with his brother, his fiancée appeared to have succumbed completely to the spell of eloquent intensity his father could create when he chose to exert himself. Unless she was a consummate actress she was totally absorbed in her host. He and Robin might not have existed for all the attention they received. Though she did not venture more than one or two mild challenges to his lordship's theories, her rapid comprehension must have pleased him, for he continued to expand on his themes throughout the delicious meal served by Marsden and one of the footmen. Nicholas, who knew all the old retainer's little ways, was cynically aware of the benevolent approval welling up behind Marsden's impeccably wooden facade as he unobtrusively carried out his duties. Kate had added another conquest, it seemed. She certainly did not appear to require any assistance from him in smoothing her path into his family. He was conscious of a faint resentment, if this was not too strong a word, that this should be so, and this feeling might have prompted his next unbecoming actions.

The earl turned from his guest to his heir, saying with a heavy attempt at gallantry, "You are to be felicitated, my boy, upon winning a bride who will do you the greatest credit."

Considering the circumstances, this was coming in much too strong! Ignoring the blatant cue, Nicholas said smoothly, "You are too generous, sir. All the credit must go to you."

His father glared at him but closed his lips after a quick glance at Kate revealed that this lack of chivalry had apparently passed unnoticed. She was calmly searching in her reticule for her handkerchief, her face serene and composed.

And so it was throughout the period of their betrothal—pleasant enough on the surface, but with each meeting producing a minute accretion in the structure of frustration Nicholas had foreseen. Perhaps the thing that chafed most was his seeming inability to overlook the unsatisfactory aspect of their relationship. He could—and repeatedly did—tell himself that a marriage such as his and Kate's was destined to be did not require that they be en rapport. The fact that between his first glimpse of Kate and that abortive first meeting there must have sprouted some semirealized but tenacious idea of what their union might mean was a clear indication that after all, he had not outgrown a romantic and unrealistic conception of marriage. In this respect, Kate, young as she was, had proved the more realistic of the two. She might have taken him in dislike, but after that involuntary revulsion, she had calmly suppressed her personal feelings and set about readying herself for her new position with a total lack of wasteful emotion.

His own efforts to do the same might have been more satisfactory had he continued to enjoy the familiar pleasures of his association with Lady Montaigne on a regular basis during his betrothal. It soon became apparent, however, that Cécile had been correct when she had protested that she would see much less of him. His imagination was inadequate to the high flight required to picture Kate demanding his attention, but certainly the fact of being an affianced bridegroom made great demands on his time. The first occasion after the announcement of his engagement when he had been able to visit Cécile had been the night he had first introduced his fiancée to his father. He had returned Kate to her home at a fairly early hour after an evening spent watching the earl monopolize her attention, in a mood to enjoy a bit of feminine attention himself. It had not improved his temper to find Cécile out when he arrived at the slim house on Green Street where she lived with a faded female dependent who supposedly lent her countenance, but was most conveniently invisible upon request. There was no question of his being admitted, of course, and he spent the next two hours awaiting Cécile's return, glancing through some periodicals in her boudoir between bouts of impatient prowling about the ultrafeminine room with its superfluity of mirrors. There was certainly no excuse for Cécile's not being familiar with every angle and view of her lovely self, clothed or naked. By the time his *inamorata* arrived home he was heartily sick of the sight of his own dark visage reflected in a dozen surfaces.

At first Cécile was inclined to be a bit difficult, and he was not enamored of the triumphant little smile she did not trouble to hide. She also displayed an irritating curiosity concerning the personality, behavior and physical attributes of his fiancée which he was exceedingly loath to gratify. He forestalled any tendencies she might be entertaining toward holding a philosophical discussion about the state of his emotions by taking her in his arms. This argument had always proved effective in the past and it did not fail him on this occasion. When he left Cécile several hours later, his usual equanimity was largely restored and he had more or less relegated his intended bride to the negligible position he had once blithely assumed she would occupy in his emotional life.

Unfortunately, as time passed, she refused to remain neatly compartmentalized. Kate would have been dismayed to learn that she was fast becoming an obsession with her fiancé, but such was indeed the case. Nicholas managed to visit Lady Montaigne twice more in the following fortnight, but on neither occasion did her beauty and abundant charms completely succeed in wiping from his mind a persistent image of the lovely, unreachable, and thoroughly maddening girl to whom he was betrothed. And then, less than ten days before his wedding, Lady Montaigne, with tears glistening in her large blue eyes, informed him that she was going to Yorkshire for a long delayed visit to her mother because she could not bear to be in town when he was married to another. Nicholas protested, but even in his own ears his protests rang rather weakly. It had not been a comfortable experience threading his way through a maze of social events as escort to his fiancée, keeping one eye and half his brain always on the alert to discover whether Cécile, who did indeed have the *entrée* everywhere, was among the invited guests. Once when Cécile had indicated her intention of attending a rout party to which he had planned to escort Kate, he found himself formulating an excuse to change their destination that night. The altered plans had not presented any real difficulty since Kate was in the habit of deferring to her mother or himself when it came to social engagements. Not that Nicholas was lulled into believing that she acted thusly because her nature was essentially persuadable; he was well aware that she simply did not give a damn where she went. Each event represented one more duty to fulfill and all were indifferently equal in her estimation.

Chapter Eight

It would have been a considerable consolation to Nicholas to learn that the period of their betrothal was fully as great a trial to Kate as to himself. Not having been acquainted with her before their contract was made, however, he had no way of knowing just how difficult she was finding the maintenance of her unnaturally emotionless behavior, so he was denied the comfort of this knowledge. She was, of necessity, involved in the details of planning her wedding, and this experience did little to reduce the strain of the relationship between the affianced pair.

Four weeks was not a particularly long period in which to plan the big society wedding the earl and Lady Langston favored, though it was most generous compared with the mad scramble that had often occurred in the past century when matches were made and finalized in an aura of quite unnecessary haste and secrecy that appeared ridiculous from a modern vantage point. It was no longer fashionable to marry a couple secretly in the dressing room of the bride-groom's mother while five hundred guests danced merrily in the ballroom, unaware that they had another cause for celebration than the ostensible reason for the ball. Over the past two decades or so there had been a growing trend toward marrying in church with a number of friends and relatives present and then celebrating the event with a reception immediately following the ceremony to which a vast multitude was invited. Since marriages could not be solemnized except between the hours of 8:00 A.M. and noon, the reception that followed was referred to as a *déjeuner*, though breakfast was a singularly inappropriate term to apply to the elaborate feasts that had become *de rigueur* amongst the members of the *ton*.

Like most other society brides, Kate would be married at St. George's in Hanover Square. The earl had tactfully requested the privilege of hosting (and financing) the *déjeuner* on the grounds that his mansion could so much more comfortably accommodate the huge numbers of persons who would have been insulted to be overlooked on such a happy occasion. Although Gunter's was hired to do the catering and would undoubtedly provide a cake, his lordship's own chef, with the light of battle in his Gallic eye, had begged for the honor of creating the main bride cake for the viscount's nuptials. None of this masterpiece of the confectioner's art would be broken over the bride's head as had been customary in bygone days and still occurred in some form in remote rural areas. This cake would be neatly boxed and sent off with each guest and to some who might not be able to attend in person "to dream on."

The traditional wedding favors of knots of white ribbon and artificial flowers for the guests were also being provided by his lordship, but he had graciously acceded to Deborah's request that she be allowed to supervise the decoration of the altar with flowers for her sister's wedding. Kate had been not a little amused at the way Deborah had captivated the allegedly forbidding earl on the two occasions when they had spent some time together. The pretty deference in the young girl's manner could not be faulted, but she did rather tend to regard the earl in the light of an indulgent uncle. It was Lord Sedgeley's unquestioning acceptance of this role that caused Kate to smile inwardly. She had been touched and vastly relieved to find his lordship's reception of herself so warmhearted and apparently sincere, especially since both his sons, without a word being spoken in his detriment, had left her with the impression that their father was a somewhat unapproachable figure. She was inclined to the view that the possession of a daughter or two might have made the earl more tolerant of his sons but readily conceded that she was not yet well enough acquainted with her prospective father-in-law to be entertaining opinions of such a personal nature. In any case she was deeply grateful that the only difficult person she had to deal with was her fiancé—always excepting Lady Langston, and long experience had taught her how best to accomplish her own ends when acting in concert with her volatile mother. With the viscount there was no such assurance of her ability to steer a safe course between the respect due to one who would soon be her lord and master and a rooted determination to achieve the greatest degree of emotional and actual independence from his necessary influence in her future life as might be possible in the circumstances.

Her initial hope that the viscount's involvement with his mistress, coupled with a natural resentment at being coerced into marriage, might work to her advantage in the pursuit of this aim had died a lingering death. It must be admitted that up to the present her laboriously maintained pose of distant friendliness had at best merely served to irritate and annoy him. She could dismiss any possibility of doubt on this point. Though she fervently hoped the vague alarums of her intuition were groundless, the uneasy suspicion had moved into her mind and taken root there that Torvil was far from uninterested in her as a person. There was a keenness in his glance and an alertness in his manner when she was speaking that warned her he was not accepting her at face value. It had not been her intention to annoy him (at least she trusted not!), but annoy him she did, and as the date of their marriage drew near she began to fear that he saw her very existence as a challenge to something deep in his nature—some instinctive urge to dominate and possess. He did not yet understand her, but he was determined to reduce her to something comprehensible so that he might then dismiss her from such intense concentration and go his merry way. The really appalling thing was that she no longer felt sure that she understood herself either. As her wedding day approached she was forced to admit that her masterly plan, so far from producing an attitude of casual acceptance of each other, had actually resulted in creating an atmosphere of tense awareness between the two. She knew that somehow she had failed to strike the correct chord. Though reasonably sure that her inability to relax and behave naturally in her fiancé's company was at fault, she seemed powerless to correct the situation. She simply did not *feel* relaxed in the viscount's presence; she was too aware of that masculine magnetism and too determined to remain unaffected by it to respond naturally to his overtures. He should *not* have another groveling victim at his feet on whom to trample unconcernedly.

She reviewed these unsatisfactory conclusions the day before her scheduled marriage as she frowned over a delicate pillow cover she was hemming. All three ladies had been working diligently on linens for Kate in the small gaps between social engagements, fittings for her hastily assembled wardrobe, and preparations for the wedding. Of course there was no possibility of producing an adequate supply in such a limited period, but by unspoken agreement they were all bound that some of Kate's finest household linens would be made by the Harmon ladies themselves.

There had been less agreement though many words were spoken concerning Kate's trousseau and other details of the wedding. From its inception, the young girl had regarded the contract as more a matter between Lady Langston and Lord Sedgeley than the two people whom it most nearly concerned. With an uncharacteristic docility, born of unhappiness, she had accepted others' suggestions as to the time and place and style in which her nuptials would be celebrated, but Kate was *not* meek, and though she might be unhappy about the choice of bridegroom, she would have been an unnatural female indeed to remain indifferent to all the plans and decisions that were being made by others with respect to *her* future.

The first indication that the elders would not have everything all their own way came when Kate flatly refused to have any other attendant bridemaiden than her sister. In recent years it had become the fashion to enlist the services of as many as six or even eight unmarried friends or relatives to act as bridemaiden; consequently, it was an agony to Lady Langston to be compelled to limit the scope of her managerial talents, but Kate remained adamant. When pressed for reasons for this apostasy, she pinned her mother with a serious look and declared herself unfit for the continuous task of acting the happy bride for the benefit of a gaggle of gushing, envious, and, after a telling pause, *talkative* females. The absolute shock on her mother's face confirmed what Kate had suspected. From a long established pattern of refusing to see what she did not wish to see, Lady Langston had convinced herself that her daughter had swiftly become reconciled to her arranged marriage and in fact was prepared to enjoy all the ceremonial trappings that went along with weddings. Reluctantly, tearfully, the mother of the bride conceded the wisdom of limiting the bridal party to her two daughters.

Kate was more amenable to advice concerning the selection of her wedding gown. She had no decided preference for the traditional white and silver over the newer pure white costume, and quite willingly accompanied her mother and sister to several drapers' establishments and modistes to look for a suitable fabric. When they discovered a length of white silk of cobweb delicacy, embroidered all over in silver with an exquisite design of acorns, leaves, and vines, all three ladies sighed with unanimous, radiant relief. Kate quailed at the exorbitant price tag attached to such a luxurious fabric, but Lady Langston did not turn a hair as she purchased it.

From the way her mother was scattering orders for expensive additions to all their wardrobes, Kate had nightmare visions of Lord Sedgeley's generous settlement being completely squandered on a costly celebration of a sham marriage. Thankfully, her mother was able to reassure her on this point. The terms of the settlement had included a lump sum for the payment of Lord Langston's debts as well as providing five thousand pounds for Deborah's marriage portion. Most of the money intended for the Harmon daughters had gone to pay debts that had accumulated before their father died so suddenly. To compound the family's difficulties, certain unfortunate investments toward the end of his life had reduced old Lord Langston's capital to such a degree that Broadwoods was more of a liability than an asset by the time Roger inherited it. It would take years of careful management and retrenchment if the estate was ever to recover from this blow. Roger had the assistance of an excellent man of business, but it was still an awesome responsibility for such an inexperienced young man.

With the removal of her fears that their prenuptial spending might result in continued straitened circumstances, Kate was able to enjoy the novel experience and somewhat guilty pleasure of choosing costumes, hats, and accessories in the plural, if not quite without any regard to cost, then her thrifty nature and earlier training in habits of economy must be held accountable.

Without doubt practically every woman of her acquaintance would make it a point to call on the new bride once it was known that she was "at home" to visitors. Since the couple was not going away she must assemble a suitable wardrobe in which to receive these visits before her wedding took place. There was always much interest in a bride's trousseau amongst her women friends.

She considered herself fortunate indeed to have the benefit of Lady Langston's advice in this prodigious task because her mother was noted for her sense of style. In only one instance did Kate have a strong enough preference to insist upon having her own way. She acquiesced readily to the design Lady Langston selected for her wedding gown, but vetoed her next suggestion of a wreath of artificial roses to wear upon her head in the current fashion for young brides.

"Mama," she said eagerly, "do you recall that beautiful shawl of Honiton lace that Papa gave you years ago? Well, if you should have no objection, I should like to wear this draped over a high comb in the manner of Spanish ladies."

Noting her daughter's air of anxious expectancy, Lady Langston's face softened immediately. Such a relief to find the child had at least *one* preference for what was, after all, the most important day in a girl's life. Still her reply was a trifle hesitant.

"I do not think there would be a problem in the effect created with your dress since it is essentially sleeveless and very simply styled, but this would be a departure from custom, my dear, and I am persuaded it would look more the thing if your hair was dressed in the Spanish mode, gathered at the back of your head. It might not be of a length sufficient to this purpose, and the style might not suit you."

"May we try, Mama, please?" begged Kate.

Deborah's clever fingers accomplished the task of drawing Kate's heavy hair to the back where she succeeded in anchoring it in a large, soft knot at the nape of her neck, not without some little difficulty, for the hair was, as feared, not quite long enough and was in addition a bit too curly to achieve the perfectly smooth effect desired.

But, as the *artiste* said optimistically, "It will be a bit longer in three weeks and the mantilla will conceal the shorter pieces on the top that have been pinned down."

The style itself was conceded by both ladies to be unexpectedly flattering in that it emphasized the perfect oval shape of Kate's face and the purity of her delicate profile. They had found a high comb in the Pantheon Bazaar and, after unwrapping the lace shawl from its layers of silver paper, draped it carefully over this ornament, stepping back simultaneously for a better look. Kate, who had remained docilely seated throughout the long process, could not conceal her disappointment at the little silence that followed this action.

"Oh, dear," she sighed. "Doesn't it become me?"

"My dearest child, you look absolutely ravishing!" Lady Langston had tears in her eyes as she impulsively kissed her daughter's cheek.

Deborah hugged her sister fiercely to the imminent danger of the fragile lace. "Darling Kate, you will be the most beautiful bride of the season, and by far the most distinctive." She seized Kate's hand and tugged gently. "Stand up and come over to the long mirror. There! Doesn't the mantilla give her added height and a lovely dignity, Mama? How fortunate that Nicholas is so tall. He will be excessively proud of you, Katie," she had predicted gaily.

Would Nicholas be proud of her, Kate wondered wryly, recalling this scene as she sat sewing quietly on the day before her marriage. Lately he had paid her only the most perfunctory of compliments and only when her family or others were present, and yet she could not think that he had simply grown accustomed to her presence and was rather taking her for granted. His assessing glance each time they met was too keen for her to entertain such a comfortable notion. Though the idea seemed preposterous, her instinct told her that he actually begrudged her the conventional compliments that their engaged status seemed to demand. For a long moment she questioned the advisability of wearing the lovely mantilla, which she conceded (not in a spirit of vanity, for Kate, dwelling in the shadow of two beauties all her life, had never much valued her own looks), did lend her an air of distinctive elegance if not actual beauty. She was serious in wondering if it might not be more politic to play down any attractions she might possess in setting the tone for future behavior toward Torvil, but somehow all her feminine pride revolted at the thought of appearing at her wedding looking less than her best. And, she reminded herself hastily, neither her parent nor her sister would countenance a change in costume at this late date. Besides, Torvil had given his word not to press his claims as her husband. Most likely nothing she wore or did to herself would serve to inflame his senses in any case when he already possessed a beautiful mistress whose favors he had no slightest intention of foregoing upon entering the married state. She had his own word for that.

One of the most uncomfortable effects of this unsuspected knowledge of her fiancé had been a regrettable tendency on Kate's part to search the premises everywhere they went for a glimpse of an unknown but unquestionably beautiful woman with a distinctive, husky voice. Though much ashamed of her inability to put the matter behind her, at least with regard to the woman's identity, Kate could not prevent herself from listening intently to each new feminine voice that came within her orbit. She also developed a violent and totally unreasonable antipathy to the color combination of green and silver. Not for a moment did she doubt that Torvil continued to enjoy amorous interludes with his mistress during the period of his betrothal, and the knowledge affected her in the same way a burr under a saddle affected a horse.

Although her thoughts seemed to have as much direction as a pinwheel in a breeze, Kate's needle never stopped the mechanical in and out movement that was slowly reducing the pile of unhemmed linens. She knew she was suffering a fit of the dismals as the crucial day was almost upon her when all chance of avoiding her fate would be past. Absurd to feel this way, of course, when the truth was that her fate had been sealed inevitably on the day she had accepted her mother's arrangement. She realized half her problem was this living in limbo that people called an engagement. Once married she would be under her own roof with all the privileges attending the married state. For the moment she would not dwell on the responsibilities that would fall on her inexperienced shoulders as mistress of a good-sized establishment. She had always got along well with Mama's servants and she did not consider that her education in the practical arts had been deficient. In addition, for the first time in her adult memory, finances would present no problem. Torvil was making her what seemed a princely allowance, and as a wedding gift his grandfather, Lord Bartram, had offered the young couple a carte blanche to redecorate the delightful house he was lending them. Once she succeeded in overcoming this temporary lowness of spirits, she would begin to find much interest and enjoyment in her new life. She had to.

At this point in her reverie the most crucial element in her new life walked into the room. So absorbed was Kate in her own musings that she was not even aware that Emmett had opened the door. It was her mother's voice welcoming Lord Torvil that jerked her back to awareness of her surroundings. She turned startled eyes to the man approaching them and summoned up a smile.

"We did not look to see you today, Torvil. How do you do?"

He made an easy reply and settled down to chat with Lady Langston. Kate continued her sewing after a brief apology for not setting it aside, but her attention, though covert, was upon her fiancé. It would be so much easier, she thought despairingly, to relegate him to the background if only he were not such a very compelling figure. His sculptured head, bent attentively toward her mother, was handsomely covered with crisp healthy hair that would wave despite his stern application of brushes. His skin looked burnished and taut over cheekbones that had already taken on a deeper color from the spring sun. As usual he lent distinction to well-tailored clothes while exuding an overwhelmingly masculine air.

Looking up, he caught his fiancée's brooding glance. "Where is young Deborah this afternoon? I miss her cheerful presence."

Kate colored up and it was Lady Langston who answered lightly, "Would you believe that she and Lord Sedgeley are at St. George's this moment supervising the decorating of the altar?"

Nicholas laughed in real amusement. "If I had not seen with my own eyes the devastating effect your daughters have on my father, ma'am, I would not, but having observed this rare phenomenon, I must accept your word for the most unlikely event I can envision. I can well believe, however, that Father will make life extremely difficult for the poor florists throughout the entire operation."

This sally produced a faint appreciative smile from the girl busily plying her needle but she offered no comment.

Lady Langston could cheerfully have shaken her daughter if it would have roused her from this ridiculous torpor. The constraint between the two young people was growing palpable. She tossed a bright suggestion into the small pool of silence that had swallowed up Torvil's remark.

"Kate, my dear, why don't you take Nicholas into the main drawing room and show him the latest wedding gift that arrived this morning."

The viscount flashed his future mother-in-law a grateful look and rose from his chair with alacrity. Up till now Kate had demonstrated a highly developed and maddening talent for avoiding his society.

Kate, casting her mother a glance of burning reproach, saw the look exchanged between the conspir-

110

ators and her lips tightened. She could not very well refuse without seeming rude but, perversely, she tried anyway.

"Stay comfortable," she replied with a sweet false smile for both of them. "I'll get the gift and bring it to you here."

"No, dearest," protested Lady Langston hastily, "it's too heavy for you and you might break it. In any case I have just remembered that I must speak to the cook immediately." She rose swiftly and glided to the door, leaving behind one thoroughly annoyed girl and a blandly satisfied man.

Conceding defeat, Kate joined her fiancé at the door he had opened for Lady Langston. Glancing sideways at him as she passed out of the room, she noted a gleam of humor in his dark eyes, and it sparked off a reluctant response in her. "Wait till you see this present," she said with a glint of pure mischief. "I promise you, you will be much impressed."

He followed her into the main saloon where a good-sized object covered with a piece of cloth reposed on a Pembroke table.

"Close your eyes," Kate ordered unexpectedly.

When the viscount had complied with this request, she whisked the cloth from the object. "*Now*, you may look," she declaimed with dramatic emphasis.

Nicholas stared in undisguised horror at the complicated and colorful creation of porcelain.

"Good Lord! What is it?"

"It's an epergne of course, a centerpiece," Kate answered, enjoying his expression of distaste while maintaining her own composure. "See all the little dishes held up by the waves? It's from Lord and Lady Tremaine, and there are matching candlesticks."

"Ahaa! Aunt Henrietta! Now I begin to understand. She has never forgiven me for locking her pet pug in

111

the still room once when I was seven." He walked slowly around the table examining the epergne from all angles. "I gather the furious figure cavorting with the dolphins on top is Neptune. There must be five hundred specimens of shells and seaweed scattered around the base. I can see I have underestimated the depths of Aunt Henrietta's spite all these years. She must have searched the length and breadth of the nation to discover something so hideous."

"Oh, you don't like it! I was sure you would find it most impressive." Bitter disappointment dripped from Kate's voice and Nicholas whirled to stare at her, to be reassured instantly by the rare and delightful sight of two beautiful amber eyes brimful of laughter in a sparkling face. This is how she was meant to look, he thought with a pang. He was most willing to play her little game—anything to prolong this mood of camaraderie.

"I'm impressed all right," he said with mock solemnity and absolute truth.

"The only problem is that I am not perfectly certain where to display it to advantage. I hoped you might have a suggestion."

"The attics? The cellar, perhaps? Or a nice dark cupboard? Take your pick." Hands in his pockets, he leaned against the table and smiled at her.

Kate chuckled but said seriously, "How odious of us to be poking fun when I am persuaded it was most kindly meant." She replaced the covering cloth and twitched it into place. "It shall go to your father's house tonight to be displayed with the other gifts."

As she prepared to lead the way out of the saloon, Nicholas said quickly, "Just a moment, Kate. I have something else for you."

"Another wedding gift?"

He drew a jeweler's box from his pocket and closed

112

the gap between them. "This is my gift to you. I wanted you to have it today so you might wear it tomorrow if you found it suitable."

Kate's face had gone blank and she clasped her hands behind her back involuntarily. At the gesture something exploded inside Nicholas, but he preserved his calm and presently proceeded to open the box and take out a double strand of matched pearls. They hung from his fingers, gleaming softly.

"*Oooh!*" The exclamation escaped Kate's lips, but she made no move to take the necklace. She raised troubled eyes to his which were now glittering.

"Don't you care for pearls? I thought all girls did, but if not, I'll get you something else." He spoke very carefully, keeping his temper in check.

"Oh, no, they are absolutely beautiful. Any girl would love them; she could not help herself, but, Torvil, I wish you had not done this. It is so unnecessary and so extravagant and . . . and, after all, you have already given me this very lovely ring." She knew she was babbling but seemed unable to stop. "I don't feel I should accept them."

"Nonsense! It is my prerogative to give you things. This is the groom's gift to his bride." He put the pearls back into their case and put it into her hand.

"But ours is not a . . . an ordinary marriage. There is no necessity for you to—"

"Oh, yes, there is!" His strong white teeth snapped together audibly. "People *expect* the groom to make his bride a gift. You had better learn to accept it. And here's another thing they expect," he ground out, seizing her roughly by the soft flesh above the elbows and jerking her up against his long length. Before the stunned girl could make a move, he bent his head and pressed a bruising kiss upon her surprised mouth.

"You'd best learn to accept that, too," he growled,

releasing her just as abruptly as he had grabbed her. At the door, he turned and with elaborate politeness said, "Don't bother to show me out. I can find my way. *À demain, chérie.*"

The girl holding the jeweler's box remained standing rigidly where he had left her until the sound of the softly closing door released her from the spell. Slowly she sagged against the table, and the proudly carried head bowed under the weight of her misery.

Chapter Nine

Kate's wedding day dawned blue and golden and late. She sat up in confusion as Deborah danced into the room behind Becky, who was carrying a tray containing a blue and white jasperware chocolate pot and two cups.

"Wake up, sleepyhead, and look outside. You won't have to worry about being a bride who gets rained on. It's a gorgeous day!" While she spoke Deb was arranging additional pillows behind her sister's back while Becky disposed of the tray on a nearby table and went from the room.

"*If you marry in the month of May, you will surely rue the day,*" chanted the figure among the pillows.

Deborah looked up swiftly from pouring the chocolate and noted her sister's unusual pallor. She achieved a light laugh. "Nonsense, nobody credits that ancient superstition any longer, but rain now is quite another matter." She handed Kate a blue and white cup and perched herself on the foot of her sister's bed in the fashion of eastern holy men. Neither girl said anything for a time while sipping slowly at the hot, fragrant brew, but Deborah was studying Kate from beneath a tangle of discreetly lowered lashes. Her sister did not appear to have slept well, and though she was pretending a deep interest in the contents of her cup, the level of the liquid did not noticeably decrease. The younger girl frowned down at her own cup. Deborah was most sincerely attached to her sister and at first she had been appalled at the idea of an arranged marriage for Kate, but somehow, from the moment of first setting eyes on Nicholas, she had been convinced that everything would be well. He had seemed so perfect for Kate.

She had waited impatiently to hear that Kate was satisfied with her fiancé, but as the time of the engagement passed she had become less convinced that things would arrange themselves happily. Just lately Kate had become so strangely unlike the merry sister she knew, and she never voluntarily spoke of Nicholas at all. Though Deborah remained persuaded that Nicholas was the right man for her sister, she had on occasion intercepted an almost fierce look that he bent on Kate when he thought himself unobserved. A little chill passed through her slight frame, but she drained her cup defiantly and replaced it on the tray.

"Finish quickly, dearest, for it will take me some little time to arrange your hair, though the added length does help it go back more smoothly."

From that moment Deborah took charge of a strangely subdued Kate and, with Becky's able assistance, contrived to have them both ready by the time the carriage arrived. Lord Sedgeley had insisted on escorting Lady Langston to the church so there would be no danger of crumpling the bride's gown, and they had already left by this time. As Lord Langston escorted his sister to the waiting carriage, she stopped short at sight of the four matched horses resplendent in white bridal rosettes. "Oh, Roger," she murmured, more touched than she could express, "four creams and so beautifully matched. What a sweet thing to do. It looks so very regal." She smiled tremulously and squeezed his arm in wordless affection.

He was studiedly offhand. "Oh, well, it seemed the least I could do. If we're going to do the thing at all, might as well do it in style. And you certainly merit the show," he added, running a critical eye over her wedding finery. "I never realized before just how good looking you are," with brotherly candor. "I like that lace thing on your head. In fact, you both do me great credit."

Deborah, adorable in palest pink satin with a white lace bodice, wrinkled her nose saucily at him as he helped her into the carriage. "Such lavish praise! I declare you'll turn our heads if we're not careful, won't he, Kate?"

"Quiet, minx!" He nipped her arm in a token pinch. "A little decorum, if you please."

Kate smiled at the byplay but said nothing. If her brother and sister eyed her white face and frightened eyes a bit anxiously, they refrained from commenting. In fact, they whiled away the short ride with a series of lighthearted admonitions on Roger's part as to how his youngest sister was to conduct herself in company that brought forth some airy and lofty denials of his right to preach to her on Deborah's behavior. Kate remained utterly silent.

The drive was all too short, but Roger and Deborah took comfort in the fact that some vestige of her normal color had returned to Kate's cheeks by the time they alighted. She was still a bit pale, but the raillery between her sister and brother had served to distract her attention, and the awful sensation of faintness that had nearly overcome her in the carriage had passed away. Outwardly composed, she was still trembling slightly, but with luck no one would notice.

The first element that pierced her dazed composure on entering the church impinged, of all unlooked for things, on her sense of smell. A delicious fragrance rose to meet her as she approached the center aisle, and she glanced in surprise and appreciation into Deborah's expectant face. How dear of her sister to plan all of this loveliness! She had ample opportunity on her way down the aisle to comprehend the scope of her efforts on Kate's behalf. Masses of graceful branches of orange blossom stood in tall green jars on either side of the altar. Arranged on white-covered stands of varying heights, they were grouped to give the impression of living trees, and the scent was heavenly. More formal arrangements of all white flowers graced the altar itself. But no, not quite all white. Here and there were pale pink blooms, carnations and peonies that dramatically highlighted the pure white. She focused all her attention on the flowers, unmindful of the dozens of faces that were following her progress down the aisle, all but unaware of the swelling tones of the organ filling the large church with music.

As she neared the altar rail where the white-robed clergyman waited, she concentrated fiercely on his tall, gray-haired figure. Most desperately did she wish not to have to look at the man who would be her husband in a matter of minutes. With the same degree of desperation had she tried not to think about him last night or about that hateful and devastating kiss he had forced upon her. And, as on the previous day, her helpless brain failed utterly to censure her wayward thoughts or compel her senses. Inevitably her reluctant glance was wrenched from the safe target of the impassive clergyman to the peril inherent in meeting the burning regard of her husband-to-be.

118

But not for long.

Her glance spun away as if ricocheting from the clash with that inflammable but unreadable force. Not again did she raise her eyes from her trembling hands, not when Nicholas's large, brown hand took hers in an unexpectedly comforting clasp, not when they repeated the ancient vows—he in a clear firm tone and she in a whisper—not even when he paused briefly with the wedding ring poised over her thumb as the bishop intoned, *"In the name of the Father,"* over the index finger, *"and of the Son,"* and over the middle finger, *"and of the Holy Ghost,"* before sliding it gently onto her fourth finger. *"Amen."* She kept her eyes on his cravat, willing herself not to flinch when it came time for the groom to kiss his bride. At the brief, butterfly-weight pressure of lips against hers involuntarily she did look up to encounter an odd expression in the dark eyes. Apology? Concern? Tenderness? She was too overcome with confusion and lightheadedness to trust her fleeting impressions. The moment passed, the warm pressure of his hand cuddling her chin was removed, leaving her with an inexplicable chill, and she found herself facing the congregation with her still trembling hand pressed firmly to her husband's right arm by his left hand, while Deb restored her bouquet to her and made a quick adjustment of her short train.

Later she could recall nothing of the return trip up the long aisle, nor of the small ceremony of signing the parish register along with Deb and Robin as witnesses to her marriage. Evidently one could still perform such ordinary tasks as walking and signing one's name in the proper place while the most vital elements of one's brain were engaged in a monumental struggle to accept the reality of what was happening. She had actually heard very little of the marriage ceremony, and whatever Torvil might have said to her in the white carriage

119

that carried them in solitary state to Brook Street went the way of lost childhood memories. Presumably she made the appropriate responses because when she became fully cognizant of her surroundings again, he seemed his normal, slightly mocking self. It was the voice of Lord Sedgeley's porter welcoming her as Lady Torvil that shocked her to a full awareness once again. She answered him hesitantly, fixing him with a wide, questioning gaze that flicked abruptly to the face of her new husband.

"It's strange, but I don't feel different," she murmured, a small frown of concentration testifying to the fact that this sentiment was expressed in a purely rhetorical spirit.

Nicholas answered her anyway after issuing a quiet command that caused the porter to hurry away. "Why should you feel different when nothing of significance has occurred?" Something about the silkiness of his tones sharpened her revivifying senses still further. "Do you think you might contrive to appear aware of the felicitations that our guests will no doubt shower upon us in the next few hours if we repair first to the study where I shall provide you with a restorative in the form of my father's best brandy? Who knows," he added with chilling affability, "a large enough glass might even enable you to produce an occasional smile so that one or two amongst the company might not take away the impression that you have been sold into slavery."

He ignored the gasp and flaring color this taunt produced and led her into his father's sanctum with a firm grip on her elbow that fitted her conception of the way prisoners were conducted from place to place. Kate was nearly goaded into a sharp retort by this deliberate attack, but with the hasty words trembling on her lips, she glared at him, and something in his tightly controlled expression suddenly reminded her of a small

120

boy, hurt but determined to hide his wounds at all costs. The retort died on her lips.

Swiftly she crossed the room to where he was pouring out the brandy and calmly took the glass from his hands, replacing it on the side table. The golden brown eyes stared steadily into his.

"I won't need the brandy, Torvil," she said in a low voice. "I promise you I shall not give anyone cause to speculate about our . . . marriage." She had to swallow hard against the ache in her throat before she could bring out the last word.

Nicholas took hold of her arms above the elbows and drew her fractionally closer, unconscious of the incongruity of the lace mantilla draping itself over his dark sleeve. He studied his bride's pale but thoroughly composed countenance.

"Kate," he began earnestly, "there's no need to——"

Whatever reassurance the viscount was about to impart was not destined to be disclosed, however.

"There you are, my boy," boomed the earl from the threshold, advancing into the room to shake his son's hand and kiss his new daughter with surprising tenderness.

In the hours that followed Kate had the dazed impression that she had been kissed with varying degrees of heartiness by nearly the entire population of London. True to her word she received the congratulations of their guests with smiling equanimity, though after a time her muscles felt stiff from the effort required to keep the smile pinned to her face. Nicholas never left her side and, truth to tell, she was appreciative of his support which, she suspected, was all that prevented some of his more roisterous friends from taking even greater advantage of the fact that brides were evidently for kissing by all and sundry. For a girl who, until the day before her wedding, had never been kissed by anyone outside her immediate family, the reception was a revelation and a sore trial. Gratefully, she clung to her husband's arm and contrived to hide her wariness and distaste behind the modestly downcast eyes permitted to a new bride. By a tacit agreement she and the viscount remained seated behind the comparative safety of the table as long as politeness allowed, though it could not be said that either did justice to the sumptuous repast that was set before the guests in the crimson and gold ballroom at Dunston House. Kate barely repressed a shudder of distaste at the plentiful array of cold meats, fowls, tongue, and cheeses of every variety, and was scarcely more tempted by the display of beautifully decorated trifles, syllabubs, jellies, and tarts that provided ample visual testimony to the caterer's skill. At Lord Torvil's urging she nibbled reluctantly at something she never succeeded in identifying, noticing that for all his insistence that she eat, her bridegroom partook rather sparingly of the breakfast feast himself.

Robin Dunston, as his brother's groomsman, proposed a graceful toast to the bridal couple that was answered by Nicholas, who said simply and with apparent sincerity that he considered himself the most fortunate man in London. Kate steeled herself to ignore the sudden pain this blatant falsehood sent shafting through her body, remaining motionless with downcast eyes until the hearty applause finally ended. She summoned up yet another smile for the assembled guests but avoided her husband's glance. Healths were drunk to the bride, the happy couple, the bride's mother, and the groom's father, to the king and queen and the prince regent among others as the abundance of food and drink induced a quickened tempo among the wedding guests. In company with the rest Kate downed sips of vintage champagne with reckless abandon until Nicholas removed her glass and replaced it with hot coffee, a substitution that she quite failed to notice as she failed to notice the quick appraising glance he bent on her. She was unaware that he had accurately gauged the effect that even a moderate amount of champagne would have on a girl whose nerves were stretched to the utmost and whose stomach was essentially empty. But she certainly became aware in the hour that followed that Nicholas had no intention of leaving her side. There was one thought imprinted on Kate's brain—smile, be agreeable—but when she attempted to translate this into an acceptance of an invitation to inspect the wedding gifts in company with a dashing young man with handsome military side whiskers, Nicholas stepped in and forestalled her with smiling efficiency. His grandfather, he explained genially to the disappointed petitioner, had just arrived and had commanded the immediate presence of his new granddaughter.

"Oh, yes, I must meet Lord Bartram," Kate declared, promptly forgetting the young officer, though she bestowed a dazzling smile of apology upon him which he received with a rueful shake of his head. Torvil had magnanimously allowed a congratulatory kiss upon his bride's cheek, but that failure to detach her from his side was going to cost him twenty-five guineas when he rejoined his fellow officers watching the tableau with derisive grins and only restraining their hooting in deference to the awe-inspiring reputation of their host. Kate was totally oblivious to this byplay or to the fact that Nicholas had acknowledged it by a slight mocking bow in the direction of his brother's boisterous friends.

When the viscount presented her to his grandfather a moment later, Kate was hard pressed to conceal her surprise at the latter's appearance. Nicholas, Robin, and Lord Sedgeley were such large men that unconsciously she had been prepared for another such commanding presence though cognizant of the fact that this was his mother's father. Not even in the full strength of youth could Lord Bartram have cut an impressive figure, for he was a small, slightly rotund man with sloping shoulders and very small hands and feet. Indeed his hand, grasping Kate's warmly, seemed scarcely larger than her own, and their eyes met on a level. His were vividly blue and crinkled at the corners, and as the expression in them warmed rapidly from intense interest to an almost childlike friendliness, it took Kate just two seconds to decide that Lord Bartram must always have commanded affection if not the respect that was extended automatically to a man of more imposing stature like her father-in-law. His balding head with its few wisps of carefully combed, rusty gray hair was almost perfectly round. His face was round, too, and so were those lively eyes. A button nose and contoured cheeks above a small mouth and indeterminate chin increased his likeness to a rather elderly child. Except for the laugh lines around his mouth and at the corners of his eyes, his firm skin was healthy looking and remarkably unwrinkled and his movements had the quick decisiveness of a much younger man. She knew he must be past seventy, but it was difficult to accept this knowledge in view of the evidence of her own eyes. He was dressed with neatness and precision in a perfectly tailored blue morning coat worn over an old-fashioned embroidered waistcoat, and his graceful bow over her hand was a model of flattering attention.

Nicholas noted with satisfaction tinged with amusement that his shrewd old fox of a grandfather had captivated his bride in short order and wondered if the process had been mutual. He was aware, as Kate could not yet be, that a cool and keen intelligence operated behind the bland ingenuous face his grandfather presented to the world.

It appeared that the attraction had been mutual for after an animated description of the various ills that had bedeviled his journey and caused him to arrive late for the wedding, told in a manner that brought appreciative laughter to brighten Kate's pale face, Lord Bartram turned to Nicholas and observed kindly, "I felicitate you most sincerely, my dear boy, on choosing a truly lovely girl to be your wife." With something of a flourish he bestowed the hand that had remained comfortably in his throughout the conversation on his grandson, patting their awkwardly clasped fingers with the air of a benevolent monarch awarding the prize to the tournament champion. "It gives me the greatest pleasure to know that you now have a companion in joy."

The old gentleman beamed impartially on the bridal pair, blessedly unaware that his last words had affected them rather strangely. The brightness had faded from Kate's face and her imprisoned fingers jerked spasmodically. Her new husband preserved his countenance but tightened his grip until the veins on the back of his hands stood out in relief. Both kept their eyes on their smiling relative who proceeded to issue a mild command.

"And now, my boy, if you will entrust your bride to me for a few moments I wish to ask Katherine about her plans for my house while you circulate among your guests." He patted the chair next to his, and Nicholas seated Kate before releasing her hand and acknowledging his dismissal with a slight smile.

As he walked away Kate was earnestly thanking Lord Bartram for his most generous gift, thanks that he waved aside. "Nonsense, the house will belong to

Nicholas eventually, so he may as well have it fixed up to suit your taste at the outset."

On turning from the engrossed pair, Nicholas espied the brash young lieutenant gazing wistfully at Kate and his expression became thoughtful. He was entangled with a succession of well wishers in the next half hour and it was not until his friend, Mister Waksworth, approached during a welcome lull that he had opportunity to check again on his bride. Kate was still engaged in animated conversation with Lord Bartram.

Mister Waksworth followed the direction of his friend's glance.

"No need to call off the army, old chap. She's been tied up nice and tight by the old gent this half hour and more. Robin's friends have been circling, but there was no break in the wall."

"Never noticed it before, but your wife's a real beauty." There was a tinge of surprise in his tone.

"Yes, she is," Nicholas assented briefly.

The merest hint of well-concealed irritation showed on his face, but it was not lost upon such an old crony as Mister Waksworth.

"No need to look like that, old chap, I assure you," he explained kindly. "Always knew she was a good-looking girl, just didn't know she was a beauty, that's all." When this produced no appreciable softening in the viscount's features, he added hastily, "It's a good thing to have a beauty for a wife, at least so I hear. Never thought much about it myself; not much in the petticoat line, you know, but people seem to agree it adds to a man's consequence to have a wife who's much admired. A real feather in your cap, dear boy." He eyed his stony-faced friend warily, aware that his well-meant remarks had somehow failed in their intent.

"What's eating you anyway? Damned if ever I saw such a Friday face!"

126

Nicholas passed a nervous hand over his hair and forced a laugh. "Don't mind me, Ollie. Getting married plays the very devil with a man's disposition. Don't let anyone talk you into it."

This strange piece of advice from a new bridegroom, moreover one who moments earlier had assured the assembled company that he considered himself the most fortunate man in London, was received with unmoved calm by Mister Waksworth.

"Well, I won't. In no position to enter the parson's mousetrap anyway. Pockets to let as usual, no expectations worth speaking of unless that old uncle of m'mother's leaves me something, and he never liked me above half. It's my belief that he's good for another ten years despite the fact he's forever calling us all to his deathbed. Never saw such a man for imagining himself at his last illness. Healthy as a horse, really."

It is doubtful if this rambling discourse made the slightest impression on the viscount who blurted out after another glance in Kate's direction: "How much longer can this affair go on?"

Though this was poised in a rhetorical spirit of desperation, deliverance was on hand in the person of his father's chef who appeared suddenly, wheeling out the elaborate creation that was his contribution to the festivities. The wedding cake must have stood fully five feet high and Nicholas was dimly aware of the concert of admiring comments and smattering of applause that greeted its almost baroque splendor. The expression of extreme self-congratulation adorning Gaston's sharp-featured face as he condescendingly acknowledged the plaudits of the guests was to remain one of the most enduring memories of his wedding day. While Nicholas stood gazing tongue-tied at the elaborately decorated four-tiered cake, he was rescued by his bride who had been escorted to his side by Lord Sedgeley. Kate gracefully accepted the task of expressing the couple's sincere appreciation for this monumental labor on their behalf. He noted that she extolled the originality of using fresh rosebuds in the palest shade of pink to decorate the top of the bottom tier which was iced with broad interweaving strokes to simulate the appearance of a straw basket, but whatever she found to say in praise of the miniature-carved swans and intricate, ribbon-tied arches that were featured among the miscellany adorning the remaining layers passed him by. It was enough to see that she had succeeded in producing a quantity of superlatives sufficient to satisfy even Gaston's gigantic ego. It only remained for him to second all Kate's remarks and help her cut the masterpiece with the aid of a sword pressed into her hands by the same smitten lieutenant.

Nicholas was not a man who liked sweets, but he endured the cloying sweetness of the thickly iced cake with good grace as the bridal couple was urged on by their guests to feed each other a sample of the bride-cake. He nearly succeeded in ignoring the gleam of mischief in the eyes of his bride who was well aware of his dislike of sweets as she fed him the concoction, but when the younger members of the interested audience set up a clamor for him to kiss his bride, the rigid control he had exercised over his actions toward Kate since that angry, punishing kiss last night snapped. Her downcast eyes and flushed cheeks would be credited to maidenly modesty, but he *knew* she was gritting her teeth in suppressed fury and his own sense of frustration which had been mounting during this interminable wedding fiasco dictated his next action.

With deliberation he gathered the white-garbed girl into a close embrace, calmly ignoring the resentful stiffening of her body.

"Remember our audience, you are supposed to be a

happy bride," he whispered in her ear in the instant before his mouth covered hers. She compressed her lips and glared defiance at him. Instead of bringing him to a sense of the situation, he was exhilarated by her opposition, and he increased the pressure of both arms and lips until brute strength conquered. The stiffening went out of her backbone, her lips parted reluctantly, and the sherry brown eyes filmed over with angry tears. Fiercely triumphant for an instant, the ribald comments and applause from the guests shocked him to a belated sense of his surroundings, helped along by the pain of a sharp pinch adminstered to his rib section by his loving bride as soon as her imprisoned arms were partially freed. He raised the offending hand, now curled into a small fist, to his lips and kissed it gently while twin devils laughed into her carefully controlled face.

"I hate you!" she hissed under her breath, then smilingly turned to acknowledge her sister's timely assistance in straightening the lovely mantilla that had gone sadly askew during that violent embrace.

His pseudo elation evaporated as quickly as it had arisen, leaving him drained and disgusted with himself. Fortunately his public ordeal was now over. It was perfectly permissible for the newly wedded pair to slip away once the cake was cut, and this pair availed themselves of the earliest opportunity to do just that, only pausing long enough for Kate to kiss her mother and sister good-bye and be kissed in turn by her new father- and grandfather-in-law.

The short carriage ride to the house on Albemarle Street in a custom-built carriage given to the couple as a wedding present by Lord Sedgeley and pulled by a top-notch team, also of his lordship's providing, was accomplished in total silence. Kate was frankly sulking in a corner, and if her sulks were designed to cover up a more basic panic at her helpless position, vis-à-vis the disproportion existing between the physical strength of a large, athletic man and an average-sized female, her husband was too wrapped up in his own emotional turmoil to bring much discernment to the situation.

As Nicholas saw it he was driving to a house where he would be spending his wedding night with a girl who destested him. And if this were not sufficient to cast any man into the dismals, this same girl was becoming increasingly more desirable in his eyes with each passing day, and he had bound himself by his word as a gentleman to refrain from making love to her. He might dislike his reluctant bride's intransigent nature, but her face and body had appealed to his senses right from the first moment, and this feeling had grown stronger despite the basic conflict that was always between them.

Today, watching Kate drift down the aisle toward him in all the freshness of youth and so incredibly lovely, he had been seized with an aching desire to claim her for his own. It wasn't love, he told himself impatiently; it was impossible to love someone who detested oneself, but he had never before experienced such a singleminded desire for a particular woman and under the circumstances it was a damnable experience. The marathon farce of a marriage celebration might have been designed for the express purpose of reducing him to a state of impotent frustration. The less he saw of Kate the better. That was the most obvious and least destructive course to pursue.

On this unpalatable decision they arrived at the house they would henceforth share. Nicholas helped Kate down from the carriage with punctilious civility. As the door opened and Mudgrave, the newly hired butler, welcomed them, he hesitated briefly, then swept

Kate off her feet and commenced carrying her up the shallow steps into the hall.

Catching the butler's approving eye, Kate stopped in midair the fist that was about to pummel his shoulder, but she hissed a low-voiced protest. "Put me down this instant! What do you think you are doing?"

Her husband eyed her expressionlessly. "Surely you have heard of the custom of carrying a bride over the threshold of her new home for luck. Can you think of a bride in greater need of good fortune than your charming self?" This last was added with an ironic inflection as she opened her lips to protest.

Evidently she thought better of what she had been going to say because she allowed him to escort her up the stairs to her new suite with no further comment. At the door to the attractive sitting room that had been refurbished for Kate's use, Nicholas bowed and wished her a formal good night. Had he been able to see the humor in anything at that moment he would have laughed at Kate's astounded expression.

"*Good night?* But . . . but, I have ordered dinner to be served here later. My mother said, that is, I understand it is customary to dine together on one's wedding day. When Roger and I were bringing some of my things here yesterday, I gave the cook a menu for tonight. What will the servants think if you do not dine with me?" She was clasping her hands together to still their trembling, but Nicholas seemed impervious to her agitation.

"I don't give a damn what the servants think," he grated. "If you are so concerned with upholding the traditions of a wedding night, may I remind you that another time-honored custom is that a bride spends her wedding night in her husband's bed." He watched her color fade.

"I . . . you promised!" she whispered accusingly.

131

He laughed without humor. "Ah, yes, sooner or later we come to that promise. Well, I did not promise to dine with you. You cannot have it all ways, my dear. The decision is yours. Do we . . . *dine* . . . or do we bid each other good night here and now?"

The little pause that followed this challenge was electric with undeclared feelings. Kate stared at the unreadable face of her husband with naked hostility before replying with stinging contempt, *"Good night, my lord."*

She turned without waiting for his reply and entered her bedroom, closing the door softly behind her.

Nicholas acknowledged his defeat with no more than a shrug of his shoulders, but his closing of the sitting room door was clearly audible to the girl in the next room.

Chapter Ten

At eight thirty that evening Lord Langston banged the knocker on the freshly painted door to his sister's new home. He explained to the butler that he had not come to call on the viscount and his bride but only to retrieve his quizzing glass which he had left on the premises the previous day.

"Lady Torvil requests that you step upstairs to her sitting room, sir," replied Mudgrave smoothly.

"Oh, no need of that. I wouldn't dream of disturbing them, so I asked my sister to set aside the glass so that I might collect it tonight."

"I understand, sir, but my lady most particularly desired me to extend the invitation. She has your property in her possession."

Perforce, Roger allowed himself to be conducted upstairs. Kate was sitting turning the pages of a magazine, when Mudgrave announced him but she cast it aside the instant the butler departed and jumped to her feet.

"Oh, Roger, I am so glad to see you!"

Her brother frowned at this fervent welcome. "Can't

see why, you saw enough of me earlier in the day," he pointed out. "I should think Torvil would be enough company for you tonight." He glanced around the cozy room that was rather dimly lit by three branches of candles on various tables.

"I don't see Torvil," he announced unnecessarily. "Don't see my quizzing glass either."

"That's just the point. He isn't here. He has gone out," Kate stated, giving the words great dramatic emphasis.

"Gone out with my glass? Why would he do that, doesn't he have one of his own? Or was he intending to return it to me? Very good of him, but he needn't have bothered. Said I'd come around to collect it."

"*Stupid!*" Kate declared, impatient with his slow wittedness. "Of course he hasn't taken your stupid glass, it's in my bedchamber. Torvil has *gone out,*" she repeated, "on our *wedding* night. I had ordered dinner to be served here and he refused to dine with me."

Roger looked acutely uncomfortable. "Maybe he had a previous engagement he had forgotten to cancel. Not good form to ignore appointments, you know."

Kate accorded this feeble offering the contempt it merited.

"On his wedding day?" She stopped the nervous pacing she had begun when her brother entered and peered up at him with sudden suspicion. "Have you been drinking?"

"Nothing to signify." Lord Langston drew himself up to his full six feet and replied with dignity, "Your wedding reception didn't end when you left, you know. That's why I'm so late coming for my glass; had to change."

"Well, it's my opinion that you are odiously cast away," stated Kate roundly. "I'm telling you my husband has deserted me on my wedding night and all you can think about is a stupid quizzing glass!"

"No, no," Roger denied, trying to soothe his agitated sister, "the eyeglass don't matter and I'm sorry about Torvil. It's deuced awkward for you, though I understood you did not want him anywhere near your bedroom. Well, never mind that," as she swelled with indignant denial. "The thing is, I don't see what *I* can do about it. *I* don't know where he is."

"Well, *I do*! He's with *that woman*!"

And to Lord Langston's astonishment and consternation, his stoical sister burst into tears.

"No, no, of course he's not." Roger put one strong arm about the sobbing girl's shoulders and patted her back awkwardly with his other hand.

"Yes, he is! He went straight from his wedding to the arms of his mistress!" came the theatrical insistence.

"Well, he didn't. Couldn't have done so in point of fact because she's out of town. So cheer up."

Kate pulled out of his hold with the speed of a scalded cat and fixed him with a compelling eye while the tears dried unheeded on her cheeks.

"You know who she is! Tell me!"

"No, I don't know," he denied, looking more harassed by the moment.

"Yes, you do. You said she was out of town so you *must* know. Who is she? Everyone in London knows the identity of my husband's mistress except me. They say truly that the wife is always the last to learn. I would not have believed that my own brother would conspire to deceive me!"

"Now, stop it, Kate!" Roger declared, revolted by this excess of dramatics in his ordinarily phlegmatic sister. "I didn't have any idea who the woman was when you told me about her, but then I made it my business

135

to find out. She need not trouble you in any way, but it will do you no good at all to learn her name. It's unlikely you'll ever meet in any case."

Lord Langston had no compunction in telling his sister this deliberate untruth because he had given some little thought to the matter on discovering the identity of Torvil's mistress. Kate had been determined to go through with the marriage, and under the circumstances, he felt it could only add to her unhappiness to be forever looking for the woman at every social gathering she attended. Best to let the fact of her existence slip to the back of Kate's mind while she and her husband came to some arrangement of their affairs. He had been prepared to dislike his prospective brother-in-law in the beginning but had found to his surprise that he wasn't the hardened libertine he might have been. Over the weeks of the engagement he had slowly inclined to the view that Torvil and Kate might be a well-matched couple in time. It was too bad about Lady Montaigne of course, but these *affaires* did not commonly last long. The least said on that head to Kate the better. He must have drunk more than he'd thought today or he would never have blurted out the news that Lady Montaigne was out of town. He cursed himself for a fool and tried to make amends.

"That is one worry you need not have. Torvil is not spending his wedding night with his mistress. Probably he's just gone to the Argyll Rooms. That's where I'm headed myself. You've had a long, exhausting day of it. Why not go to bed early and get a good night's sleep? Everything will look better in the morning."

This interesting bit of advice to a new bride was wasted on Kate whose doleful expression had become remarkably alert.

"Argyll Rooms? Do you mean you think Torvil may

136

be attending the Cyprians' Ball?" Her eyes glittered strangely.

Roger groaned at his careless tongue. "What do you know about the Cyprians' Ball?" he demanded. "Young girls like you shouldn't be aware of anything of that nature."

"Young girls like me are aware of a great deal more that goes on in the world than people think fit to tell us." Kate's irony was almost absentminded because she was doing some rapid calculation in her mind. Her brother did not much care for the speculative look she cast at him. Just so had she looked as a child when about to propose some activity guaranteed to land them both in the basket. He braced himself for certain disaster.

Kate did not disappoint him.

"Roger, take me with you," she begged eagerly.

"Take my sister amongst the Fashionable Impures and the muslin company? Are you mad? I'd have to be more than a trifle cast away—I'd have to be completely disguised before I'd help you to ruin yourself!"

She cut into his disgusted retort. "Naturally I'll wear a mask and alter my appearance. No one will recognize me."

"You'd never get away with it. Why, half the men there will have been at your wedding breakfast today, and not just the unmarried ones either." As Kate's eyes grew round, he tacked hastily, "Well, never mind that, the thing's impossible and even if it weren't, you'd hate it. The manners and behavior won't be at all what you are accustomed to at Almack's, let me tell you." He watched her closely, but she displayed no sign of maidenly shrinking at this warning. "The men won't keep the line tonight, they'll expect you to be pretty free with your favors, and if you acted missish they'd spot you, mask or no mask. In fact, a mask would make you appear all the more intriguing. You'd have all the rakes in town sniffing after you. Besides, Torvil would have my head on a platter and it would give him a real disgust of you, mark my words."

Kate had grown increasingly thoughtful during this masterful speech, and Roger congratulated himself on having avoided disaster by a hair's breadth.

He now said softly: "I'm sorry, Katie girl. I know what a disappointing day this has been for you, but you'll be the better for a good night's sleep."

"No, Roger, wait!" Kate cried as he turned away. "I am confident of my ability to ward off the advances of any men save those completely lost to all sense of decency, and you will be there to shield me from such as these. If I can convince you that no one will recognize me, will you take me, please?" She laid a pleading hand on his sleeve and looked at him through hard-bright eyes that had recently known tears. "Torvil has humiliated me before all the servants. You may be assured my solitary dinner while my lord left the house has been the talk of the servants' hall tonight. He deserves this retaliation. You may take me away from the ball immediately if he isn't there. At least the servants will see that I have not languished in my room awaiting my lord and master."

Roger stared into his sister's quiet bitter face and knew an urge to murder his brother-in-law for bringing that look to her eyes. Kate was too young to know such disillusion. He hesitated and was lost.

Kate's expression changed to pure mischief. "Just give me twenty minutes to make myself over," she said gaily, and whisked herself into the bedchamber before he could marshal his defenses against her.

Not that he had ever had much chance against Kate when she was determined on a course, he mused ruefully when he was alone in her pretty sitting room.

138

Even as children her will had generally been the stronger, and she invariably enlisted his aid in her escapades. Right from the moment that crafty butler had enticed him upstairs he'd had a premonition of danger. He should have heeded his instincts and flown without the damned quizzing glass. It was nothing but an affectation anyway. He never had succeeded in achieving the correct supercilious air to carry the thing off. Now Torvil could wield the eyeglass like a rapier to depress pretension. He'd seen him stare at an encroaching mushroom at the Daffy Club with the air of a scientist studying a rare specimen until the fellow had turned beet red and effaced himself completely, after which Torvil had calmly continued his conversation without the least reference to the episode. In point of fact his brother-in-law, for all his reputed affability, would be a dangerous man to cross. He would not take kindly to meeting his wife in a place where no lady would dream of presenting herself. Roger had been wishing himself elsewhere for the past half hour and would have cravenly stolen down the staircase and made good his escape if the habit of standing by Kate had not been so ingrained. To prevent himself from sinking deeper into a melancholy conviction of disaster he picked up Kate's magazine and tried to concentrate on the contents. He was deep in an article arguing the benefits to the complexion of nightly applications of Denmark lotion versus the regular use of extract of pineapple when a seductive voice aroused him.

"*Bon soir, Monsieur,* 'Ave I kept you waiting? *Je vous demande pardon.*"

A vision in diaphanous red stood poised in the doorway, one hand extended to touch the door in an attitude that displayed a shapely white arm to great advantage. The other was slowly unfurling a black lace fan that matched her black half mask. From the fan

139

resting coquettishly beneath a rounded white chin Roger's bemused eyes traveled up to a pair of smiling lips whose natural color had been artfully deepened, lingered on a tiny heart-shaped patch beside her mouth. Patches were no longer worn by well-born ladies of fashion, but there was no denying that this one enhanced the attractiveness of a slight dimple in her right cheek. Roger noted the highly colored cheekbones before his fascinated gaze was irresistibly drawn to the barbaric earrings that hung nearly to her shoulders, shoulders which were almost totally exposed, along with a generous amount of curving white flesh, by the brevity of the red bodice.

"Good Lord! Where did you get those earrings? Never tell me Mama approved that purchase, and I'll go bail she never ordered that dress either. You look like a . . . like a . . ." Words failed him.

"An opera dancer? A game pullet? One of the muslin company?" Kate supplied, her smile deepening to reveal perfect teeth. "As a matter of fact Mama did order this dress, but it had some ruffling inserted at the bodice that I removed. Also it looks quite different when teamed with the black lace. The earrings were bought for a masquerade. I was tempted to dampen the muslin to make it cling but decided against it." She laughed at his expression of horror. "Will I pass for a Fashionable Impure?"

Roger was studying her thoroughly now that the initial shock had worn off.

"Yes and no," he concluded finally. "I do not fear that you'll be recognized. That hair style, drawn back like that, changes your appearance somewhat. The lacy thing you wore today concealed it so I don't think that will give you away, and that costume is certainly a far cry from your usual style, not to mention the patch and the war paint and feathers," he added, eyeing the three

140

black ostrich plumes arranged on her head. "Despite the revealing nature of your outfit though, there is still something about you that sets you apart. Perhaps it is only the mask," he finished doubtfully.

"I shall be a lady of mystery," declared Kate regally, "a Frenchwoman with an imperfect command of the English tongue. That should serve to get me out of any difficult situation."

"You'd best remove your rings," warned Roger dryly. "That topaz bauble could precipitate you into a more than difficult situation. There's not another like it in the world." He arranged a black silk cloak over Kate's finery while she took off the topaz and diamond ring and her plain gold wedding band. "I'll have the porter call a hack. You stay out of sight until it's time to leave, and keep that dress covered. We don't want the servants speculating about a mistress who is a painted hussy by night."

Kate laughed and allowed him to give the order to the porter while she locked her rings in her jewel box. She would remove the mask for the moment and rely on her fan to conceal her painted lips when they left.

Their exit went without a hitch as did their arrival at the brilliantly lighted Argyll Rooms. Roger had agreed with Kate that it would be advisable to pretend they were unacquainted, though he promised to keep his eye on her and be ready to lend assistance if required. Kate was in a reckless mood that was more defiance than gaiety but resembled the latter closely enough to pass muster.

The ball was in full swing when they arrived. The setting was definitely more impressive than Almack's, Kate agreed, noting the classical statues in their high niches ranging around the walls between decorative pilasters. The large orchestra was placed on a dais at one end of the glittering room. Though most of the gentlemen were correctly attired in black and white evening dress, the female contingent ran the gamut of colors, fabrics, and fashions, with tastes ranging from opulence and display to those styles expressly designed to reveal as much of the female figure as decency and the law would allow. Kate's diaphanous red muslin had seemed to fit into the latter category at home but was now shown to be on the modest side when compared with the costumes of some of the women. The jewels that glinted around the throats and at the bosoms of a number of these charmers would rival those of a duchess. Evidently their admirers were moved to reward them in a most lavish manner for their favors. Kate herself had worn no jewels that could later be identified with her.

Roger had not overstated the case when he warned her not to expect the style of this gathering to resemble Almack's select assemblies. Kate scarcely had time to assimilate the very free manners of some of the women and to accustom herself to their loud voices and immoderate laughter before she was besieged with would-be partners. Once again Roger had proved correct. Her mask lent her a sense of mystery in an assemblage where female charms were only too obvious. In a sense her popularity was a great asset in that she was able to parry her partner's queries as to her identity in a lighthearted manner, knowing a new petitioner would rescue her from the importunities of the present one. She danced a great deal in that first hour, noting with inward amusement that three of her partners had been guests at her wedding that afternoon. One was the young lieutenant who had wanted to inspect the wedding gifts with her. Her heart moved into her throat when he muttered that he was certain they had met before. He asked probing questions and did not seem satisfied with her denials of previous encounters. Since he was slightly the worse for drink by this time, she turned with relief to a dark-visaged stranger who claimed her for the next dance.

By the time she met up with Roger again she had parried dozens of intimate questions, refused two offers of carte blanche from gentlemen who were anxious to set her up in a snug little house, and turned down several invitations to go on to private parties at the close of the ball. To all of these eager cavaliers Kate replied in her assumed accent that she already had a protector to whom she was devoted. It served quite well, though one or two gentlemen showed disturbing signs of interest in the identity of the absent lover.

She had spotted her husband almost at once, and though convinced he would not be able to penetrate her disguise, she prudently kept as much distance as possible between them at all times. He seemed to be very well entertained by a succession of dashers including the notorious Harriette Wilson, who with her bright auburn hair and voluptuous figure was even more attractive at close range than she had appeared in her box at the Opera when Lady Langston had pointed her out to her fascinated daughters.

The darling of half the *beau monde* (the masculine half) seemed to find Nicholas highly amusing company for he kept her in a continuous ripple of laughter, and she playfully rapped his knuckles more than once with her fan. Kate was too preoccupied with her own evasive responses to a number of highly persistent escorts to spare much thought for her husband, however. Though buoyed up initially by an emotional recklessness totally foreign to her nature, the accumulated strains of a very eventful day were beginning to take their toll. She was tiring rapidly and had just made the surprising discovery that she was famished. Actually, it should not have been a surprise considering the fact that she had eaten nothing since her breakfast chocolate, save a morsel of something or other at the wedding reception. She had been too upset to eat later and had thrown her solitary dinner out of the window to some prowling cats, so reluctant had she been to provide any more evidence of a languishing bride such as an untouched plate would have been for the delectation of the servants.

Whirling in the too tight embrace of an inebriated gallant, Kate cast her glance rapidly down the room, hoping to catch Roger's eye, but her gaze met that of a dark, saturnine stranger who had partnered her earlier. His manner had been perfectly civil, but she hadn't cared for the look in his eyes. For that matter she hadn't cared for the looks the majority of men present bent on her. It had certainly come home to her tonight that gentlemen even of the highest ranks of society (perhaps *especially* of the highest ranks of society) wore an entirely different face toward women who were not their social equals. She would have preferred another rescuer, but the dark man whose name she had not learned earlier was heading purposefully toward her as the music ended. He bowed politely and requested the pleasure of the next dance.

Kate watched her present partner weave his unsteady and reluctant way across the floor. Roger was nowhere to be seen.

"You are very kind, sir, but I would be most grateful if you would conduct me into supper instead. I missed my dinner and am monstrous hungry."

He responded to her supplicating smile with a slight widening of a thin but well-shaped mouth and offered his arm. "I have never yet been accused of allowing a lovely lady to starve in my company." His deep voice was pleasant enough, but something about him had sent off warning bells in Kate's head on their first encounter and they were still clanging. She would hate to be the woman he wanted if she did not want him, she decided with a slight shiver as she permitted him to seat her at an empty table in the almost deserted supper room. She hoped Roger had noted her exit from the ballroom and would soon follow. Meanwhile her escort was inquiring her preferences before giving an order to a hovering waiter. This accomplished, he joined her at the table, keeping his chair at a reasonable distance from hers and bending toward her attentively.

"Do you realize that you have created something of a sensation tonight, *Mademoiselle?*" Kate remembered her accent, nervously aware that she had allowed it to slip earlier, hoping it had escaped his notice.

"A sensation, *Monsieur,* among so many so beautiful women? You are—how do you say—flattering me, *non?*"

"No, indeed. They are calling you *La Belle Inconnue.* There is intense speculation as to your identity and place of origin. You are a woman of mystery."

Kate chuckled richly in genuine amusement. "*Mais, non, Monsieur,* there is no mystery. My name is Desirée St. Germain and I am born in Paris. This is my first visit to London, but I 'ave lived in England for ten years and I speak very well the English."

"You do, indeed."

Kate pretended to accept the ironic compliment at face value. When her inquisitor switched to fairly creditable French for a few remarks, she had cause to be grateful to the martinet of a French governess who had presided over the Harmon schoolroom for a dozen years. Since her French was better than his, she felt safe from discovery. If he was disappointed in the results of his little test, nothing of the kind was allowed to manifest itself in his expression which remained tolerantly amused.

"And how are you called, *Monsieur*?" she asked with wide-eyed innocence, having decided that attack was the best form of defense.

"I am Ralston," he answered carelessly.

Kate hoped the shock that rippled through her on learning the identity of her companion was not reflected on her face. A French girl recently come to London would not be expected to know of the reputation of Henry Bond, Marquess of Ralston, but even girls as sheltered as Kate and Deborah knew that his lordship had caused so many scandals dating back to his youth that he was no longer received by respectable hostesses. Well into his forties now, he showed no signs of abandoning his dissolute life-style.

"*Enchantée, Monsieur* Ralston," she murmured, keeping to her role, but now she was hoping Roger would not put in an appearance. According to gossip, the marquess had twice killed his man in duels over women.

"It's Lord Ralston, actually, but no matter," he replied. "Tell me, my dear, who is your protector?"

"I am sorry, milord, but he wishes to remain an . . . anon . . . er . . . unknown."

"Oh? I gather then that he is not present tonight since there are no masked gentlemen amongst the company. He must trust you implicitly, my dear. Quite a compliment to you."

Too late Kate realized that she had been backed into a corner, but she hotly resented his suave implications and had no intention of allowing him to think her unescorted.

"*Malheureusement, non,* he was unable to be present, but he entrusted me to the care of a friend."

"Now that is a true test of loyalty," the marquess said affably. "A man who can be entrusted with the

146

safety of a beautiful woman. And who is this devoted friend, my dear?"

"I doubt you are acquainted, milord." Kate preserved her calm demeanor, refusing to let Lord Ralston's hypnotic regard unnerve her, but she greeted the arrival of their waiter at that moment with as much relief as pleasure.

During supper, which Kate enjoyed immensely, devouring lobster patties and creamy crabs and chicken with the gusto of a dainty gourmande, the talk remained light and impersonal. The marquess drank several glasses of champagne and ate little, seeming to regard the sight of a young woman enjoying her food with the same slightly cynical air of detached amusement that had set her hackles rising earlier. She did not allow it to disturb her while she was repairing the ravages of an exhausting day, however. With luck they would never meet again and she had every intention of terminating their tête-à-tête at the first opportunity. Consequently, when she had polished off a delectable orange ice, she raised her untouched wine glass with a slight gesture in her companion's direction.

"*Mille mercies,* milord, for providing me with a most delicious supper. I am most grateful. Shall we return *maintenant* to the ballroom?"

"Not quite yet, my dear," the marquess interposed smoothly, raising his glass to her. "I should like to drink to a most charming dinner companion." He proceeded to toss off the rest of his glass in one gulp, but when Kate started to rise from her chair he put out a restraining hand. "I would beg a small favor of you first, *Mademoiselle,* in return for the supper."

A tickle of alarm squirmed its way down Kate's spine. "And what might that be, milord?" she inquired with a coolness she was far from feeling.

147

"I have an overwhelming desire to gaze upon *La Belle Inconnue* without her mask."

"*No! Je regrette mais c'est impossible!* I 'ave promised." She rose abruptly, intending to lead the way out of the supper room, but he stopped her with a hand on her arm.

"You won't be breaking your promise if *I* do the unmasking, my dear," he replied with sinister softness. "I'm afraid I must insist."

Kate jerked her head back in alarm as his hand reached for the strings of the lace mask.

"And *I* must insist that you respect the lady's wishes in this matter."

The cold voice that slashed between the pair caused Kate to jump visibly, but though her antagonist slowly lowered his arm, his slightly bored expression did not alter. He did, however, glance quickly around, noting a half-dozen newcomers to the supper room who were looking curiously at the trio before he replied in his smooth, slightly acidic voice, "Your timing is so perfect, my dear Torvil, one might almost suspect you of waiting in the wings as it were. Would I be redundant in offering to present you to the lady? Perhaps you are already acquainted with Mademoiselle St. Germain?"

"I have not had that pleasure."

"Then pray allow me to repair the omission. Mademoiselle Desirée St. Germain, Viscount Torvil, who was just married today and has chosen a most original way of celebrating his nuptials."

Kate emerged from her stupor long enough to breathe a soft reply in French. Nicholas sent a glance of pure dislike at the marquess, who continued to display a sneering little smile on his lined countenance, before he bowed and expressed his pleasure at the introduction.

"May I have the honor of the next dance, *Mademoiselle*?"

Kate's brain, which had stalled dead at the shock of coming face to face with her husband, was functioning again and bent on arranging an escape. She bestowed a brilliant smile on him.

"I am so very sorry, milord, but it grows late and I must not keep my friend waiting. *Au 'voir,* gentlemen." A brief impersonal smile for both and she slipped away before either man could react.

"Mademoiselle, wait—"

She ignored their protests and attained the doorway, dodging around a couple entering the supper room. She was safe for the moment but dared not waste an instant in locating her brother. Both of the men she had left behind were quite capable of pursuing her and she did not want them to see her with Roger. Although she thought herself undetected by Nicholas, his face gave nothing away. Flight was imperative, but where was Roger? She dared not remain any longer in the ballroom.

Evading the approach of a gentleman bent on detaining her, she edged toward the hall leading to the cloak rooms and slipped outside. Thank heavens, it was deserted. She would wait five minutes then slip back into the ballroom for a few moments to search again for Roger. There was no possibility of going home alone; she had not thought to provide herself with the money to pay for a hackney cab. Her thoughts kept pace with her nervous movements up and down the hall. It was certainly true that young women of her station were raised to be helpless. They never left home without a male escort or a servant to arrange the mundane matter of transportation. One might as well be an imbecile for all the control a grown woman had over her own movements, she raged silently. Were the five minutes up? Dare she go back into the ballroom? It was a moot point which of her late companions she most dreaded to meet again. An encounter with Nicholas would result in a lively quarrel if he recognized her, but she was not so naive that she failed to sense the danger in even a minimal association with Lord Ralston. The fact that he might embarrass her by disclosing her identity would not weigh with such a self-indulgent type if curiosity about her piqued him enough. Such a man would admit no interests save his own.

At this point in her mental gyrations a hand descended on her shoulder. She froze for an instant while her heart zoomed to her throat; then she forced herself to turn slowly, still unsure which man represented more trouble. Her guarded eyes met the angry gray orbs of her husband.

"You wish to speak to me, *Monsieur?*"

"I don't trust myself to speak to you at the moment," he replied grimly. "Come on, I'm taking you home."

Kate still hesitated, unsure whether or not Nicholas knew her. He took her arm and propelled her impatiently toward the cloakroom.

"If it will set your mind at rest, I have known your identity since before you blithely accepted the escort of the most notorious rake in London. Lord, I thought I'd never shake off my partner so I might follow you in there, and it was none too soon, either."

Kate stopped dead and faced her husband. "How did you recognize me? I made sure my disguise was perfect."

"Oh, it was very good, but you cannot entirely disguise your profile even with a mask. Come *on;* the sooner we get out of here the better."

150

"What about Roger? I must let him know I am leaving."

"He knows." If possible his manner became even more forbidding. "I'll have something more to say to your idiot of a brother when next we meet."

After this caustic threat there was no conversation exchanged while Nicholas retrieved Kate's cloak and escorted her outside where their carriage awaited. Nor did he have anything to say to her during the entire length of the drive to Albemarle Street. If he wished to quarrel, Kate was more than willing to oblige him but she had no intention of initiating the battle. Still under the influence of the cold rage that had overtaken her at what she considered her husband's treachery at humiliating her in front of the servants, she was totally unrepentant. Though well aware that no female who could lay claim to even a modicum of delicacy of principle or who valued her reputation would have dreamed of doing something so crassly vulgar as must sink her quite beneath reproach should it be discovered, she would not hesitate to repeat her masquerade given the same conditions. Submerged in this mood of defiance, she was totally unprepared when the carriage pulled up in front of the door.

Nicholas, looking at her for the first time in her corner, said coldly, "Unless it is your intention to set the household on its ear, I suggest you remove that ridiculous mask before we go in."

A hot flame of rage licked through her body. How dare he accuse *her* of setting the servants talking after what he had done! Her trembling fingers ripped off the mask, sadly disarranging the smooth hair style. Nicholas was momentarily nonplussed at the incendiary quality of the glance returned by his cool, emotionless bride, but whatever enlightening and undoubtedly blazing retort trembled on her lips, it was forestalled by the appearance at the open door of the omnipresent Mudgrave, and by the time the bridal pair had made their way up the stairs to Kate's suite in palpitating silence, she had herself well in hand.

At the door she wished him an abrupt good night and entered her sitting room, but if in a moment of cowardice she thought thus to avoid a confrontation, she had seriously misjudged her man. Nicholas was beside her, closing the door gently behind him before she had taken two steps into the room. There was a faint but genuine smile of amusement on his hard-featured face.

"Whoa there! You and I have some unfinished business before we say good night. Sit down." He gestured toward an inviting bronze green *fauteuil*.

Kate, already regretting her momentary lapse, was once more carefully expressionless as she ignored the chair he indicated and seated herself on an armless chair with a cane seat and back. She smoothed the red muslin skirt with deliberation and directed a calm stare at her husband. His anger was well controlled, but she knew he was seething behind that stern civility. For a moment, blinded by her own rage, she had forgotten that her most effective weapon against him was that determined imperturbability she had so assiduously cultivated during their engagement. She was remembering it now.

He broke the hostile silence. "Well," he said curtly, "I am awaiting an explanation for this extraordinarily ill-advised—to set it no higher—escapade of yours."

"It's quite simple, really. I had no wish to spend my wedding night alone, so when Roger called to collect his glass I persuaded him to take me along with him." She appeared to think no further explanation was required.

He frowned. "Did not Langston tell you where he was bound this evening?"

"Oh, yes."

"Assuming he was too foxed to exercise any rational judgment, surely you must have known that affair was no place for you." His frown deepened. "In fact, you did know it; otherwise, why that highly improper rig out, why the mask?"

"For the first because I did not want to appear different from the rest of the *ladies,* and for the second, to conceal my identity. I thought I fitted in quite well," she added with deliberate provocation. Roger had warned that this escapade would give Nicholas a disgust of her and, watching his face darken with anger at her cool admission, she saw with a perverse satisfaction that her brother had been in the right of it. But even while she stared defiantly into his dark, angry countenance, a reluctant gleam of humor lighted the gray eyes and there was the merest twitch of the compressed lips.

"Oh, you looked the part well enough, but even that deplorable French accent could not disguise the fact that you did not belong in that company."

On the point of retorting that *he* seemed at home to a peg in that same company, sanity or self-preservation prevailed and she contented herself with a careless toss of her head. "I enjoyed myself excessively."

"The devil you did!" All trace of softness had vanished. "Now I want to know what prompted you to do such a foolhardy thing, and don't bother spinning me anymore bamboozling tales of not wishing to spend your wedding night alone for I cut my wisdoms years ago and I won't swallow that one!"

Kate put up her chin. "I was furious with you for humiliating me so by going out tonight. What would you wager that such behavior wasn't the prime topic of conversation amongst the servants this evening?" She had the satisfaction of seeing a tinge of red creep up under Nicholas's bronzed skin at this frankness and could only hope that slight shifting of his severe gaze was due to shame at his own conduct. "When Roger suggested that you might have gone to Argyll Rooms—without realizing it would mean anything to me, you understand—I decided I would pay you out by appearing there myself." Her eyes dropped to the black lace fan in her lap which seemed to engage all her attention as she played with its folds. A thought brought her head up again almost immediately. "Don't hold Roger responsible. He would never have consented if he had thought my disguise could be penetrated."

"Well, I hope you are pleased with your little revenge. You'd have been well served had I let Ralston unmask you. In the future if you try anything so grossly improper I shall know how to deal with you. The least I can expect from you is that you will act in public with due regard to your position as my wife."

"Your wife?" Kate's resentment at this peal being rung over her, unjustifiably as she considered, erupted into unwise speech. "I find that most amusing. We may share a roof and a name, but I am *not* your wife."

The brief silence between the pair vibrated with danger. Kate experienced a chill of fear even as she managed to convey contempt. Nicholas was white around the nostrils and his fists were clenched with the effort to control his fury. His voice, however, was quite level, a travesty of pleasantness.

"That situation, my dear Kate, is not without remedy. May I suggest that you bear this in mind. As for sharing a name, the name is mine, I'll remind you; and the day you do something to damage it you will have gone your length. And now I'll bid you good night—*wife*."

154

Chapter Eleven

After this sadly unpropitious introduction to the married state, Nicholas and Kate settled into a surprisingly easy routine with a minimum of friction. They had only a day or two to themselves because the wedding announcements sent out by Lady Langston had proclaimed the young couple "at home" to those of their friends and relatives who might wish to pay visits of congratulations to the newly wedded pair. This grace period was spent in a homely fashion, checking on supplies to meet the projected demands of hospitality and taking stock of the charming house which was to be their home.

There had been no time before their marriage to initiate any but the most urgent of decorating necessities and order a general cleaning and polishing. Lord Bartram had not lived in the house since the demise of his wife some twenty years before, and with the exception of his occasional visits to London, which became shorter while the intervals in between stretched out over the years, the house had been closed up, its once elegant furnishings perpetually swathed in holland covers.

In the last several years the rooms had undergone no more than a cursory annual cleaning under the direction of his lordship's housekeeper who did not care to remain away from Kent for more than a few days at a time.

Early in their engagement Nicholas had gone to the registry office to engage the services of a full staff with the exception of his own valet and Kate's dresser. Kate had been conducted over the house during the bustle and disorder of the subsequent cleaning spree and had been able to do little more than assimilate the layout of the rooms and decide on the most essential areas of repainting. By tacit agreement the couple left the question of furnishings till after their marriage, except for Kate's personal suite. In the back of her consciousness was the knowledge that much of the furniture was decidedly old-fashioned, some even dating back to Queen Anne's reign, but she had not given the matter much consideration.

Now, as she and Nicholas strolled on a leisurely tour of inspection of their domain, they had no difficulty in coming to an amicable decision that they rather liked the lines of many of the large cabinet pieces and tables with their beautifully polished surfaces of inlaid woods and handsomely formed ormolu trim. The craftsmanship was superb in most instances, and there was only the occasional item that seemed too large or ornate for the moderate size of the rooms.

Nor, after one good look, did they experience the least difficulty in deciding to consign the greater portion of the window hangings to the attic storerooms. Though none were actually shabby from wear, most had faded unevenly and no longer presented a pristine appearance. Only in the ground floor room, with the wall of book shelves that Nicholas had selected for a study, had the process of time resulted in a happy mellowing of a once garish brocade (judging by a glimpse of the seam allowance showing through a tear) into a muted rose blended exceedingly well with the blue turkey carpet on the floor and the dark oak paneling on the walls. In general the rugs had fared better than the draperies, including a lovely Aubusson in which shades of peach and beige predominated. Kate had not seen this prize unrolled on her first visit to the house, and she was delighted with its delicate beauty. Nicholas agreed that it would make a perfect focal point for the dining room and that once the seats had been re-covered in a complementary fabric, the mahogany chairs after a design by Thomas Chippendale would take a new lease on life. Their open backs with lattice work in the Chinese manner had an austere grace that pleased the eye.

Kate's eager eye had dwelt with surprise and pleasure on a charming lacquer ware cabinet on an ornately carved and silvered stand in the main saloon. The interior of the piece was even more beautiful than the exterior with a profusion of small drawers to house "collections," all covered in an exquisite fashion with Chinese patterns and motifs. Nicholas smiled indulgently while she exclaimed at some length over the good fortune that allowed them the enjoyment of such a rare and beautiful example of the cabinet maker's art.

On the other hand, the chairs and settees in the grand saloon seemed too stiff and uncomfortable to provide an inviting prospect for guests. Nicholas concurred with Kate's suggestion that they purchase some more modern pieces and readily agreed that an early visit to a showroom was indicated. At this point she had glanced a little uncertainly at her husband, wondering if all the discussion about furnishings was boring him. She had no wish to abuse his indulgence or try his patience, yet she felt a natural diffidence at making unsupported decisions regarding a house that actually belonged to his grandfather. Perhaps there were pleasant associations for him with the present furnishings. Nicholas might secretly resent her interference. She broached the subject timidly to be reassured immediately by her husband in hearty tones, the sincerity of which could not be called into question, that he was eager to modernize the house and found himself so far in complete agreement with her thoughts on the subject. Upon hearing this, Kate's sense of well-being burgeoned, and she smiled more warmly than usual at the viscount before resuming her tour of the main rooms with an increased pleasure.

Their dealings with regard to those initial congratulatory calls proceeded with similar ease. For the most part Kate played hostess to the ladies who chatted briskly over tea and sweetmeats in the main drawing room while Nicholas entertained gentleman callers in his study, supplying them with more hearty libations culled from a cellar that was still fairly well stocked. His callers were as willing to advise him on what to add to his liquor supply as Kate's visitors were eager to discuss decorating schemes for the main rooms. If there was still abundant curiosity and speculation concerning this surprise marriage, it encountered nothing in the atmosphere of the pleasant house on Albemarle Street to sustain it. Kate and Nicholas appeared like any other newly married couple, a little diffident, a trifle self-conscious when referring to each other before friends perhaps, the bride sometimes thrown into adorable confusion by the distinguishing attentions of her new husband. In short, this bride and groom provided no new tidbits for gossiping tongues to savor. Each night the viscount dined at home with his wife or provided her with an attentive escort at one or more evening parties. If their demeanor struck a more comradely than loverlike note, it could certainly be argued that they were merely conforming to the niceties of a social code that called for a strict propriety in public manners. It was considered very bad *ton* to display one's heart on one's sleeve, as the saying went.

A week or so of being more or less on public display produced the unlooked for benefit of a gradual reduction in the tension that had built up between the young people during their engagement and culminated in the bitter scenes following their wedding. Though Kate had certainly derived a momentary satisfaction from flaunting herself amongst the *demi-monde* under her bridegroom's incensed eye and thus avenging her wounded pride, a night's reflection had brought her a saner perspective on her actions with regard to her original plan to coexist on distantly friendly terms with her husband. It would never do to make a habit of enraging Nicholas whenever her feminine sensibilities were exacerbated; in fact, where he was concerned she must have no feminine sensibilities. Consequently, she had steeled herself to greet him with determined affability the following morning for their first shared breakfast. To her secret relief Nicholas responded in kind, and in a surprisingly short span of time the friendliness on her part was completely unfeigned. She had found him easy to deal with over the question of furnishing the house and an unfailing support socially. When relaxed he displayed a dry masculine wit that put her forcibly in mind of her grandfather. Exposed from early childhood to a good deal of masculine company, she responded unreservedly to this aspect of his personality and suffered no missish qualms about answering him back on his own terms.

It was not to be supposed that even a newly married couple would be forever in each other's pockets, of

159

course. All members of the Polite World kept up a hectic social schedule during the short Season, but naturally the ladies had little part in the gentlemen's more active pursuits. Ladies of quality did not attend race meetings, nor did they go to Tattersall's to buy horses or place bets on races. Naturally they took no part in shooting practice at Manton's or sparring at Gentleman Jackson's select establishment on Bond Street. They witnessed no boxing matches at Cribb's or the Fives Court for such violent sports were anathema to a female of breeding, though less than one hundred years previously there had been quite a vogue for boxing matches featuring female combatants. Needless to say, these contestants were not from the upper levels of society, nor were ladies present among the audience in the provincial towns where such contests were held. Such sporting events as curricle races at Epsom where the Corintheans pitted their knowledge of horseflesh and driving abilities against those who aspired to leadership in these fields were talked about amongst the ladies of course, but although a few members of the fair sex could boast of being very pretty whips themselves, they did not engage in racing against each other in public to prove their skills with the reins.

The one activity pursued with almost equal avidity by men and women was gambling. The craze for gambling had reached its peak in the previous century when huge fortunes were won and lost at the turn of a card or a throw of the dice. It reached such an extent that it was not unknown for the titles of properties that had been in one family for generations to change hands at the gaming tables. Though not quite so prevalent now, gambling was still a popular pastime with both sexes, but here, too, there were restrictions on the participation of females. Ladies might play whist for chicken stakes at Almack's and indulge their passion for gaming at private parties. Some few daring individuals might even visit gaming houses run by hostesses with some claim to respectability, where admission was by card only, but ladies of *ton* did not frequent gaming halls where they were in danger of rubbing elbows with the scaff and raff of society. In fact, a lady who valued her reputation would not so much as drive down St. James's Street, that masculine province where the gentlemen's clubs as well as several of the more notorious of the gaming hells were located. Even Bond Street, which was a shopping mecca for females in the morning, was considered by high sticklers to be off limits in the afternoon when unescorted ladies might be exposed to the unwelcome attentions of the so-called Bond Street Beaux on the strut.

With male and female pursuits so clearly defined, it would have been extraordinary indeed if Nicholas and Kate had continued to be for long in each other's exclusive company. Nicholas was soon drawn back into the company of his sports-minded friends and Kate was reabsorbed into her mother's schedule. Lady Langston and Deborah were thrilled with the opportunity to assist in decorating an entire house without needing to regard the cost, and the three ladies became happily involved in this ambitious undertaking.

Kate's marriage produced one additional benefit in the estimation of Lady Langston. She enjoyed the company of a select group of friends and delighted in an occasional visit to the theater or opera, but she found the constant round of social activities engaged in by the mothers of unmarried girls to be excessively fatiguing to one of her delicate constitution. Though she had undertaken the task of presenting her daughters in an heroic spirit of selfless maternal devotion, she now discovered that the rigors attendant on a month-long spree of social engagements arising from her elder daughter's betrothal, combined with the exertion of arranging a big society wedding, had so debilitated her slender resources of stamina that she was at present unable to exert a similar effort on behalf of her younger daughter. In short, now that Kate, by virtue of her new status as a young matron, was considered an adequate chaperone for Deborah at Almack's and private parties, Lady Langston took to her couch to recruit her flagging physical strength with a new tonic and a bland diet prescribed by Doctor Abbott for those unfortunates like herself whose digestive systems were particularly sensitive to stress. Unless an affair promised to be uncommonly entertaining, Lady Langston turned the task of accompanying Deborah over to Kate while she endeavored to repair the excesses of the season by limiting herself to no more strenuous an activity than perusing the latest novel from Hookham's with a box of sugar plums at her elbow for nourishment.

The viscount escorted the ladies to occasional private balls and rout parties, but he considered Almack's pretty poor value as entertainment, so on Wednesday and Friday evenings the more accommodating Lord Langston or the Honourable Robin Dunston was prevailed upon to act as escort. Kate and her good-natured brother-in-law had gotten upon easy terms in very short order, and since Miss Deborah Harmon was exactly the sort of girl to appeal to his taste, it was no hardship for Mister Dunston to gallant the young ladies to the subscription balls.

Watching Robin flirting audaciously with her sister, Kate smiled to remember her own brief *tendre* for him which, fortunately, had not survived a closer acquaintance. It would certainly have complicated an already difficult situation to be striving to conceal hopeless yearnings for another man while sustaining the image of a happy bride before the interested gaze of the Polite World. Assessing Robin with a more analytical judgment than formerly, she conceded that he was definitely handsomer than Nicholas by virtue of a more regular alignment of features and a less forbidding jawline, but his face lacked something of the strength of character that gave his brother such an arresting quality. Nor did the workings of his intellect strike responsive sparks from hers. Robin's company was pleasant and restful, but Nicholas challenged her to meet him on another level.

So far from fading into the background in accordance with the defensive design she had devised from the moment they contracted to marry, she found herself aware of all his plans and increasingly more a part of his life. When she thought about the situation, she was dimly aware that matters had not fallen out the way she had planned and that it was her husband's persistent interest in her daily activities that made it impossible for her to remain aloof. This would have seemed more a matter for concern had not Nicholas treated her in their home with the unself-consciousness of a friend who had known her from her cradle. She would not have believed a month ago that she could be so comfortable and content in the company of such a man, but so it was.

When Lady Langston ventured to ask her daughter how she and the viscount were dealing together, Kate was able to reply that they were rubbing along tolerably well, which remark caused Lady Langston to direct a penetrating stare at her daughter's unrevealing countenance. She opened her lips, paused briefly, then made some commonplace observation, evidently having decided against pursuing the subject, for which forbearance Kate could only be grateful. In her view nothing was to be gained by a discussion of the relationship between Torvil and herself with her mother, and somehow the very idea of such a discussion smacked of disloyalty to her husband, though why this should be so she would be hard pressed to explain.

What Kate in her understandable preoccupation with the daily events of her new life did not realize was that the present situation and her complaisant acceptance of it had been neatly maneuvered by her husband, following a plan of action no less determined than her own had been, though its inception was of a later date. Nicholas, too, had had much with which to occupy his mind during the sleepless night following the tensions and quarrels of their wedding day. He had tried initially and unavailingly to get upon comfortable terms with Kate during their engagement, until his annoyance at her intransigence and his wounded masculine vanity had brought his good intentions to a crashing halt. Then had followed a period in which he vacillated between striving for retaliation and conciliation with no appreciable reaction from Kate to any change of tactic.

Not until his wedding day, however, had he admitted to himself that he wished above all things to turn his sham marriage into a true union. He had stupidly tried to compel Kate's agreement by issuing an ultimatum about that cursed bridal dinner, and like the spirited girl he had known she was, she had defied him, even going to the lengths of hitting back by appearing at the Cyprian's Ball. Prevented by his word as a gentleman from claiming his husbandly rights, he had determined during that long night of frustration to gain his ends by winning her acceptance. He did not deceive himself that it would be an easy task; he would have to overcome Kate's instinctive, and to him, unreasoning dislike, and this would take time—how much time he dared not predict. Up to the present he had never been compelled to exercise patience or restraint in his pursuit of a woman. Without conceit he could say that the

164

women he had made the objects of his gallantry had displayed a flattering willingness to submit to his advances. Patience had never been numbered amongst his few virtues; he was by nature impulsive and impatient. More importantly, though, he had inherited some of his father's cast iron determination, so if patience was what was needed to achieve his objective then he was prepared to go slowly and carefully about the task of winning Kate.

He acted with the deliberation of a general initiating a military campaign. Of the first importance was the breaking down of the wall of distrust and dislike his bride had erected. He proceeded slowly, missing no opportunity to breach the wall. If she wished to discuss rugs and curtains, then rugs and curtains were his main interest. If she desired his opinion on furnishings, then he was willing to give this matter his fullest consideration. He advanced by inches and restrained himself from making any moves to touch her. When she smiled that adorable, mischievous smile, he jammed the fingers that itched to trace the lovely curves of her mouth into his pockets and smiled back lazily. Wary of him at first, she gradually learned to relax in his company and, he hoped, to enjoy being with him. Sometimes when they were discussing some topic unrelated to their personal situation, he felt they had been friends for years, so receptive to each other's opinions were their minds. Not until this point when Kate could forget herself enough to laugh helplessly at some nonsense of his did he dare to proceed to the next step.

He would have had to be insensitive indeed to fail to recognize Kate's reluctance to have the slightest physical contact between them. On the three occasions when he had kissed her she had gone absolutely rigid. He had seethed at her reluctance to take his hand or lean on his arm. It was essential that he accustom her to his casual touch before trying to make love to her. The first time he seized her hand and pressed it lightly in a complimentary fashion she stiffened slightly, but he had already released the hand and was off on another topic before she could react further. The first time he strolled casually into her bedchamber on some pretext, her startled expression had almost caused him to lose countenance, but he had controlled his twitching lips and blandly exhibited a small tear in the sleeve of his shirt. Kate's woman had been experimenting with a new hair style for her mistress at the time and had looked extremely put out at the interruption, but Kate had immediately volunteered to mend the tear. He had been confident of just such a response from one of her generous nature and had calmly proceeded to strip off the shirt under the scandalized nose of Miss Elsie Hawthorne, his wife's lofty abigail. His laughing eyes had invited Kate to share the joke and, although her color was slightly heightened, her lips had curved irrepressibly as she accepted the shirt from his hands, carefully looking away from Hawthorne's outraged face. Whistling a gay tune, Nicholas had sauntered back to his own bed chamber very pleased with himself, but hopeful that the incident would never come to the ears of his valet. Perkins would expire of chagrin at the suggestion that any garment in his care would ever be permitted to appear in less than perfect condition. He might even leap to the correct conclusion that his lordship had caused the damage to one of his fine cambric shirts for reasons of his own.

His lordship lost no time in consolidating his gains. The next day he had the good fortune to meet his wife almost on the doorstep as he returned home from a most satisfactory session at Manton's Gallery. She was accompanied by a footman whose arms were piled high with parcels. Never one to lose an opportunity, Nicholas began to unload the packages.

"I'll carry these up for her ladyship, James. You may go."

Kate blinked at this maneuver and quickly seized two of the packages from the pile now balanced precariously in her husband's arms and held them out.

"Wait, James. Please take these to Mrs. Clarke. They are items she ordered." She bestowed a warm smile on the young footman and headed up the stairs, followed by her husband. "You are very gallant, Torvil," she observed lightly, a mildly quizzical gleam in the amber depths.

"Nonsense, my dear," came the bland response. "It's all part of my new job."

Kate laughed gaily. "I may remind you of those words one day." She turned at the door to her sitting room and thanked her husband prettily, holding out her arms for the packages, but he ignored the gesture and followed her into the room. He walked over to the door to her bedchamber.

"In here?" he inquired, and paused expectantly as Kate hesitated for an instant before opening the door for him.

"What have you been buying?" Nicholas asked, cheerfully oblivious to any atmosphere as he deposited the parcels on the bed. He had good reason to congratulate himself as Kate completely forgot her embarrassment in her eagerness to display a sample of the fabric she had selected for the seats of the dining room chairs. After gratifying his wife by agreeing that the color was perfect, he was called upon to admire a new shawl of a silver gauze that she had been unable to resist. Kate was draping it over her elbows to display it to advantage when a dreadful cacophony claimed their attention.

"Good God, what is that infernal yowling?" demanded the viscount, striding to the window that faced onto the alleyway leading to the stable mews. Kate joined him, peering anxiously out of the window Nicholas had thrown open.

"Oh dear, it is that poor little cat again. Look, Torvil, the gray and white cat! See, those big cats have cornered him. I have noticed them before. He doesn't stand a chance against those bullies." She gripped his sleeve imploringly. "Please, Torvil, do you think you might rescue the poor little thing? They will surely hurt him. Bring him to me."

Nicholas spun about in astonishment to confront two wide, anxious amber eyes edged by a thick fringe of straight brown lashes. He swallowed the jeering words trembling on his tongue and, obeying an insane impulse, kissed the tip of her shapely nose before loping out of the room. Five minutes later he returned carrying a cringing, spitting excuse for a cat. When Kate exclaimed happily and tried to take the animal from him he warded her off.

"Take care! He isn't in the least grateful for my intervention; in fact, he has already clawed me. If you'd like a kitten I'll find you something better than this mangy specimen."

"Nonsense!" Kate had petted and crooned over the shivering creature and now took him in her arms where he lay passive, totally spent but with huge eyes still fixed unblinkingly on the viscount. "Naturally he isn't very handsome at the moment—"

"The understatement of the year!" Nicholas gave vent to an exasperated laugh as he assessed the scrawny feline with extreme disfavor. "He is undoubtedly loaded with fleas. You cannot—"

"I think he's finally stopped trembling," interrupted his wife, paying no heed to his dire prediction. "Look, he's starting to groom himself in my arms. He must trust me already," she added with satisfaction.

"He's at least half grown and has always been homeless by the look of him. You'll never tame him," warned the viscount.

"Let me try, please, Torvil. See, he's licking my hand; he likes me."

Nicholas was not proof against the earnest face with pleading eyes raised to his. He sighed gustily. "Very well, sweetheart, but not until we get him cleaned up." He reached for the cat again. "James will see to it for you, unless he offers his resignation rather than so demean himself." This last was added with gentle irony for he was well aware that the footman cherished an almost worshipful regard for the young mistress who always had a kind word for him and never failed to inquire after his ailing mother. On more than one occasion she had exhorted James to bring his parent some delicacy from the kitchen in the hope of tempting her failing appetite, with the result that James was Kate's devoted slave.

Now she twinkled saucily at the picture of her elegant husband holding a dirty, cowering example of a breed he regarded with little liking under the best of circumstances. A faint dimple unexpectedly dented one smooth cheek. Nicholas stared in fascination, allowing his bold gaze to roam along the enchanting curve of throat and neck where it lingered for an instant on the shadowed little hollow at the base of her neck where a tiny pulse beat enticingly. Bemused, he took an unthinking step forward to close the distance between them when a startled flash of alarm darkened Kate's eyes and brought him to a belated realization of his actions. At the same instant the forgotten feline in his hands, resentful of the sudden tightening of those hands, reached out a paw and clawed one of them.

"Damned little ingrate!"

The mild tone in which this pejoration was uttered scarcely accorded with the sentiment thus expressed but was more allied to the relief and gratitude Nicholas was experiencing at the timely intervention of the wretched cat. His wife's instinctive recoil was completely eclipsed by her concern for his wound as she alternately scolded the cat and expressed anxiety over his scratched hand.

"It's nothing," he assured her, "but take care with this little brute until he gets used to being handled. What are you going to call him?" This was added with the intention of giving Kate's thoughts another direction lest she feel impelled to comment on what had transpired.

She smiled ruefully. "After that clawing he should probably be called Attila the Hun, but I think, because he's been such a wanderer, that Ulysses would suit him."

Nicholas laughed. "It's to be hoped he lives up to his noble name. Come, Ulysses, you are totally unfit as yet for a lady's boudoir." He nodded a friendly goodbye and got himself safely out of Kate's bedchamber, thankful to avoid any repercussions from his ill-judged action. His face wore a thoughtful frown as he descended the staircase and went in search of James, unmindful of the protesting cries being uttered by one tightly held small cat. That had been a close run thing! He was finding it increasingly difficult to keep to his chosen role of platonic friendliness when Kate exhibited any additional degree of warmth in his company. The longing to take her in his arms and kiss her until she responded to his ardor was taking on all the aspects of a physical ache, sometimes rising to a crescendo of agony, at other, busy moments scarcely noticed, but always present on some level of his consciousness.

"Go slowly, you fool."

The muttered words reached the ears of the young footman standing in the hall.

"I beg your pardon, my lord?"

"It was nothing," disclaimed the viscount hastily as he thrust the protesting animal into James's surprised arms with the most unusual orders that young man had yet received during his brief sojourn in the household.

The following day when Nicholas knocked on Kate's door for the purpose of restoring to her a cat much improved in appearance but still vociferously protesting his lot in life, he did so with a dogged determination to maintain an air of casual friendliness. He need not have bothered to put a conscious check on his ardor, however, because upon entering at her command, he found Hawthorne bustling about getting her mistress ready for an evening party. It soon become apparent from that lady's offended air that the wanton introduction of wild animals into a boudoir was an experience she had never been called upon to endure in all her years of waiting upon ladies of the highest social rank. Kate's airy portrayal of someone completely oblivious to any atmosphere of ill feeling was much less convincing. She made a wry face at her husband behind Hawthorne's rigid back when she caught his expression of wicked appreciation of the situation, then bent all her attention on Ulysses, who was conducting a thorough investigation of every corner of his new domain. After satisfying himself that no hidden peril lurked in the shadows, he submitted politely to Kate's caresses, accepted her compliments on his improved appearance with exemplary *sang froid,* and selected the best chair in the room as his due. When the viscount removed him with insulting promptitude, he directed a long unblinking stare at him, wreathed himself around Kate's legs once or twice to show he did not hold her responsible for the unfortunate prejudice of her husband, and settled himself on a warm spot on the rug at a safe distance from the small fire. A few moments' scrutiny served to convince him it was not actively hostile, and he closed his eyes with a little purr of contentment. All action in the room had remained suspended during this short interval. A disgusted sniff from Hawthorne caused Kate to grip her lower lip firmly between her teeth, but one glance at her husband's face proved too much for her composure and she dissolved in helpless giggles.

Nicholas had to laugh himself but confessed, "I would not wish my life or my fortune to be hanging on the chance that that fur-covered rogue won't immediately climb back onto that chair the instant I close the door behind me."

Kate wiped her streaming eyes and promised shakily, "Indeed, I won't permit him to presume, Torvil, though after this performance, I'm inclined to suspect his pedigree is at least equal to yours."

"Wretch!" Her husband chuckled and left the room to resume his own toilette.

Nicholas and she had been in perfect charity with each other lately, and they always seemed to have a lot to say to one another Kate was thinking several hours later as their luxurious carriage rolled smoothly toward Albemarle Street. She cast a covert glance at her husband sitting quietly in his corner and wondered uneasily what might have occurred to cause this uncharacteristic silence on his part. It had been a very ordinary party with dancing and cards, and Nicholas had displayed no reluctance to attend. The lighthearted conversation had never been allowed to lapse on the short drive to Lord Selwyn's town residence, but since he had collected Kate and they had bidden their hosts good-bye not one unnecessary word had been exchanged. He had assisted her into the carriage, inquired mechanically for her comfort and made brief polite replies to her opening remarks. Since then he had volunteered nothing in the way of conversation, and gradually Kate's flow of chatter had dried up as she searched her memory for some incident that might have upset or annoyed him. She was impeded in this task by the fact that except for one dance early in the evening and a word or two exchanged later when Nicholas sought to assure himself that she was partnered for supper, she had spent almost no time in his company. It had been a mildly enjoyable affair; though her mother and sister were not present, she had no lack of friends to converse with and several of her favorite partners had sought her hand for a dance. As had happened frequently of late, the young lieutenant whom she had met at her wedding had singled her out for attention. Although she could not deny she found Lieutenant Mason's open adoration quite flattering, she was most careful not to go beyond the line of ordinary civility with him because she had gathered the impression that for some reason Torvil did not like him above half. After noticing her husband's brooding eye on them during a waltz, she had rather avoided Lieutenant Mason for the remainder of the evening, choosing instead to stay within Robin's orbit in the belief that Torvil would prefer to know she was safely attached to his brother so he might feel free to join the whist players in the card room.

She frowned in perplexity. Something must have occurred during the card game to have produced this unnatural silence. Kate was about to inquire more closely into his reactions to the evening when they drew up to the house. Nicholas leaped out of the carriage before the coachman had completely stopped the horses. He let down the steps and gave Kate his hand, still without speaking. A welcoming glow of light flooded out of the door that Mudgrave had opened. One of the viscount's peculiarities, Kate had discovered, was an ingrained dislike of returning to a dark house.

She acknowledged a pleasant drowsiness as they ascended the staircase together and was deciding that whatever had caused Nicholas's silence would probably loom less important after a good night's sleep, when he broke his silence at the door to Kate's sitting room.

"I wish to talk with you. Get rid of your maid in good order; I'm coming in."

"You wish to talk with me?" echoed Kate in some bewilderment. "But you had nothing to say all the way home. Can it not wait until tomorrow?"

"No, it cannot," he answered curtly. "If you don't get rid of her, I shall." With that he pushed open her door for her and walked on down the hall to his own room without troubling to see her inside.

On the instant Kate's mind was a seething mass of conjecture. Something dreadful must have happened to cause Nicholas to deviate from the impeccable courtesy that characterized his manners. Unconsciously she gnawed on her lip as she walked slowly toward her bedchamber. Could he have lost a great deal of money in the card room? She could not know for certain, of course, but she had rather gained the impression that Nicholas no longer cared to play for high stakes. It had always been a case of enjoying the thrill of pitting his skill against another's more than the acquiring of money that had attracted him to gaming. In any event he had spent less than two hours in the card room. He could not have done anything too terrible in that length of time. Sudden, unreasoning fear slashed through her mind. Unless he had challenged someone to a duel or been challenged himself! But that was nonsense, her saner self argued. Nicholas was noted for his even temper amongst his friends; besides, though her knowledge of the rules governing dueling was scant, she was positive gentlemen never made any reference to an affair of honor to a female so that could not be what he wished to discuss.

She reached this comforting conclusion and her bedchamber at the same time and had her thoughts jerked back to the immediate problem, that of getting rid of Hawthorne, by the sight of that individual preparing to carry out a long bedtime routine. Hawthorne rather prided herself upon being more scrupulous than the ordinary run of dressers when it came to maintaining a strict regimen concerning the health and beauty of her ladies. Feigning the sleepiness that had deserted her with Torvil's announcement, she yawned delicately behind her hand and addressed the abigail who was starting to examine her mistress's discarded garments for stains or rips.

"Never mind about the hair brushing tonight, Hawthorne, or all those clothes. They can wait till morning. Just help me with my stay laces and you may retire." She aimed for a casual, offhand manner, but had to remind herself to breathe in a normal rhythm.

Judging from the absence of all expression on the maid's gaunt features as she obeyed these commands, Hawthorne considered the elimination of a nightly session of hair brushing as much a social solecism as tying one's garter in public. Kate sighed inwardly; she feared she would never be able to live up to Hawthorne's standards for a lady of fashion. She barely restrained her impatience while her stays were dealt with methodically and an absurd but delightful concoction of ruffles of misty green silk was tenderly slipped over her unbrushed head. While tying the ribbons of a

175

matching dressing gown, she regarded out of the corner of her eye Hawthorne's deliberate motions in removing the discarded clothing and accepted that they were in the nature of a silent protest. Just as silently she awarded the palm to the abigail in this contest of wills. She didn't have much time to wonder if she would ever prove a match for Hawthorne, however, for the moment the maid closed the door behind her there was a sound from the adjoining room and Torvil stood in the doorway attired in an extremely elegant dressing gown of deep green brocade.

Kate wasted no time admiring his sartorial perfection, however; she was on tenterhooks to discover the reason for this interview. She flew across the carpet on bare feet and clutched one green-clad arm in both hands, unthinkingly giving it a little shake as she demanded, "Well, what is it, what happened tonight? Are you in trouble?"

She sustained a searching look before her husband laughed softly, without mirth. "Thank you for your concern, my dear. No, I am not in any trouble, except perhaps for the fact that you appear not to have guessed the reason for this meeting." As Kate merely looked more bewildered than before, he went on evenly, "I thought it only fair to warn you that I am ending that ridiculous bargain between us here and now."

176

Chapter Twelve

"Bargain? *What* bargain?" Kate echoed blankly, but even as she searched her husband's curiously watchful countenance, horrified enlightenment swept across her own. She turned fiery red and dropped his arm abruptly while retreating a step or two back into her room.

"But . . . but you can't be serious! You *promised* not to try to make this a real marriage for a year or two!"

"No, my dear," replied the viscount calmly, smiling tenderly at her truly ferocious scowl, "*you* said for a year or two; I agreed, most reluctantly, to leave you untouched for a *while,* and so I have, difficult though it's been."

"But that's dishonorable!" Kate fairly shrieked in her fury and disbelief.

"Where is the dishonor in wishing to see what I've bought?" His tone was still equable but Kate's angry accusation caused a tightening of lips and he took a step toward her that added the first measure of fear to her anger.

177

Kate's chin took on a classically belligerent tilt and her voice lashed with contempt. "You mean what your father has bought, do you not?" Her backward progress had halted and she flung any thought of caution or conciliation to the winds in favor of a toe to toe battle.

Strangely enough this last jibe had the effect of relaxing the stern lines of his mouth. He laughed with genuine amusement.

"You little hellcat! Think you a little din will daunt mine ears, sweetheart?" The soft caressing tones brought a look of perplexity to her outraged face.

"You . . . you are quoting *Shakespeare* at a time like this?" Her brows drew together again and her chin went back up. "And I *think* you are calling me a shrew."

"No, no, I am calling you a darling, my darling." His slow forward motion had forced her back another step until the proximity of the bed perforce halted her retreat. "You are my darling, you know." The seductive quality of the soft murmur had a hypnotic effect on Kate for a moment as she stared into compelling, night-dark eyes.

Not until his hands had gone to the ribbons at the throat of her gown could she summon a voice to deny breathlessly: "No, I am *not;* I am not anyone's darling, I'm just plain Kate."

He smiled at her with immeasurable tenderness. "Plain Kate? You mean bonny Kate and *never* Kate the curst, but always Kate, the prettiest Kate in Christendom, Kate of my consolation."

"You . . . you are mangling Shakespeare," she protested illogically.

He had succeeded in removing the dressing gown now and was holding her loosely by the shoulders while his devouring gaze roved over creamy flesh barely concealed by the almost transparent night rail.

"I always knew you were beautiful," he declared in tones made husky by rising passion. His mouth descended to the pulse in the hollow of her throat and the burning touch brought her completely out of her semihypnotic state. Frantically, her hands beat against his chest and she struggled distractedly in his tightening grip.

"No, no, you must stop. I won't let you . . . I'll fight you!"

He held her firmly, allowing her to wear herself out with her uncoordinated struggles. His voice was now soothing, persuasive.

"Don't fight me, sweetheart. I don't want to hurt you. I want you to enjoy this." He continued to press little kisses all over her throat and neck while she twisted her head continuously in a vain attempt to evade his mouth.

"*Never!* Perhaps I cannot stop you, but if you do this I promise I'll hate you till the day I die!"

"Will you, Kate? Will you hate me?" Nicholas didn't wait for an answer to this but proceeded to wrap his arms more securely about her, drawing her struggling form suffocatingly close to the hard length of his muscled body. He abandoned her throat to set his lips on her protesting mouth in an extended kiss that progressed from rigid denial on her part to reluctant softening, to outright cooperation as the magic penetrated her entire being. When he finally raised his lips from hers an inch to draw in a very necessary breath of air, she gave a little moan of protest, but since this was accompanied by an unconscious lifting of her quivering mouth toward his face, Nicholas was encouraged to repeat his actions, which he promptly did, to the mutual satisfaction of both participants.

179

By the time that second marathon kiss ended it was obvious that Kate had been betrayed by the weakness and delights of the flesh. Even a month ago Nicholas might have experienced a thrill of triumph at overcoming her resistance so completely, but all he was aware of as he gathered her pliant body into his arms and deposited her gently on the bed was an immense swell of gratitude for her generous nature. When Kate gave, she gave with both hands. Inexperienced she might be and still shy with him perhaps, but she was no prim, overbred female submitting to her husband's caresses from a sense of duty. He gloried in the intuitive knowledge that he had the power to arouse and thrill her, and, heaven knew, she was his chosen companion in joy. That vaguely familiar phrase came to him later as he gazed down at the soft lines of his wife's face as she slept sweetly beside him, her head nestled confidingly against his shoulder as though she had always possessed the knowledge that she belonged to him. He smiled at his own fanciful imaginings as he eased her into a more comfortable position in his arms and presently drifted quietly into sleep himself.

Kate's eyelashes fluttered slowly and her heavy lids opened just far enough to see that sunlight was flooding the room. She smiled dreamily and closed her eyes again, snuggling deeper into the bedclothes in perfect contentment.

"Good morning, sleepyhead."

The soft words came from close by and succeeded to perfection in alerting her sleep-drugged senses. Her eyes flew open and her gaze focused instinctively on the empty pillow beside her before turning to meet her husband's smiling eyes just inches above hers. He was already dressed, she noted in the instant before his face blotted out everything else as he placed a hand on each side of her on the pillow and bent to kiss her gently.

"Good morning, Nicholas." She smiled at him drowsily but with a hint of shy confusion in her look and more than a hint of rose in her cheeks. Her arms went of their own volition to entwine themselves around his neck as he lightly traced the line of her jaw with a caressing knuckle. "I didn't hear you get up," she volunteered breathlessly to dispel the sense of languor that was stealing over her at his touch and the look in his gray eyes. His little chuckle told her he knew the reason for the ruse, but all he did was kiss her again lingeringly before answering her unspoken question.

"I tried not to rouse you and I told Hawthorne to let you sleep this morning. If I hadn't promised to go with Ollie to Tatt's to check out a three-year-old bay gelding he's interested in, nothing would induce me to leave this room today." He watched with delight the hasty lowering of those incredibly thick straight lashes that reminded him of an artist's paint brush, and bent again to kiss both shadowed lids before straightening up with a mock groan. "At this rate I'll end with a broken back. You should not look so enticing so early in the morning, sweetheart. It's bad for my resolution, not to mention my back. I'll see you here for luncheon, shall I?"

"Oh, yes . . . at least . . . I think Mama planned to have a luncheon with Aunt Agatha today, but she will understand if I cry off."

"I trust not."

Her cheeks, in which the rose had faded somewhat, took on a deeper hue again at this dry comment, and he laughed teasingly.

"You blush so delightfully, my bonny Kate, that it is a constant temptation to my baser nature." He strolled over to the door connecting their bedchambers and paused with his hand on the knob to add with an air of discovery, "Do you know, that is the first time you have ever called me Nicholas." His smile kindled an answering warmth in Kate's. "I like the way you say it. *Au revoir* until lunch."

The room seemed less sunny somehow with Nicholas gone. Kate stretched lazily and sat up, hugging her knees with her arms while she relived the startling events of the past night. It still seemed nearly incredible that she could have been unaware that Nicholas had been determined to make their marriage real right from the beginning. She had been going along happily from day to day, pleased with the success of her plan to achieve a friendly relationship with her husband, and then in the span of one evening Nicholas had turned her fool's paradise into a real one. His determined pursuit of her and ultimate conquest had been singleminded enough to strike terror into her heart if the results had not been so marvelous instead. Having discovered even before their marriage that an average-sized female was totally at the mercy of a strong young man, the wonder was that she had not at any time experienced the nerve-chilling fear that would have assailed her if, for example, Lord Ralston had ever been in a position to compel her submission. Nicholas might have been inexorable in his determination but his arms had been gentle, his smile tender, and the look in his eyes had proved irresistible. Kate had been unable to sustain her resistance against the magnetism of that compelling regard which dissolved her bones, and she had been rewarded by a glorious defeat.

She tossed back her tousled hair, recalling with pleasure her husband's comments and behavior when she had wakened this morning. It might have been acutely embarrassing had not Nicholas been so sweetly solicitous. And he wanted to return to the house for luncheon when surely it would have been understandable if he had gone on somewhere with Oliver and his friends. Kate hugged her knees tighter and produced a triumphant little smile, making no effort to rise out of the lovely lassitude that had overcome her at the look in her husband's eyes when he had bid her *au revoir*.

A knock on the sitting room door interrupted her pleasant reverie. Two figures entered her bedchamber at the same time, but no one could have judged their proximity to be voluntary. The tall, gaunt, eternally disapproving dresser was looking less amiable than ever, and it was not hard to discover the reason. Pattering at her side with innate dignity and conveying a rather inflated attitude of self-importance was Ulysses, looking sleek and well groomed. He mewed an ingratiating greeting and promptly jumped up on the bed to receive Kate's caresses as his due before curling up at her side where he began to wash a paw he had evidently overlooked earlier.

After the shortest of greetings Hawthorne disappeared into what had once been a powder cabinet and now served as a dressing room and wardrobe holder. Kate was dreamily watching Ulysses' ablutions from the exact same spot on the bed when the maid returned a few minutes later to lay out a charming walking dress of rose-colored French muslin worked with hundreds of tiny tucks. She glanced at the enameled clock on the bedside table and reminded her unmoving mistress that she had made plans to go out with Lady Langston that morning. This remark galvanized Kate into action.

"Oh dear, Hawthorne, I must send a note around to Mama to tell her I won't be coming today." She swung her legs off the bed, slightly disturbing Ulysses who glanced reproachfully after her departing form before resuming his grooming. Kate grabbed the dressing gown Nicholas had thoughtfully laid at the foot of the bed and disappeared through the door without further explanation. Hawthorne, appearing at the doorway to the sitting room a moment later, discovered her engaged in this task, seated at a beautiful little rosewood writing table. She took in every detail of Kate's appearance but remained ungratified by the charming picture her mistress presented in extravagant green ruffles with an abundant cloud of ruffled brown hair framing her intent face. The abigail's dispassionate scrutiny succeeded in piercing Kate's concentration for she glanced up after a few seconds.

"Yes, Hawthorne?"

"I beg your pardon, my lady, but what garments would you be wishing me to get ready?"

"Oh, it does not signify; I shall be staying home for lunch today. You decide, Hawthorne." Kate sent a propitiating smile in the maid's direction, guiltily aware that once again she had manifested a regrettable lack of interest in her appearance.

Hawthorne's pinched mouth thinned even more as she moved away from the door without replying.

Kate stared after her for a thoughtful moment. She was fast coming to the conclusion that Hawthorne would elect to serve a bad-tempered mistress who would make unreasonable demands on her time and talents and never utter a word of appreciation, so long as her appearance reflected constant credit on her dresser. Kate's tentative advances toward a less formal relationship had been not so much repulsed as ignored by Hawthorne. She shrugged her shoulders slightly and returned her attention to the pink paper in front of her for a moment, then folded the sheet carefully and affixed a pink wafer to it. She walked over to the bell pull to summon a footman to deliver the note and floated back into her bedchamber to inform Hawthorne of this. If her feet actually touched the floor she was unaware of the fact. Today she was too happy to allow Hawthorne's moods to affect her. She hummed a catchy tune, danced a few dizzy steps, and stopped to tickle Ulysses under his complacent chin before divesting herself of her ruffles with one fluid motion and approaching the wash basin.

When Nicholas joined her for lunch he had no complaint to make about her appearance which was not surprising since she never left her bedchamber without enduring the most minute examination by Hawthorne. Kate often had to restrain a naughty impulse to hold out her hands so that her dresser might pass on the cleanliness of her nails as their old nurse had been wont to do in the past, but that was the unfortunate effect that the abigail had on her. Later, back in her boudoir with her husband, she was reduced to a fit of giggles when Nicholas deliberately ruffled her smooth coiffure and, not content with that, removed the pins and observed the tumbled effect with supreme satisfaction.

"I shan't be able to face Hawthorne until I have repaired the damage," scolded Kate, but her attempt to look severe was greatly hampered by the presence of the elusive dimple he found so enchanting.

"A sweet disorder in the dress, kindles in clothes a wantonness," quoted Nicholas softly into her ear since her gaze had faltered, unable as yet to meet the blaze in his.

"First Shakespeare, now Herrick. You are indeed erudite, my lord."

"With such an inspiration I am ashamed to be reduced to quoting the ancients. I should be able to compose an original tribute to such glowing loveliness." As he looked deep into the amber eyes in her rapt face, all trace of lighthearted foolery vanished; in fact, all efforts at speech ended. He cupped her rounded chin in long fingers and studied the soft curves of her lips before yielding to the temptation they had always represented to him.

Kate was ecstatically happy in those early June days, experiencing a joy in Nicholas's company and in his love-making that she had never looked for in marriage, pleasure of an order she had never dreamed of in her ignorance. In the early days of their acquaintance she had steeled herself against the easy charm of manner that she was persuaded concealed a selfish, callous streak. Even when she made the surprising discovery that he could be supremely companionable and had a mind that could reach out to hers, her opinion of his basic nature had not been challenged. From the moment he had put their marriage on a regular basis, however, her fears had started to evaporate in the warmth of his concern for her. She had been totally unprepared for such generous consideration and was wholly disarmed. All the barriers she had erected against him fell before it like a line of toy soldiers swept by a gleeful, rampaging arm. In the beginning her response to his pervasive charm had been reluctant and tentative but now she could deny him nothing. The unguarded warmth of her own nature triumphed over her initial caution.

The rewards were certainly fulsome. Kate blossomed and grew lovely in the sunshine of her husband's attentions. She exuded a radiance that could not be mistaken. Lady Jersey, chatting away nonstop on various topics during a morning call in Albermarle Street, remarked on it.

"Marriage certainly suits you, my dear. You are absolutely blooming these days. Torvil is to be congratulated."

"Th . . . thank you. After all the bustle attending our engagement and wedding, I am finding the more moderate pace of life since our marriage a great relief,"

186

said Kate, unsure just how to answer the implications of this flattering observation and annoyed that she could not control the sudden heat in her cheeks.

Lady Jersey noted the blush and laughed indulgently, but whatever embarrassingly candid comment she might have produced next was forestalled by the arrival of another caller, much to Kate's relief. In her gratitude at the interruption she greeted her brother-in-law with more than ordinary warmth, concealing her surprise at the unexpected visit. The trio continued to converse lightly on some upcoming social events. Kate could not imagine that Robin would find such frivolous chatter entertaining, and after nearly half an hour spent in this manner, had arrived at the conclusion that he was bent on outstaying Lady Jersey. She contained her curiosity and presently had the satisfaction of seeing the Queen of the *ton* off the premises after an offer to take Mister Dunston up in her carriage had been courteously refused. The door had scarcely closed behind Lady Jersey when Robin rose from his chair as if on wires and walked restlessly over to the window.

"Lord, how that woman prattles! She can prose on about nothing for hours. Small wonder they call her Silence." He gave a crack of laughter and fell silent himself.

Kate tilted her head on one side and studied her brother-in-law with a thoughtful air. "Did you have something of a particular nature to say to me, Robin?" she prompted in an attempt to help him begin.

"I'm not sure, perhaps not; in fact, most probably not, but I thought I'd best prepare you in case events don't fall out the way they ought." He lapsed into silence again and Kate waited patiently, admiring the set of his olive brown coat across the broad Dunston shoulders. Robin was not quite as tall as Nicholas but he had a fine, athletic build that set off his clothes to

187

advantage. He also possessed a tendency toward moderate dandyism, unshared by his more casual brother who declined to be made uncomfortable by the stiff shirt points and more elaborate arrangements of neckclothes favored by Robin. Today's version Kate judged to be the Waterfall, most difficult to achieve and in imminent danger of being ruined as Robin tugged nervously at its constricting folds.

"You may not know—in fact, I'm dead certain you don't know because Nick wouldn't go blabbing, but he pulled me out of a hole a couple of weeks ago—lent me the blunt to pay off a bet. I promised him I wouldn't take that kind of chance again." He paused and looked straight at Kate for the first time. She had never seen her insouciant brother-in-law with such a serious expression. "I meant to keep my word, believe me, but I was at the Fives Court the other night and fell into a discussion with some sporting types that think they're top of the trees Corintheans when they're nothing of the sort." He tugged again at his neckcloth and finished miserably, "The upshot of it all was that I engaged to race against one of them who fancies himself a top sawyer with a curricle and pair. That was all right if I'd let it go at that, but they were all egging me on, and I got so hot under the collar that I laid a big bet on the outcome before I remembered my promise to Nick. Couldn't back out then, of course, point of honor."

"Of course not," Kate said soothingly, touched by his shamefaced air. "You were most likely all drinking too much blue ruin, too, and forgot discretion."

"Fireballs," Robin corrected with a grin, "but it's all the same thing in the end."

"Do you wish me to explain it to Nicholas?"

"Lord, *no*! I don't want Nick to know anything about it."

188

"Oh." Kate was puzzled. "I do not think I perfectly understand then why you are telling me, Robin."

He looked even more guilty. "Wouldn't be if I was sure of winning the wager, but my friend Wolford was telling me Gantry, the chap I'm racing against, has just bought a tidy pair of bays from Ellsworth's stable. Gantry's a cowhanded driver, but these horses have never been beaten."

Enlightenment began to dawn on Kate. "How much was the wager for, Robin?"

"Three hundred pounds."

"Do you have the money if you lose?"

"Just over half. That's why I thought I'd best warn you in case I had to hit you up for a loan." Now that the sorry tale was told he looked much more himself. Kate could not forbear smiling at the absurdity of men and their egos, but she solemnly assured her anxious brother-in-law that she could afford to make him a loan in the unlikely event that it should become necessary.

"And you won't tell Nick anything about it?"

"I shan't even mention that you came to see me," she promised.

Robin went away reconfirmed in the belief that his new sister-in-law was a very good sort of girl, handy to have in the family, and Kate, recalling that Nicholas had once used that very phrase "cow-handed" to describe his brother's driving, went off to check the state of her finances in the firm conviction that a loan would indeed be required.

The viscount came home for lunch that day, eager to talk over plans for the summer months with Kate but, as usual, he inquired how she had spent her morning. When she reported Lady Jersey's call, he grinned and remarked that at least the conversation would not have flagged. Beyond inquiring whether or not her guest had

189

had some new tidbit of gossip to relate he did not display much interest, being more concerned with his own news. Kate was more than willing to change the subject. She felt a trifle uncomfortable about concealing Robin's visit from Nicholas, although it seemed a small matter. However, her husband's news was of sufficient moment to drive all thoughts of his brother's problem from her mind.

"Do you think you might care to spend the summer by the sea?" Nicholas asked casually, but with a look of anticipation enlivening his features.

"At Brighton, do you mean?"

This fashionable waterhole had become a summer playground for the Polite World ever since the Prince Regent had shown such a marked preference for the resort town. The fabulous Pavilion he had built there had become a source of lavish hospitality which set the tone for summer revels amongst the privileged class. Nicholas had mentioned hiring a house for several weeks but had not seemed overly enthusiastic at the time.

"No, not Brighton unless you particularly wish it. My father has a small estate near the sea in Sussex. It has been neglected of late, but I thought you might enjoy spending a quiet summer, just the two of us, in the country. We can ride and drive about the area, and I can teach you to fish and sail. Father keeps a small yacht in the harbor at Rye. It can be sailed by two persons so you may crew for me."

Kate's face was alive with pleasure. "Oh, Nicholas, what a lovely idea! I would prefer it above anything. I have never even been on a sailing boat."

Her husband looked as pleased as a small boy on his birthday. "It's settled then. I'll see Father today and tell him you like the plan. If it should become too slow for you we can always invite some friends down for a visit. The house is not large but it is comfortable enough, and the couple who run it are good people and very accommodating. They enjoy company."

"Perhaps later, but I think it would be delightful to be by ourselves for a bit, don't you?"

Since Mudgrave came into the room just at that moment to remove the dishes, Nicholas contented himself with an enthusiastic verbal agreement in lieu of hugging Kate for her sweetly serious air. She was losing some of her shyness with him, and although he must still initiate any affectionate exchanges, he was thrilled with the warmth of her response. He was confident a few weeks in his exclusive company would overcome the strict upbringing that turned young women into unnaturally formal creatures with a boring sameness about the majority of them. He was convinced that Kate's was a warm, impulsive nature and looked forward with impatience to getting her all to himself in the country.

To forward this end he presented himself in Brook Street that same afternoon to complete arrangements with his father. As he exited from his paternal home, a familiar carriage came down the street. He doffed his hat politely but was not best pleased to see the coachman pull in the reins. He presented himself to the two ladies within the barouche and greeted them with flattering deference. The Countess of Lieven merely inclined her head graciously, but Lady Jersey had summoned him for a purpose.

"I called on your little bride today, Torvil, and found her in radiant looks. If this is the effect marriage has on her, you are to be congratulated."

If the viscount found her archness difficult to stomach, he disguised it with suave civility.

"Much as it would suit my male vanity to claim all

the credit, ma'am, honesty compels me to demur. My wife, quite simply, is a lovely girl."

"Very prettily said," approved Lady Jersey with one of her trilling laughs. "Your brother would no doubt agree with you. I left him in your drawing room determined to enjoy a private chat with Lady Torvil."

"Robin is not the only one who would agree with me," Nicholas countered smoothly. "Kate has captivated all the members of my family including my grandfather." He bowed smilingly to the ladies and proceeded on his way, a bit surprised that Kate had not mentioned Robin's morning call when she had told him of Lady Jersey's visit. He recalled then that he had been so eager to tell her of his plans that he had rather passed over her report of the morning's activities. Most probably his proposition had driven everything else from her mind. He smiled to himself as he strolled toward his club. Her reaction to his suggestion of spending the summer alone and away from society had been as enthusiastic as any bridegroom could wish.

Like Kate, Nicholas was finding the early weeks of his married life to be a time of unexpected happiness. He congratulated himself on having knocked down the barriers his wife had erected between them during their engagement. Kate with her defenses down was an unending delight to him. Strangely enough, he actually begrudged the time he was forced to spend away from her by the demands of his friends. He had good-naturedly endured their ragging when he had left them early on several occasions to return home, and he admitted willingly that the life-style of a bachelor was hardly compatible with that of a newly married man. This summer was going to be a wonderful opportunity to consolidate his gains and bind Kate to him even more closely.

A few days after taking the decision to retire to the

192

country at the end of the season, the complacent glow that surrounded Nicholas like a warm breeze was diminished abruptly by an icy draught. Rounding a corner onto Bond Street one fine afternoon, he suddenly came face to face with Lady Montaigne. Cécile had been so far from his thoughts for weeks that he stopped and gaped at her in blank surprise for a second until he could gather his wits and make a recovery. Fortunately, her enthusiastic greeting covered his hesitation.

"Nick! How lovely to see you so soon, darling. We just returned from Yorkshire yesterday. I was planning to send a note around this evening telling you of our arrival."

Nicholas ignored the implications of this and offered his hand first to Cécile and then to her mouselike cousin, Mrs. Rafferty.

"You are looking as charming as ever, Cécile. I trust you enjoyed your visit and found your mother well?"

"Oh yes, but I am delighted to be back in London. I missed you, Nick." There was no misunderstanding the husky, seductive tone.

"Flattering but unlikely, my dear Cécile. You will not easily convince me that every man within a radius of thirty miles was not scheming for an introduction once the news got around that the beautiful Lady Montaigne was in residence."

Cécile smiled perfunctorily at this blatant piece of flattery but her eyes had narrowed, and the viscount was aware that her regard never left his face while he listened with a fixed smile to Mrs. Rafferty's diffidently expressed concurrence with his remark. He could only hope fervently that his profound discomfort was less apparent than he feared.

"When shall I see you, Nicholas?" Cécile cut across her cousin's effusions abruptly. She was still smiling, but now there was also a challenging glint in the light blue eyes.

"I will do myself the honor of calling upon you in the next few days," the viscount replied readily, and brought the meeting to a close with exquisite courtesy that masked a craven urge to flee.

As he increased the distance between himself and his mistress, Nicholas was reeling mentally from his second shock in as many minutes. It had just struck him that the sight of Cécile had proved so unnerving only because he had not given her a moment's consideration since his marriage, perhaps not even since she had departed for Yorkshire before his marriage. And the reason for this was to be found in one word—Kate. The fact that the sight of a beautiful woman with whom he had only recently enjoyed the most satisfactory intimacy should be productive of no other emotion than intense embarrassment was mute testimony to the thoroughness with which Kate had invaded his life. How could she have moved in and filled his world without his being aware of the process?

Nicholas gave up trying to answer the unanswerable in favor of addressing his mental energies to the complication that had arisen out of this unanticipated meeting with Cécile. She obviously expected their *affaire* to continue unchanged, and for this he had only himself to thank. With distasteful clarity he recalled promising her that his marriage would make no difference to their relationship. They had parted on the best of terms, and here she was expecting, with good reason, to continue as before. How had he managed to get himself enmeshed in such a coil? Never before had he experienced the least difficulty in extricating himself from an entanglement after the novelty had worn off, but he acknowledged with ruthless honesty that this time his sins had come home to roost. He could ignore her invitation, of course, but that was the coward's way out. He must see Cécile and try to explain to her that his marriage had changed him; certainly he owed her the truth. She was assuming nothing that his behavior had not encouraged her to assume, and it was not of the slightest use to tell himself he was not Cécile's only admirer. She had repudiated all her numerous *cicisbei* when their *affaire* had intensified, and no matter how he tried to excuse his conduct on the grounds that promiscuous women got what they deserved, he felt a complete cad. He also felt a decided unease. Cécile was a woman of strong passions; it was something he had admired in her formerly. For a certainty she would not ease his path; in fact, he rather guessed she would adopt the role of the woman scorned and play it to the hilt.

He was in for a deuced rough voyage, and this reflection brought a black scowl to his face as he approached his grandfather's house. James, opening the door to his master, needed but one glance to assess the situation and quietly effaced himself without venturing the least remark. Ulysses, too, glanced up from his comfortable position in front of the fireplace in Kate's sitting room and immediately returned to his slumbers without making his customary welcoming circuit of the viscount's legs. A slight wry smile replaced the scowl at this ability of his household to gauge his mood despite his efforts at concealment. At sight of the glad radiance in Kate's face as she came through the door from her bedchamber the mood vanished and his smile became real, but he caught her in his arms with a tightness that verged on desperation, as though something had threatened her.

The forthcoming interview with Cécile preyed on his mind over the next few days, but he had not yet called at Green Street when he accidentally met Robin as he was coming out of Rundell and Bridge one afternoon. The brothers strolled along together for a bit making casual small talk. Nicholas received the definite impression that Robin would prefer to pass over his own current activities so determined were his efforts to keep the conversation on impersonal matters. He eyed him consideringly but followed his lead.

"What were you doing at Rundell and Bridge, Nick?" the younger man asked, groping for a new topic when a pause had lengthened beyond what was comfortable. "Going to deck Kate out in jewels?"

"As a matter of fact I have just purchased a little trinket for her that they made up to my design." He slowed his footsteps and dived a hand into an inner pocket of his coat.

"That's pretty." Robin admired the gold pin gleaming on the viscount's outstretched palm. "May I?" At his brother's nod he picked it up to examine the workmanship. The pin was no more than an inch and a half long and was in the shape of two overlapping hearts. A single fine ruby was set in the space where the hearts intersected.

"Very nice indeed," repeated Robin, returning the pin to the viscount, "and so is the message it conveys." He laughed at the slight discomfiture on his brother's face. "No need to color up, old boy, nothing wrong with being happily married."

Nicholas passed this off with an acknowledging smile, but the truth was that his embarrassment was due to the fact that another piece of jewelry with a "message" was also reposing in his pocket at that moment. He had purchased a costly diamond and pearl bracelet for Lady Montaigne to assuage the pain of parting. It didn't make his conscience a damned bit easier, but he thought he owed her something for a pleasant association.

Cécile was not a member of the muslin company, but he entertained a shrewd suspicion she would not be averse to accepting the costly bauble. No doubt his delay in visiting her had given her cause for thought, but he dared not count on this making his task easier. In any case he must not postpone the meeting much longer.

He jerked his mind back to the present and made some tentative approach to discovering what Robin had been up to lately, but again found his usually loquacious brother reticent on the subject. They parted shortly and Nicholas headed home, eager to see Kate's reaction to the little heart brooch.

Had he been privileged to witness his brother's next accidental encounter, however, it is unlikely that he would have postponed his visit to Green Street for even one more day.

Robin was strolling toward his own lodgings when he very nearly bumped into Lady Montaigne on the flagway. He had been presented to her on one occasion but they were on no more than bowing terms. He doffed his hat and smiled a greeting with the intention of walking on, but Lady Montaigne stopped her companion with a touch on her arm and returned his salutation with a degree of civility that surprised him.

After inquiring about each other's health, the beautiful redhead said with a casualness that did not quite ring true, "And how do you find your brother these days, Mister Dunston?"

"Nicholas is quite well, I thank you, ma'am," replied Robin, beginning to experience a slight wariness.

"And the new Lady Torvil, is she also well?"

"Kate is in splendid health also." Robin's unease deepened as it occurred to him that his brother's mistress was intent on pumping him about his marriage. Nick must have stopped seeing her, the Lord be praised, and she was hoping to discover if there was any chance of resuming the *affaire*. If it would help Kate he would do his best to discourage her efforts along those lines. Consequently, when Lady Montaigne, with superb nonchalance, asked if all was well with the married couple, Robin took pains to answer in some detail.

"If the pin Nick has just purchased for Kate is any indication, I would say the marriage is prospering."

"A gift for the bride? But how charming." Lady Montaigne's voice was still elaborately casual and Robin hastened to hammer home his point.

"Yes, Nick designed it himself, two gold hearts intertwined with a perfect ruby linking them." That should make things clear to her.

It seemed he was correct if the sudden veiling of her eyes and thinning of her mouth were any indication of her feelings. "A delightful expression of sentiment even if a trifle obvious for a man of Nick's experience."

Robin gave her full credit for keeping her voice light and even under the circumstances. He passed on with polite farewells, rather pleased with his good deed on behalf of his sweet sister-in-law. It was eminently satisfying to know, should the need of that loan arise, that he had been able to make some small return to Kate even if it was something she would never learn about.

Chapter Thirteen

"Nicholas, how exquisite! I just love it and it's so light and graceful I'll be able to wear it with almost everything, even this ball gown if I remove the garnets." Suiting the action to the words, Kate unclasped the string of garnets from her neck and pinned the brooch to the ivory lace of her gown. "There, is that not perfect?" She whirled to display the effect for her smiling husband.

Nicholas had called Kate to his bedchamber while he finished dressing and had presented the small pin.

"It's merely a piece of trumpery, you know, not very valuable," he replied indulgently, mentally contrasting her pleasure in the little pin with her reception of the pearls he had selected for her wedding gift. How everything had changed since then!

"It's valuable to me," Kate declared, entwining her arms about her husband's neck and smiling tenderly into his eyes, "especially since you designed it yourself. I'll treasure it always. Thank you, Nicholas." She pressed her lips to his in what was intended to be a brief salute, but he wrapped his arms around her and gathered her in a close embrace that threatened to crush both Kate's silk ball dress and the cravat he had just painstakingly tied.

"I wish I were going with you tonight, but I promised Ollie I'd appear at his card party," he sighed, releasing her reluctantly while he prudently removed his coat from the back of the chair that Ulysses had just selected upon following his mistress into the room to watch the proceedings. "That cat thinks he owns the place!"

Kate smiled at his resigned tone. "He is really very well behaved. You know you don't truly object to him," she defended coaxingly, as she assisted him to shrug himself into the garment in question.

"I strongly object to finding cat hairs on my coats, however," he replied, standing still while his wife hastily removed several from the lapels of the blue coat.

"I'm rather sorry I accepted for the Mendlesham's ball," Kate admitted. "It is bound to be a terrible crush and I don't know them very well, but Mama wished to go, and I'll have Deb to talk to, of course."

Several hours later Kate's doubts of the wisdom of attending the Mendlesham's ball for their twin daughters were all in a strong way to being confirmed. None of her particular friends were present and she was finding the affair dreadfully flat despite the presence of her mother and sister. In the interests of truth it must be reported that she would probably have found even the most brilliant gathering flat without Nicholas. Not that this might by any stretch of the imagination be described as brilliant, she reflected waspishly as she headed closer to one of the long windows, searching for a breath of air, though the evening was so warm and sultry that the effort was in the nature of a forlorn hope.

From somewhere close behind her came a lovely, low-pitched voice.

"Why yes, thank you, I have been looking forward to meeting the new Lady Torvil."

At the sound of that well-remembered voice, Kate froze to absolute stillness for a second, or an eternity, before her trembling limbs would obey a command to turn around issued by her brain in defiance of a mad impulse to flee through the open window out into the safety of darkness. She knew the blood had drained away from her brain because she felt so light-headed, but she was momentarily powerless to conceal her plight from the redhaired woman whose ice blue eyes were glittering with triumph as they surveyed her person coolly. She concentrated fiercely on focusing a polite regard on the acquaintance who was performing the introduction. *Lady Montaigne, so that was her name!* How odd that it didn't come as a surprise! She had always known she would be beautiful, of course, so that wasn't a surprise either. Why then this muscular paralysis, this refusal of her limbs and brain to function except at a dragging pace that belonged to a nightmare? It seemed an inordinately long time before she achieved a conventional murmur of acknowledgment, but the two women did not seem to notice, and her voice, though strange sounding in her own ears, apparently passed as normal also.

Lady Montaigne extended two fingers and Kate forced herself to meet them with her own for the bare minimum of time demanded by good manners.

"I have been acquainted with your husband for an age and I'm delighted to meet you, Lady Torvil."

"You are too kind, ma'am," Kate murmured, watching in helpless horror as their mutual acquaintance drifted away, doubtless to perform another good deed. Her paralyzed tongue seemed unable to

201

form even one of the polite remarks suitable to the occasion—if there were suitable remarks when a woman met her husband's mistress for the first time. A faint, bitter twitching of her lips accompanied this insight, but Lady Montaigne was continuing with perfect ease in a tone which nicely blended casualness and condescension.

"Not at all. I consider Nicholas to be one of my dearest friends."

"Indeed?" Kate managed the one word and hoped desperately that it conveyed complete indifference to this sweetly uttered shaft.

"Oh yes," Lady Montaigne produced an attractive trill of laughter. "I see you are wearing the little gold brooch. Isn't it the most charmingly elegant trifle? I was persuaded it was just what you would most like." The beautiful redhead nodded smilingly but her light blue eyes held an alert, watchful expression.

Kate's dazed intelligence was struggling to cope with what her senses were reporting. This could not be happening! Lady Montaigne could *not* be smilingly intimating that *she* had selected the little heart pin for her lover's wife. This was nightmare material. She had to stop her hand in midair to prevent it from covering the brooch with an instinctive protective gesture.

From somewhere she found the resourcefulness to transform this action into a wave as she said to Lady Montaigne in a low voice in which she tried without measurable success to infuse some warmth or regret, "I do beg your pardon, ma'am, but I fear you must excuse me. My sister has been trying to attract my attention for some few moments. It may be that my mother is feeling unwell. She had a touch of the headache earlier this evening." She nodded to the woman, uncaring now whether or not Lady Montaigne believed her invention so long as she succeeded in escaping from her presence. She had spied Deborah across the room and now headed purposefully for the spot, but her brisk pace slowed as she widened the distance between herself and the other woman.

The numbness was starting to wear off now, leaving a throbbing mass of anger and pain in its stead. How *dare* Torvil allow his mistress to select a gift for his wife! The callousness of such a gesture was almost beyond comprehension. If Lady Montaigne had been unsure whether or not Kate had learned of her relationship with Nicholas, she had certainly chosen the most effective and humiliating way possible of conveying that information short of a public announcement. *And she was every bit as beautiful as Kate had feared!*

Her shining globe of happiness shattered beyond repair by a few well-chosen malicious words, Kate strove to blot out her feelings and focus her attention on what she must accomplish in the next few minutes if she was to escape from this place without making the world privy to her desolation. She knew she was pale; since she could do nothing about this, let her pallor work for her. Accordingly she approached her sister, and when Deborah exclaimed at her appearance, she explained in a weak voice that she had a raging headache. Her complexion bore mute testimony to her claim. Deborah located Lady Langston and managed their departure with a minimum of fuss and a good deal of quiet efficiency, so that the three ladies were driving through the streets toward the young couple's residence within fifteen minutes.

Lady Langston subjected her elder daughter's face to a rather unnerving scrutiny, but Deb was merely gently solicitous. Kate sat quietly in her corner keeping the door shut on all thoughts but the practicalities of attaining solitude. Her eyes burned with unshed tears but she forced herself to respond to Deb's inquiries, touched and faintly comforted by her sister's concern. She gave an involuntary shiver. Strange, she had found the ballroom overpoweringly stuffy, but now she felt leaden and cold to the tips of her fingers. She hastened to reassure her relatives that she was certain the headache would have gone off by morning and endured a lecture on the strength and duration of migraines from Lady Langston.

The short ride seemed to take forever, but at last the carriage drew up in front of Lord Bartram's house. She declined—politely, she trusted—her mother's offer to have Deborah stay with her overnight and bade both a relieved good night. Thankfully, Mudgrave was the only servant in view as he opened the door for her. At his faintly questioning look, she explained again that the ballroom had been hot and stuffy and had given her a slight headache. There was now only Hawthorne to face before she could hope to be alone. Nicholas would not be in for hours, thank goodness. *Nicholas!* She decided she would not think about her husband tonight. It was essential to concentrate on taking one step at a time. Hawthorne was next, and there was no one in the world she would liefer avoid with the exception of Nicholas himself, but there was never any evading of Hawthorne. She submitted to the dresser's ministrations with exemplary patience, meekly accepting the powders she pressed on her to relieve the alleged headache, and enduring a shortened version of the nightly routine. Her control was superb, but that was because she felt nothing. She tested this absence of feeling by questioning herself and found it perfectly true. Tears no longer threatened and the burning sensation behind her eyelids had ceased. The poets were mistaken about hearts breaking. One might sustain a severe emotional shock and hardly miss a beat physically. She was living proof of that. Though still cold, she was experiencing no aches or pains at all, not even in her head. Most probably everything would be fine once Hawthorne left. She was tired, she would sleep and defer the problem until morning.

Finally Hawthorne was gone and the longed-for solitude achieved. Kate climbed carefully into bed, arranged two plump pillows with meticulous care, and disposed her limbs for sleep. Five minutes later she admitted the futility of denying her problem through this avenue of escape. Her eyelids refused to remain closed and her spine persisted in retaining the rigidity of a bar of steel on the bed. She stared dry-eyed into the darkness, seeing again the beautifully carved features and gorgeous red hair of her husband's mistress. Odd, she had been almost exclusively concerned with maintaining her composure in the face of a devastating shock, yet she carried an image of Lady Montaigne in her mind's eye that was detailed enough to serve as a model for her portrait. She closed her eyes tightly in a vain attempt to erase that image. She didn't *wish* to think about Lady Montaigne! She wanted to forget about her very existence, to pretend they had not met at that accursed ball. If only she had never accepted that invitation!

Life with Nicholas had been so wonderful lately that she had allowed the fact that he had a mistress to slide from her memory. Incredible as it seemed at this moment she had completely forgotten the existence of a mistress. It was a bitter irony to recall how she had searched each gathering before her marriage wondering if the unknown mistress would be present. At that period she had almost expected to be confronted with the woman daily. There would have been very little surprise attached to the event then, but tonight's encounter had left her stunned, violently bereft of the quiet joy that had welled up in her when Nicholas had presented her with the pin of linked hearts. It had seemed to mean so much and her rival had helped him select it. *Oh, Nicholas!*

And now the enormity of her error in believing that Nicholas had come to love her burst over her head like waters released from a dam. Without warning the tears flowed, unresisted now, as Kate surrendered to her misery and wept unrestrainedly. She cried until sheer exhaustion caused a halt to her tears. She wept for shattered dreams and lost illusions but also for her own colossal stupidity in allowing her husband's charm and apparent sincerity to overcome her carefully erected barriers. It would have been sad but understandable had she known nothing of her husband except what anyone could see, but *she* had possessed special knowledge from Nicholas's own lips. Kate writhed among the now sodden pillows, her weary brain trying unsuccessfully to reconcile the picture of her husband's tender pride tonight in her pleasure over the gold pin with that of a man who could permit his mistress to advise on a gift for his wife. It made no sense, but the facts could not be denied. Lady Montaigne had been quite odiously explicit. At this point the tears she thought totally spent began afresh. Were all men like this then? Could they pretend to be wholly in love with one woman yet still desire another? Her own happiness these past weeks could never have existed had she not seen it reflected in all her husband's actions. He *was* happy; that was obvious to the dullest eye, but it would now appear that his joy arose not from the love of one woman but from the satisfaction of having two women in love with *him*.

These unhappy conclusions were squirreling around in her head when a soft sound in the next room pierced the cloud of misery that pressed down on her like a physical weight. Her exhausted body stiffened instinctively and she rolled onto her stomach, allowing her hair to cover her tear-stained face while she strained to follow the faint sounds issuing from the other room. She held her breath when the door opened, then forced herself to breathe lightly and evenly as she felt Nicholas approach her bed.

"Kate, Kate darling, are you awake?"

His whisper caused two more tears to squeeze out from under her closed lids, but she continued the desperate pretense of sleep, and after a long instant of dead silence that made her nerves crawl, she was aware of a light touch as her husband pulled the blanket more securely over one shoulder. It was a prodigious discipline not to shrink away from the hand that rested warmly on her shoulder for an agonizing interval. Her senses remained stretched as she strained to follow the tiny sounds as he crossed the room and softly closed the door.

In the silence that succeeded, her own sobbing breaths rang harshly in her ears for a few minutes as she struggled to bring the hopeless weeping under control. It was hours before she succumbed to her exhaustion and slept.

Morning brought no alleviation of her misery nor solution to her problem, which was not to be wondered at since Kate had not progressed so far in her thinking as to formulate a distinct problem in her mind. She was still quivering from reaction. For the first time since her marriage she stayed away from the breakfast parlor but she was too cowardly to question her motives. However, she had barely summoned up the strength required to order Hawthorne to choose her attire and begin the process of preparing her mistress for the day's schedule when Nicholas entered her bedchamber. The brush in Kate's hand halted momentarily, then resumed a slow, rhythmic motion. After one quick look she avoided his glance, feigning an absorbing interest in her task.

They exchanged quiet greetings, then Nicholas added with an assessing stare, "Mudgrave told me you returned early last night with a headache. How are you today?"

"Tolerably well, thank you."

"The shadows under your eyes give the lie to that assertion," he replied with seeming concern. "Promise me you'll not try to go the pace today, sweetheart. Have a quiet day."

"Mama invited me to lunch but I have no other plans."

"Don't let your mother quack you with her eternal remedies either," he ordered. The grin that accompanied this remark brought forth no responsive smile from Kate.

"No, I won't," she promised tonelessly, still concentrating on her hair brushing.

Nicholas frowned slightly. "Perhaps you had best remain home after all until you feel more the thing. Maybe Doctor Baillie should see you."

At this she glanced at him fleetingly, then away again. "I am fine, really, Torvil. Don't have me on your mind."

The viscount looked undecided and was opening his mouth to add something when Hawthorne bustled in carrying a dress and a pair of half boots. Her presence had the effect of causing him to feel *de trop* as usual, and he bowed himself out hastily.

Kate placed the hair brush on the dressing table with infinite concentration while she struggled to overcome the tightened feeling in her throat, but her muscles refused to relax. Though she had brushed through this first meeting with Nicholas, it was a mere reprieve, of course. There would be daily meetings for the rest of their lives and how was she to bear the pain of it? She stared dully at her reflection in the mirror, trying to convince herself that it would not always be like this; at present she was suffering all the pointed agony of discovery, but this piercing pain would certainly subside to a dull ache in time. After all, nothing had actually changed. She had known of Lady Montaigne's existence even before her marriage and she had accepted her relationship with Nicholas as one of the more unpleasant facts of the arrangement. Nothing was different now, *nothing*!

Defiant amber eyes stared back at her, scorning to dignify the feeble protests of her heart that everything had changed from the moment she had become Nicholas' wife in all respects. Suppose for the sake of argument that she *had* thought herself loved and in love for a couple of weeks; people got over being in love, didn't they? Look at Deb. She had fancied herself in love several times in the past three months and had recovered each time. Kate's fingers crept up to massage her temples. The apocryphal headache of last evening threatened to become reality, but she could not face a day of solitude with only her thoughts for company. All the thinking in the world, even from a Solomon, was powerless to alter the situation. It existed and she would have to live with it, but how could she ever welcome Nicholas into her bed again?

With dull eyes she followed Hawthorne's deft movements as she cleverly arranged the burnished brown curls, but she was seeing instead an endless succession of empty days stretching before her. The maid felt the shudder that went through her mistress and paused with a pin in her hand.

"Did I hurt you, my lady?"

"No, Hawthorne, it was . . . just a momentary chill. That looks fine. Thank you."

The abigail gazed with satisfaction upon her creative efforts, but Kate could only hope the new hair style would draw attention away from her washed-out complexion and bruised-looking eyes. She turned from the mirror and accepted the kid gloves Hawthorne was holding out to her, impatient all at once with her own lack of pride in allowing her misery to be written on her face for the whole world to see. She squared her shoulders and prepared to meet the demands of the day with as much dignity as she could assume.

It was not in Kate to take to her bed as her mother had fallen into the habit of doing, but she discovered in the next week a more compassionate understanding of the factors that had contributed to turning Lady Langston into the hypochondriac she had become over the years.

For there was no denying that first day was difficult, and the ones that followed grew no easier. Kate got through them one at a time by mustering up the pride necessary to keep her head high and present a serene appearance in company. The radiance was gone; that was beyond mending, but she felt she managed to maintain an air of smiling good humor before others. This was actually less of a strain than that of carrying through her pose of normalcy with her husband. Though she tried not to make it obvious, she cudgeled her brains to devise ways to avoid his society because she was aware that she was unable, despite her frequently taken resolution, to relax in his presence. She was aware, too, that Nicholas was watching her closely behind a formal manner. For a day or two he had been concerned for her health, but her nervousness in his company and the physical withdrawal she could not suppress must have become evident almost immediately because he was at first puzzled, and very shortly, cold and watchful. He had come to her room that first night and, though despising her cowardice, she had pleaded a remnant of her headache as a reason for needing unbroken sleep. Nicholas had been tenderly sympathetic and had kissed her gently before withdrawing. Despite her resolve to remain unmoved she must have stiffened slightly because he had searched her face intently before straightening up. To avoid a visit from the doctor the next day it had been necessary to abandon the headache once and for all. However, her attempts at brightness had only served to intensify his quiet study of her, and the tension between them built slowly and wordlessly until Kate almost hoped for an explosion to clear the air.

There were times when she would have loved to scream and hurl accusations at him, but what accusations, and to what end? Unfaithfulness? She had always known he did not intend to be faithful to a bride he had had no hand in choosing. Should she then accuse him of not loving her? He had never said he did, she recalled now with bitter clarity, despite his behavior to the contrary. Their bargain had never mentioned love and fidelity. Hopefully, she possessed too much pride to charge him with the one thing he was indeed guilty of—having caused her to fall in love with him and thus expose herself to certain heartbreak. It was unlikely he had even intended any such unhappy result. Piqued by her indifference, he had probably been challenged to compel her acceptance of a conventional marriage of convenience for his own comfort and incidental pleasure. So Kate leveled no accusations and created no scenes. She and Nicholas met daily at breakfast and appeared at previously scheduled social functions together but they no longer discussed future plans. Nothing further was said about spending the summer in the isolation of Sussex. In fact, nothing passed between them that did not pertain directly to their daily activities.

In the midst of this strained situation Kate returned from a boring round of social visits late one afternoon to find among her usual pile of calling cards and invitations two personal notes. Recognizing Deb's schoolgirl hand on one, she laid it aside for the moment and commenced to break the seal of the other as she wearily climbed the curving staircase and walked down the carpeted passage to her sitting room. Glancing at the signature, she ascertained that the writer was her brother-in-law, but she had to read the brief communication twice before the meaning penetrated. Lately she was finding it difficult to concentrate on anything outside her own problems. Robin had written:

My Dear Kate,
I'm afraid I lost that race I told you about last week. If you can let the bearer have one hundred twenty pounds I will be eternally grateful. I shall need it by Friday at the latest since I am leaving that evening for Ireland to look at some hunters with Wolford. With many thanks to my dear sister, I remain your obedient servant,

Robin

She looked up from her second reading and frowned. *This* was Friday and it was already almost evening. With her hand on the bell pull, she desisted from her first impulse which was to question the servants as to why she had not received this note before today. It was advisable surely to avoid calling something to their minds that they might later report to Nicholas. She had promised Robin that she would not reveal his breach of the promise he had made to his brother. For that reason also she dared not dispatch one of the footmen with the money. She must go herself and there was very little time in which to accomplish her errand. She should be dressing for dinner within the hour. With no wasted effort Kate located the key to the tooled leather jewel case in which she had laid aside the sum Robin would need over a week before. In order to free both hands she put down the post which she still carried. Deb's note took her eye. She had intended to ignore it for the moment, but it occurred to her that if for any reason Deb had requested her presence at home, she would have provided herself with a reason to order the carriage. Quickly she skimmed over her sister's letter, noting with satisfaction that Deb desired to show her the new ball dress that had just arrived from the modiste's. Her sister would be surprised to find her invitation accepted so quickly. She pulled the bell to order the carriage brought round again and made swift repairs to her hair and face while she waited for this to be accomplished. It would never do to drive to Robin's lodgings in her own carriage, of course. She must send John Coachman back to Albemarle Street from her mother's house and hire a hackney cab to take her to Robin's and return her home. Her mother's footman would find the hack for her with no questions asked. She would tell her own coachman that she would return in Lady Langston's carriage and trust to luck to slip in unobserved.

As it turned out everything went quite smoothly with Kate's careful arrangements except that she hadn't taken her sister's chatty disposition into account. Deb kept prattling on about her new gown and then insisted on modeling it for Kate. At her sister's feeble protests that she herself should be changing at that very moment, Deb laughed merrily and offered to shoulder all her brother-in-law's wrath at the delay. Kate produced the expected smile at the very idea of Nicholas being angry with his adorable sister-in-law whom he indulged prodigally, but she was hard pressed to conceal her impatience to be gone. Fortunately she had requested the footman to order a hack on her entrance. As he had glanced in some surprise at her carriage going off down the street, Kate rapidly invented a friend to whom she had lent the conveyance, mentally reflecting that the practical difficulties attendant on a career of deception must keep more people on the straight and narrow path of virtue than their consciences.

At last she was seated in the musty-smelling hired vehicle for the short drive to Robin's lodgings. This time her errand was dispatched quite promptly. She found Robin on the point of coming to see her himself and explained about not receiving his message until that afternoon. He escorted her to her waiting hack with profuse expressions of undying gratitude tumbling from his lips, accepted her wishes for an enjoyable stay in Ireland, and on impulse flung an arm about her shoulders and pressed a grateful kiss on her cheek as they said good-bye. Robin watched the hack start up and then went back into the house. Neither he nor Kate had noticed the figure of a man who had halted abruptly on the flagway a scant fifty feet away to watch the leavetaking. The man now turned and retraced his steps so that he did not pass Robin's house after all.

Kate settled back in the cab and acknowledged the tiredness that came sweeping over her in a flood tide now that the need for sudden action was over. Lately it was an enormous effort just to get dressed for each day's pointless round of activities. She was weary in the depths of her soul. Part of it was the feeling that matters could not continue long as they were. Nothing was being said between Nicholas and herself at present but sooner or later the situation would explode around

214

them. *Or would it?* Perhaps the fates had decreed that she and Nicholas would simply spend the rest of their lives making polite conversation when others were about and lapsing into tense silence when they chanced to be alone. She shuddered violently at the thought, but at the same time knew there was nothing she would be able to say to her husband about her feelings.

At this stage of her unhappy musings she became aware of the cessation of motion and her brain began to function normally again. She was able to pay off the jarvey and dismiss the hack without attracting any attention from inside the house. With that little adventure successfully completed she steeled herself to ignore Hawthorne's reaction to her lateness and began a necessarily hasty toilette. By leaving her hair style untouched and scrambling into her gown, she was able to congratulate herself on being only five minutes late for the dinner gong.

On the point of leaving the room, she froze as a knock sounded at the door connecting her bedchamber with her husband's. He entered before she recovered animation and said evenly, "I should like a few minutes of your time before we go down." He nodded dismissal to the abigail and kept his eyes on her as she left the room soundlessly.

Kate was experiencing a sinking sensation in the pit of her stomach. So, the reckoning between them had come at last! One glance at Nicholas's rigid jawline and glittering eyes had warned her that the limits of his patience had been reached. He was going to demand an explanation of her coldness, and there was nothing she could say. Her pride refused to grant him the satisfaction of knowing she had been mortally hurt by his continuing liaison with another woman. Could she have been assured of the requisite composure to inform him she knew of his infidelity without revealing her own misery she would have allowed herself the revengeful pleasure of seeing him squirm at being found out long since, but she had known with dismal certainty that she would betray herself in the telling.

As the door closed behind Hawthorne, Nicholas turned to study his wife's pale, set face; he flicked a lambent glance to her white knuckled hands gripping the back of the chair that had been the nearest object to her at his entrance and returned his gaze to her face. The cold contempt in his eyes caused her own to drop, though deep within she was furious at her inability to bear that scorn without flinching. After all, *she* was the injured party, not Nicholas. Some tiny spark of courage animated her chin and eyes to raise both to return his stare calmly.

"Sit down."

She ignored his curt command and remained standing, looking steadily back at him.

"I prefer to stand," she replied quietly.

Nicholas's voice was also quiet and so even that at first Kate did not take in the full sense of his next words.

"I'm here to correct a slight misunderstanding you seem to be laboring under concerning the terms of our bargain. If you thought I would be so complaisant as to countenance unfaithfulness on the part of my wife, arranged marriage or not, you were never more mistaken."

In the silence that followed this bombshell Kate's gasp was clearly audible as was the ticking of the bedside clock. She could not be hearing correctly. It sounded as though he were . . .

"Are *you* accusing *me* of being unfaithful?" she croaked. Her eyes never left that dark, cold visage staring relentlessly at her as she groped her way around to the front of the chair and sank onto its seat.

"Do you intend to deny it?"

She could, with great pleasure, have slapped the unpleasant travesty of a smile from his lips and she curled her fingers into her palms to prevent them from stiffening into claws.

"Of course I deny it; it is utterly preposterous!"

"You're a cool one, I must admit," he said with what sounded absurdly like grudging admiration, "but it won't wash, my dear. I saw you with my own eyes."

"You *saw* me?" Kate floundered, not understanding him at all.

"Very well done," he applauded with mock appreciation. "Your pose of bewildered innocence would be quite convincing had I not witnessed that tender parting just now."

Kate was still completely at sea. "What parting?"

"Oh, come now, my dear, a good actress never overplays a scene." He paused suggestively, but his taunting suavity had succeeded in rousing in Kate an anger as great as the one he was concealing. She gritted her teeth and glared wordlessly at him, refusing to swallow the bait.

He looked away from her and once again the rigidity of his jaw struck her.

"Neither you nor Robin was aware that you had a witness this afternoon, but—"

"Robin!"

The involuntary exclamation brought his dark, opaque stare back to her face and he did not miss the two spots of color that flared on her cheekbones.

"Did that jog your memory, my dear?"

"Stop calling me your dear in that odiously sneering way!" she cried raggedly. "You must *know* I am not having an *affaire* with your brother!"

"You deny it then?"

"Of course I do."

217

"Then perhaps you'd care to explain the meaning of that tender scene I witnessed?"

This time the silence was a nervy, palpable entity. Kate's shoulders sank and she slumped slightly from the petrified position she had been maintaining on the edge of her chair. She could see how that scene must have appeared, of course, and she could never explain it without betraying Robin's confidence. Her voice reflected the helplessness that was beginning to creep over her as her mind raced ahead.

"I am sorry, Torvil, the meeting was perfectly innocent. But I cannot explain why I visited Robin without breaking a confidence." She looked up, unconsciously pleading for understanding, but realized from his uncompromising attitude the futility of such a plea under the circumstances.

"Do you deny that you have been meeting Robin in the afternoons when your *busy* social schedule has kept you from home until almost dinnertime?"

She clasped her hands together tightly in her lap, knowing she was committed to playing out the whole dreadful farce to its inevitable conclusion. All emotion was erased from her countenance as she moistened dry lips with the tip of her tongue before answering, "Yes, I do deny it. Today was the first time I have been to Robin's lodgings, and it was not for the purpose of making love."

"And do you also deny that Robin has been visiting you here?"

"In your own house with your servants present? Really, Torvil!"

"Do you deny it?"

"Of course I do," she repeated dully.

"Even when I remind you that on one occasion at least there was another witness?"

She looked at him questioningly.

"Have you forgotten the day Robin had the misfortune to call while Lady Jersey was here?"

She *had* forgotten of course, and she bit her lip before admitting it, while protesting, "A simple morning call. Any number of gentlemen pay calls on me as well as on every other lady in town."

"Perhaps, but you did not cherish a *tendre* for any number of gentlemen before your marriage, did you?"

"Of course, I did not. What are you implying?"

He made a weary gesture with his hand as if pushing something infinitely distasteful away from him. "Perhaps it will serve to cut this unpleasant discussion short if I tell you something you haven't known before. That day in your mother's drawing room was not the first time I had seen you."

Kate flashed him a startled look, wondering suddenly if he might have seen her behind those palms at the Westerwood ball. Before she could begin to cogitate on the implications of this, however, he was proceeding, "I had gone to Almack's the previous evening for the express purpose of making your acquaintance. Robin pointed you out to me and was preparing to perform the introduction when you looked up and saw him. *I* saw your expression, and it did not require extraordinary sensibility to realize that you were far from indifferent to him. It was there for anyone to see."

Hearing him say this, Kate was surprised to find she could barely recall having once been very taken with Robin's charms. So much had happened since those days of innocence. She could not begin to deal yet with all the ramifications of Nicholas's revelations, but one question flashed into her head and demanded immediate utterance.

"Then why, if you thought I loved Robin, did you make me an offer?"

Nicholas smiled in that peculiarly nasty way he had.

"I asked Robin later that night if he returned your affection. I was prepared to step aside, no matter what my father wished, if this were so, but he assured me that you were not in his style." The obvious intent to wound caused Kate's color to rise again, but she met his contemptuous gaze unflinchingly.

"I see. You believe I have pursued your brother then?" she inquired.

"Shall we just say that perhaps he feels a safely married woman is less dangerous and more interesting than an impressionable girl?"

It must run in the family.

Did I actually say that? Kate wondered frantically, then relaxed as Nicholas remained silent, watching her relentlessly as she struggled to absorb all that he had flung at her in the last few minutes. She withdrew her glance. One thing had become unavoidably apparent. Nicholas had built up such a case against her in his own mind that even if she broke faith with Robin and told her husband of his brother's debt, there was no guarantee that he would believe her in the face of what he thought was evidence of her perfidy. In any case some of the things he had said were quite unforgivable. If there were any indication that it was his heart and not his masculine vanity that was bruised, she would tell him the truth, knowing that Robin would understand the necessity, but as things were she no longer felt any inclination to defend herself. Solely for Robin's sake she repeated, "I can see that nothing I might say will convince you that you are wrong; nevertheless, for the sake of your brother's honor, if not my own, I must tell you again that you are quite mistaken in all your conclusions." She straightened her shoulders and looked squarely at him. "What do you intend to do?"

Her question, or her utter calm, seemed to unsettle him a bit. He looked undecided for a moment, then answered harshly, "First, let me hasten to reassure you that in future it will not be necessary for you either to endure my touch or pretend a headache to evade it. I trust I make myself clear?"

"Very clear."

"On the other hand, this is not an unmixed blessing for you because I really cannot bring myself to the indulgence of permitting my wife to have a lover. Quite a Gothic attitude I freely admit, my dear, but there you have it. There will be no need for you to warn Robin of this; I intend seeing him myself tonight."

"You won't, you know," she replied conversationally. "He has already left on a trip to Ireland."

"The devil he has!" For the first time the control Nicholas had imposed on his temper cracked a bit and Kate caught a glimpse of the fury simmering below the sarcastic exterior. With respect to herself it seemed he could contain his natural anger because she mattered little to him, but Robin was his brother and *his* betrayal hurt. It was just one additional and quite unnecessary proof of how mistaken she had been when she had believed that Nicholas had come to care for her. She stood up, grateful that her legs would support her, and presented an expressionless mask to the man who had briefly been her husband.

"I would not expect you to take my word for this, of course. You must do as you see fit. Now, if you will excuse me, I find I do not, after all, desire any dinner. May I bid you good night?" She stood politely, waiting for him to go, and after an instant when she wondered if she read murder in the smoldering glance he bent on her and braced herself for whatever came next, he bowed stiffly and went out without a word.

In the next two days conversation between Nicholas and Kate was strictly limited to those times when the servants were in hearing distance. Through good luck, or more probably good management, they did not even meet on the day following the showdown in Kate's boudoir. She was grateful for the breathing space this afforded her to reassess the whole situation. The attack Nicholas had launched against her had been so totally unexpected and so groundless that she had experienced the greatest difficulty in accepting that he was indeed serious in the accusations he had hurled at her. Her cool reception and refutation of the charges stemmed in part from this lingering disbelief. Nicholas had never manifested the least suspicion that he disliked or distrusted the friendliness between his wife and brother, and his attitude last night had evidenced more of the cold scorn of disgust than the hot flame of jealousy.

The more Kate dwelt on the situation in retrospect, the greater the sense of absurdity. She was still of two minds as to whether Nicholas actually believed the charges he had made against her. One fact, however, had become glaringly apparent. No one save a colossal hypocrite could have created that scene while indulging in the exact same behavior himself. Perhaps society always judged errant wives more severely than philandering husbands, but somehow she would not have expected Nicholas to be guilty of this particular brand of hypocrisy. Still, in a way it had helped ease her own heartache. Today she found it quite easy to dislike her husband intensely, and there was certainly a sense of relief that all need for pretense between them was over. He was now as anxious as she to avoid the intimacies of marriage with a partner whose affections were not exclusively directed toward the only person entitled to them. After the turmoil and torment that had followed upon her meeting with Lady Montaigne, Kate found the next few days strangely bland and serene. She went about her ordinary routine with a quiet composure that

222

resulted quite naturally from this present feeling of insulation from emotional stress.

The season was rapidly drawing to a close now as families began to withdraw from town in increasingly greater numbers. Her mother and Deborah were scheduled to leave for an extended visit to a favorite cousin of Lady Langston's in a few days. Roger had already departed for Broadwoods, and Lord Sedgeley was making plans to spend the summer months at his principal estate in Hampshire. Nothing further had been said about their own tentative visit to Sussex but Kate scarcely gave the matter a thought. She was existing in a carefully maintained vacuum where no additional slings and arrows of fortune might penetrate her hard won immunity. She paid farewell visits to her departing relatives, smilingly referred their requests for definite news of her plans to her husband, and lightly parried all invitations to pay visits later in the summer.

On the third day following their quarrel, Nicholas sent word by a servant that he would like to see her in his library at her convenience. In due course Kate presented herself. After the briefest of greetings Nicholas came directly to the point.

"I have just received a communication from my grandfather. He was thrown from his horse last week and sustained a broken leg." He paused at Kate's sympathetic murmur, then continued, "The leg has completely immobilized him, of course, and judging by his letter, he is feeling quite persecuted by a cruel fate. He suggests we might like to pay him a short visit to raise his spirits." Again he paused, aware that Kate's air of concern had changed to a slight look of perturbation. His knowing smile succeeded in erasing all expression from her face as she waited for him to continue.

"My reaction was very like yours. It might be a bit awkward, to say the least, to try to project an image of newly married bliss in front of a shrewd old fox like Grandfather. However, it might answer if only *one* of us were to pay him a visit." He waited until her averted gaze swung back to his face.

So far she had voiced none of her reactions, but now she asked, "Which one?"

"Well, if I went we should have to make new plans for you. I suppose you could join your mother and sister for the summer, or your brother even, but this would be bound to give rise to certain conjectures that you might find . . . uncomfortable at this point." He paused again, saw he had her silent and undivided attention, and proceeded to detail his thinking on the subject.

"On the other hand, Grandfather took a great liking to you at the wedding, which I believed to be mutual." He raised questioning brows and accepted her affirmative nod with satisfaction. "If you were to pay him a visit, there would be no need to explain that our change of plans did not include me. We can simply allow everyone to accept that we have both gone to Kent for the summer months."

"Which leaves you where?" Kate inquired, meeting his eyes directly.

"I am flattered that my whereabouts should be of interest to you, my dear."

"It would be as well to have something to say in case your grandfather should inquire." Kate's voice matched her husband's in mocking civility.

He answered shortly, "The estate in Sussex still needs some attention, and I'll come up to Kent occasionally to keep Grandfather from getting suspicious."

"And of course you can always cite business as a reason for coming back to town at any time," she suggested smoothly.

"If I needed a reason," he concurred affably. "May I

consider the matter as settled then? You are willing to go to Kent?"

"*I* am, but I have a hunch that Hawthorne will balk. She was none too pleased at the idea of being immured on the estate in Sussex even with the promise of a house party as an enticement."

The viscount permitted a trace of impatience to show. "I'll dismiss her with a big bonus and a sterling character to stop her tongue. You've not been comfortable with her superior airs right from the start. Why should you be forced to endure her notions of what your relationship should be? You may find someone here or let Grandfather's housekeeper select a temporary abigail for you when you get to Kent."

"You make it sound so simple," said Kate wryly.

"It is simple. You and Hawthorne are incompatible so Hawthorne must go."

On hearing this pragmatic sentiment, Kate's glance fell and there was another pregnant little silence which Nicholas ended by proposing a tentative schedule for Kate's short journey. She sat in an attentive posture, but her real attention was concentrated on an inner voice that persisted in likening his efficiency in getting rid of an unsuitable maid to the dispatch with which he was divesting himself of the unwanted presence of an unsuitable wife.

Chapter Fourteen

Less than twenty-four hours after Kate had bidden Lady Langston and Deborah an affectionate farewell, she was preparing to follow them into the country. The luxurious carriage that had been a wedding present from her father-in-law was being loaded with baggage as she checked off the items on her list. An hour before, she and Hawthorne had come to a final parting of their ways with punctilious civility and no regrets on either side. Since the drive to Lord Bartram's estate could be accomplished in under three hours, Nicholas had agreed that she could dispense with the services of a maid until she reached Hickory House. With exquisite detachment she watched her husband giving final instructions to the outrider who would accompany the carriage on the short journey. An unmistakable hiss of annoyance drew her attention to the closed basket at her feet where Ulysses unreservedly expressed his feelings at being thus confined. The delicate alliance between Nicholas and Kate in the matter of her smooth departure had trembled on the brink of disintegration when the question of Ulysses' future residence had arisen. None of Nicholas's logical arguments, delivered in carefully reasonable tones, about the disinclination of the feline species for traveling in wheeled vehicles had made the least impression on Kate's stubborn insistence on carrying Ulysses off to Kent with her. For an instant the air had hung heavy with portent, but then Nicholas had shrugged in defeat, having no longer any taste for brangling with the pale-faced girl who had briefly given him such joy. His sole desire now was to see her off the premises so that her face would not be a constant reminder of what he had lost. He didn't even want to think about his marriage for a time until the wounds Kate had dealt him had scarred over.

At last, vehicle, horses, and passengers, both human and animal, were ready. Nicholas assisted his wife into the coach with an air of devotion that was assumed for the benefit of the servants, kissed her hand in an old-fashioned gesture, and mouthed a few platitudes about a good journey. Kate's replies were barely audible and the amber gaze looked anywhere but at her husband. As the coachman gave the team the office to start, Nicholas stared after the departing carriage and felt nothing save a great relief. He turned on his heel and walked back into the house whereupon he shut himself up in his library for the next several hours. He managed to get through a good deal of work, but eventually the silence became oppressive and he decided against dining at home. Changing to evening rig became a process to dawdle over while he debated what to do with the evening that stretched ahead of him. On a sudden impulse he opened the door to Kate's bedchamber and stepped over the threshold. The room looked strangely barren, though a swift glance around assured him that there was nothing missing but a set of crystal-backed brushes from the dressing table and the miniature of her father that she kept on the bedside table. He took a deep breath and inhaled a faint scent that he associated with Kate, light and sweet and reminiscent of some flower that he could not quite identify—and didn't wish to identify, he reminded himself savagely. His brows drew together and his lips thinned somewhat as he ran a finger idly over the smooth surface of a mahogany chest. Unthinkingly, he pulled open the top drawer. It was empty save for a silver gilt jewel casket which gave him pause. A strange item for a woman to leave behind. With one finger he pushed up the lid and stood staring at the string of matched pearls and the heart-shaped pin that gleamed within. An expression of pure rage distorted his features as he dropped the lid and shoved the drawer closed before striding back into his own room where he crossed purposefully to an ebony highboy. There was a jeweler's box in the third drawer which he removed. A quick glance reassured him as to the contents before he put the box in a pocket and left the room by the hall door.

Cécile was dressing for an evening party when he arrived, but she received him in her boudoir, garbed in a black lace dressing gown that complemented her red hair and emphasized the clear whiteness of her skin. She smiled slowly at the viscount in the mirror of her dressing table, and when her maid had discreetly withdrawn, turned to him with both hands extended in an invitation that he accepted after an imperceptible hesitation.

"Nick, darling, how wonderful you look!"

Nicholas was flatteringly prompt in returning the compliment. Cécile exclaimed with delight over the diamond and pearl bracelet and immediately donned it, demanding his assistance in securing the clasp. She studied his dark head bent over this task with an enigmatic little smile that he did not see.

"It has been so long, Nick," she murmured, allowing

a faint hint of reproach to creep into the beautifully pitched voice. "Your 'few days' turned into a fortnight almost. I missed you terribly."

Nicholas straightened from his task and smiled lazily into the pleading blue eyes. "My time is not so much my own these days," he offered by way of explanation.

"Then why are we wasting any?" she demanded, moving closer and placing two small hands, sparkling with rings, on his shoulders. This gesture caused the wide sleeves of her gown to fall back, revealing shapely white arms that slid around his neck as he gathered her pliant body into a light embrace. "Have you missed me, Nicholas?" she whispered, pressing closer to him and raising a provocatively curved mouth toward his.

"Yes," he answered untruthfully, and proceeded to kiss her long and deeply, recognizing her instant and total response with an impersonal pleasure at the ability of an experienced woman to arouse and satisfy passion. He was aware, too, of the heavy French scent Cécile favored, but with less pleasure. He had come to prefer a lighter, more subtle fragrance. He drew back slightly to study the flawless face that looked back at him with naked hunger, jolted to discover that he was analyzing his reactions instead of losing himself in the sensual experience. Almost instantaneously Cécile pulled his head down with a little growl of yearning to bring his mouth back into contact with hers.

This time he was carried along on the tide of her desire and his hands were untying the ribbons at the front of her gown when she raised her head and demanded softly, "Can your little bride make you feel like this?"

"What?" Nicholas was slow to grasp the meaning of her challenge.

Cécile traced the shape of his mouth with one finger and smiled triumphantly into his eyes.

229

"No one knows how to please you as I do, Nicholas," she purred. "How could that child with her pedigreed background and her insipid ways possibly satisfy a man like you?"

Even before Nicholas opened his mouth she was aware of her tactical error in attacking his wife. Her eyes fell before the coldness that appeared in his and the tip of her tongue made a quick circuit of her bottom lip. His hands paused in caressing her throat and she felt his withdrawal.

"We won't discuss my wife, if you please, Cécile. Never having met her, you can know nothing about her."

Resentment at the curt finality of his tones plus the ever-present jealousy of the girl who had married the man she wanted caused Lady Montaigne to compound her initial error.

"It isn't necessary to meet her to know she's too terribly well brought up to have any red blood in her veins. I have seen her. Can *she* fire your blood the way I do?"

"Where have you seen Kate?" he shot out, and now his hands were gripping the soft flesh of her arms above the elbows.

"Nick, you are hurting me!"

The strong fingers relaxed their hold but the expression in his eyes remained forbidding. "Answer my question."

"She was pointed out to me at some large gathering or other." Lady Montaigne was deliberately vague. She had no intention of confessing that she had engineered a meeting with her lover's wife. Somehow, despite the promising beginning, this first assignation with Nicholas since his marriage was not progressing according to plan, and she abandoned argument in favor of an appeal to his senses that had never yet failed.

"Love me, Nicholas," she whispered urgently, twining her arms about his neck and pressing her body against his.

It failed this time. He smiled directly into her eyes, but his eyes remained hard. "To answer your original question, yes, Kate can rouse the same passion as you do . . . *and gratify it*!"

Cécile recoiled slightly and her expression stiffened. "So, she is not so milky as she appears?"

"Your claws are showing, my pet. She is not 'milky' at all. My wife is every inch a woman."

"Then I am amazed that you are not with such a paragon at this very moment. Why did you come here, Nicholas?"

The instant this challenge was uttered Cécile regretted the hasty words, but they hung in the air between them. As the silence lengthened she was filled with a sense of dread, but there was no retreat possible.

Nicholas laughed softly and gently removed her arms from around his neck. "You have me there, my sweet," he replied with unimpaired affability. "The unanswerable question. Enjoy your bracelet." He bowed formally and walked out of the room before she could recover from the shock.

"Nicholas, come back!" If the hoarse cry reached him, he gave no sign. The sound of the closing door was her only answer. She stood rooted to the floor for another few disbelieving seconds, then dashed over to the window and twitched the curtain aside. She watched him emerge from the entrance way, settle his hat more firmly on his head, and saunter down the street, his walking stick under his arm as he replaced his gloves. He did not look back.

The viscount at that moment was looking neither back nor forward as he set a swift course for Brooks's and some reliable and undemanding male companionship. He was kicking himself mentally for having allowed his fury (he was not willing to call it heartbreak) at Kate's treatment to send him to Cécile looking for . . . what? Not love, surely. He had never encouraged her brand of possessiveness under the easy guise of love. Physical satisfaction then or for some agreeable feminine ministering to his male vanity? Certainly Cécile was eminently capable of satisfying both cravings, but he'd forgotten how spiteful and jealous she could be toward her own sex. Supposing she had not disgusted him by overplaying her hand just now, though, what would have been the result of his visit? He examined his own behavior with ruthless honesty and did not care for what he discovered. He'd have used Cécile for his own transitory pleasure and, more importantly, as a weapon with which to strike out at Kate, which was patently absurd since she would never have known anything of the matter. But in what more favorable light could he consider his sudden decision to seek out a woman he had not thought about in weeks within seconds of discovering some additional action on Kate's part that demonstrated her desire to have done with him? By the time he arrived on the doorstep and confronted the porter with an unsmiling mien, he was disliking Cécile, hating Kate, and thoroughly disgusted with his own idiotic foolishness in allowing any woman to get under his skin.

His luck was in in one area at least, and he returned to the quiet house on Albemarle Street just before dawn, enriched by several hundred pounds won from various unfortunate acquaintances, enlivened by the prospects of a congenial party for the upcoming Ascot races and with his spirits considerably heightened by the benevolent effects of enormous quantities of wine and brandy consumed with unusual dedication during the lengthy session at his club. Several hours later after a minimum of sleep he was still richer, the prospect of a group party for Ascot was still pleasant, but the beneficent effects of the alcohol had proved to be merely temporary. Perhaps the presence of a dull pain in his head contributed to the jaundiced view he took of his home this fine summer day, but regardless of the reasons, the viscount wandered morosely from bedchamber to breakfast room to library, after ordering his valet to pack a bag for him. It was with a sense of release that he mounted his spirited chestnut in the late morning and rode off without a backward glance.

Nicholas enjoyed a modest financial success at the race meeting and for the most part disported himself pleasurably amongst his cronies. The pace was fast and hours at a time would go by without his giving a passing thought to his personal problems. Then some small thing such as the line of a girl's throat as she bent over some task would trigger a memory of Kate in a similar pose, or perhaps he would note some amusing incident with the intention of repeating it for Kate's enjoyment before he remembered that they had very little to say to one another these days. At these moments a bleakness would settle over his countenance and his friends would have to speak to him more than once to gain his attention. He had been so intent upon pursuing Kate as a suitor after their marriage that it came as a surprise to him now to realize that in addition to being a most desirable creature she had been uncommonly companionable for a girl. He was beginning to feel the lack of this attribute even amongst the company of good friends.

Of course he'd be a liar to deny he missed above all her warm presence in his bed. There was no scarcity of females in the immediate locale, several of whom, judging by the invitation in their bold glances, would have been well pleased to remedy the lack. He surveyed the straw damsels who frequented sporting events of this type with appraisal, disliking the coy assumption of gentility that characterized their approach to prospective protectors as much as he deplored their over-rouged cheeks and the exaggerated style of their clothing. An unflattering comment made in the hearing of his cronies provoked loud guffaws and a crude reminder that he had not used to be so nice in his requirements. He had grinned at that, his good humor restored by the good-natured ribaldry of friends.

Through Mister Waksworth, he received invitations to evening parties at the homes of some of the local landowners. The company was decidedly more select, but he found the respectable females present at these events of even less interest than their wayward sisters, and he grew weary of explaining that his bride was in devoted attendance on his grandfather who had recently sustained an injury. He saw himself observing the behavior of those around him and was conscious of all his own replies and reactions to others as well as theirs to him. The feeling was growing within him that he was a spectator at his own life and it was faintly disturbing. He wanted to stop observing his life and return to merely living it, but the knack seemed to have eluded him. A strange restlessness invaded his being, causing him to make increasingly frenetic efforts to keep active. He'd agree to any plan to avoid solitude because once he was alone his angry thoughts would not be kept at bay, nor would the underlying misery.

A sennight of trying to escape his problems by denying them attention left him drained of all energy, mental and physical. Suddenly he could no longer face another evening of doing the polite to a bunch of faceless strangers. He excused himself from his friends' plans and returned to his bedchamber at the inn, knowing all at once that it was the sense of something incomplete between himself and Kate that was preventing him from putting her out of his mind permanently. He missed her abominably, but who save an idiot could long for the presence of a woman who loved another man? He was slumped in a chair staring at a blank wall, seeing Kate's face as she denied being unfaithful. After her first surprise at being accused, there had been no emotion in her manner at all; her denials had seemed almost mechanical. and how could this be so if she were telling the truth? And yet he would have been willing to stake his life that Kate had loved him just a few weeks ago. Nothing made sense anymore if he accepted that Kate had loved him once, and yet how could he have been mistaken? Every moment with her, discovering new facets of this unwilling bride of his, had been a joy. It would take an abysmal lack of sensitivity to others to be so completely happy himself if she were not. If she were telling the truth about not loving Robin, then something else must have occurred to spoil their enjoyment of each other. He must see her and demand that she tell him the truth. He had half risen to his feet as if to implement this decision immediately, but now he sank down again in the hard chair. Though he no longer more than half believed that Robin was the cause of her coldness, the facts still pointed in his direction, so he must start with Robin. And his brother was in Ireland! Well, that was not an insurmountable obstacle.

The remainder of the evening was devoted to making his plans, and he was away at crack of dawn the following morning, leaving a deliberately ambiguous message for his cronies. He dared not contemplate his next move should Robin fail to convince him that there was nothing warmer than brotherly feelings between himself and Kate, but at last he was committed to action, and this of itself was a significant improvement on his behavior of the last few weeks.

Chapter Fifteen

A persistent beam of sunshine plodded painstakingly across the rug in the silent room, eventually coming to rest on the open pages of the book balanced on the knees of a girl perched atop a set of library steps. For a second her eyes were dazzled and her attention shifted from the printing to the light itself. She appeared lost in fascinated contemplation of the dust motes dancing in the sunbeam; then, her concentration shattered. she shifted position and returned the volume to its place on one of the shelves behind her. She stared through the long windows at the sun-dappled hedges enclosing a rose garden. Another in a seemingly endless succession of lovely summer days made just existing lazily a pleasure. On an impulse the girl descended the steps and crossed to the window doors and pulled them open. Immediately the silence was invaded by a muted chorus of humming as the bees went about their vital tasks among the flowers. The fragrance of hundreds of late roses drifted in and she sniffed appreciatively. Never in recent memory had there been such a perfect July. She stood by the open doors watching a hard-working robin tugging at an insect buried in the grass until he flew away with his prize, then she retraced her footsteps and remounted the steps, but not to return at once to her reading. With elbows on knees and chin in cupped hands, she surveyed her surroundings with pleasure.

Hickory House was a fair-sized gentleman's residence of mellow red brick set in extensive grounds. It was not of interest to antiquarians, having been built in the early days of George the Third's reign, but there was a pleasing symmetry and grace about its proportions, and Kate thought it absolutely charming. All the main rooms were well lighted and beautifully proportioned with attractive but not elaborate ceiling moldings and designs of painted plaster work. This room, containing thousands of volumes accumulated over the years, was Kate's favorite. It was not a particularly large room, and except for windows, fireplace, and door, the entire amount of wall space was given over to book shelves. A good-sized library table stood diagonally across one corner and there were several stuffed chairs for comfortable reading. Much of Kate's time in the fortnight that had elapsed of her visit had been spent in this room, for she had undertaken to set about the formidable task of cataloging Lord Bartram's library for him. He readily admitted the need for such a catalog but confessed to a dread of having someone disturb the organized confusion of a lifetime of collecting. Kate had solemnly promised to make no major upheavals and Lord Bartram, thinking to give her an additional interest besides catering to the whims of an old man, had accepted her offer with alacrity.

The task was proceeding at a snail's pace, however, since Kate spent the major portion of this time browsing compulsively amongst the books, which just exactly suited both Lord Bartram and his granddaughter-in-law. It had been a most enjoyable visit so far. Kate and the young-thinking Lord Bartram got on famously together. If he was disappointed at the continued absence of his grandson, he allowed nothing of this to spoil his pleasure in getting to know his new granddaughter.

The only factor to strain the amicable tone was the attitude of Lord Bartram's lugubrious hound, Hamlet, toward the presence of Ulysses in his bailiwick. It was a case of instant hatred on Hamlet's part for the feline interloper, and Ulysses' habit of strolling unconcernedly past the door of whatever room Hamlet was inhabiting in faithful attendance on his master only added fuel to the dog's burning outrage. Kate found it necessary to keep her pet safely closed in her bedchamber when she was in company with her grandfather-in-law, and when she worked in the library, she would transport the cat in his despised basket and make sure that the door remained closed against a prowling four-footed enemy.

Could she but have put her husband entirely out of her mind, Kate's residence at Hickory House would have been completely serene and untroubled. But thoughts of Nicholas refused to stay submerged for long; they could surface in the midst of an animated conversation with Lord Bartram or intrude as now when she was enjoying a peaceful interlude amongst the books. And with the thought of Nicholas would come the vulnerable look to her eyes, the brooding curve to her mouth. She wore that look now as she gazed unseeingly at Ulysses' sleeping form on the deep blue carpet.

For the first week of her visit it had been enough to savor the absence of the tension that had built up in the atmosphere of the house on Albemarle Street dating from the meeting between Kate and Lady Montaigne. She was relaxed and quietly content in the

239

company of her husband's grandfather. No longer might the sound of a door opening herald the possible entrance of an expressionless Nicholas with the concomitant sense of strain that any contact between them had produced. The serene existence at Hickory House was precisely what Kate required to help her regain her healthy appetite and enable her to sleep more restfully at night.

Strangely enough, though, once she was feeling more her former self, it became more difficult to exclude her husband from her thoughts. Even before she had fallen in love with him, Nicholas had come to take the place her brother had occupied in her childhood, that of an easy companion whose company was always welcome. They had laughed at the same things, had seemed to share so many opinions and tastes. The realization had come to her gradually that not only had she lost a lover, but a friend as well. Friends were people you trusted, and she could no longer trust Nicholas. Her revolving thoughts always stuck at this point—she had come to believe Nicholas loved her because all his actions had been designed to convince her of this. That was why Lady Montaigne's revelations had proved so overwhelming.

He need not have been so blatantly false, she mourned wretchedly. He had coerced her acceptance of a normal marriage, there had been no need to pretend she was the sum of all his desires. Of course he could not have guessed that she would actually be confronted by a jealous mistress determined to vent her spleen. More likely Nicholas had never intended to hurt her. He liked her well enough, and she had been so obviously head over ears in love with him that it was possible he had deemed it kinder to let her continue in her delusion. Wearily she pushed a lock of hair back from her forehead. She never got any further on her

240

ratiocinations. It always came down to a betrayal of her trust. It was queerly apropos that Nicholas, too, should be suffering from what he believed to be *her* betrayal, but of course in his case it could only be his ego that was bruised since she had not touched his heart. Sooner or later, though, he and Robin would meet, and she felt sure Robin would be able to convince him of their innocence. The brothers had a careless affection for one another though they were not close companions. It must have hurt Nicholas deeply to be forced to think ill of Robin. She shifted her position somewhat uneasily as it occurred to her that perhaps the final reckoning between herself and her husband was yet to come.

The ray of sunshine had advanced across the room and was now illuminating Kate. Its warmth was delightful, and she shook off her melancholy mood and returned her interest to the books behind her. So engrossed did she become in turning the pages of an old folio edition of Shakespeare that the sound of the door opening did not reach her. Ulysses opened one eye, then stretched himself mightily and ambled over to the quiet figure standing just inside the door. Kate continued to pore over her book, unaware at first that Ulysses had been picked up and was being absentmindedly stroked by the man whose eyes never left her profile bathed in a golden shower that brought out the highlights in her shining brown hair and bestowed a soft glow on her cheeks. Something in the atmosphere reached her shortly, however, for she glanced up, turning toward the door.

"Nicholas!" she gasped, and fell silent, staring at the man holding the gray and white cat.

He had been studying her fixedly but could detect nothing save surprise in her reaction to his unexpected appearance. With a wriggle, Ulysses indicated that he

241

had had sufficient of tribute, and the viscount set him down before slowly approaching the girl perched above him on the steps. He stopped abruptly a few feet from her as he noted the wariness of her regard. Did she imagine he had come to continue their quarrel in his grandfather's house?

"Hallo, Kate. You are looking well."

"So are you, Torvil. You have acquired a tan." For the life of her she could not produce anything less banal to say to the unsmiling man who seemed to be devouring her with his eyes, though he stood absolutely still. The familiar tension filled the space around them. Nothing had changed. She shifted her gaze to Ulysses, who was wreathing himself around the viscount's legs.

"He's glad to see you," she commented absently.

"And you, Kate, are you glad to see me?"

"Of . . . of course. Lord Bartram will be delighted to welcome you. I'll tell him you're here."

She extended one foot to descend the steps, then retracted it as he announced, "Grandfather knows I'm here. I have already spoken to him. He told me where to find you."

"I . . . see."

"I have just arrived from Ireland."

"Oh." After a pause she said again, "I see."

"Do you?" he replied quietly. "Can you guess why I went to Ireland, Kate?"

"Did you . . . see Robin?"

"Yes, of course." Nicholas unclenched one hand and thrust it through his crisp hair in a gesture that was habitual with him when he was ill-at-ease. "I went because I had to know the absolute truth."

"And did you find out?" she asked evenly.

"Yes. I owe you an apology, Kate, and I do apologize, most humbly."

"It does not signify," she replied with indifference,

and watched the color drain from beneath his sun-bronzed skin as his tight control snapped.

"No, it doesn't signify, does it?" he ground out. "Because something had happened before I accused you of being unfaithful, had it not—something that had turned you cold? I jumped to the conclusion that it was Robin because it seemed to fit the evidence—what I thought was evidence," he corrected, and continued, making an obvious effort to speak without inflection, "Was it another man then, not Robin?"

"There was no other man."

Husband and wife looked levelly at each other, and Nicholas had the queer notion that she was totally inaccessible to him, but he refused to accept defeat. It mattered too much and desperation rang in his next question.

"Then what happened? What went wrong between us? Can't you be honest with me, Katie?"

Her response to this plea took him completely by surprise. Seeing Nicholas again so unexpectedly had undermined all her recently achieved serenity. Kate was at the end of her emotional tether and she flared like straw at the touch of a torch.

"*Honest? I* be honest with *you*? When were you ever honest with me? Do I not deserve the same consideration as your mistress? At least you told *her* why you were getting married *and* reassured her that *her* status should not be affected by such a small matter as your marriage to another. Could you not have been equally honest with me? Why did you have to pretend to care for me? Why could you not have left me in peace?" She subsided at last, trembling with reaction but with her head high.

A white-faced Nicholas attempted a swift gathering of his wits after this amazing tirade and tried to marshal his arguments.

"I have never been dishonest with you, Kate," he began earnestly, and raised a silencing hand as she opened her lips to refute this. "No, let me finish, please. A man doesn't generally tell his wife about the women he knew before their marriage. They don't concern her. It's what happens after marriage that is important. I don't know what busyhead told you that I had a mistress once, but I assure you that—"

"I have known about Lady Montaigne since before I knew your name, Nicholas," Kate interrupted. "I was present when you told her of your prospective marriage *and* your plans to continue your *affaire* with her."

"What are you talking about?" he demanded.

"At the Westerwood ball you chose a spot in front of some palms in which to make your announcement. I was seated behind the palms fixing my stocking. I heard every word."

In the silence that followed this blunt declaration Nicholas searched back in his memory for details of that almost forgotten incident. Kate watched the changing expressions of astonishment, comprehension, and chagrin chase across his countenance, but she was unprepared for his next words.

"So that accounts for the way you looked at me at our first meeting." He sighed deeply. "No wonder you could never bring yourself to use my name." He seemed to be talking half to himself in soft, weary tones. Kate felt the swift tears of reaction crowding her eyelids and she turned her head away to hide them. In the next instant her hand was gripped tightly and she was eased down the library steps.

"Kate, my darling, look at me. Ours got off to as bad a start as any marriage could and I realize it was my fault entirely, but surely you must have sensed very early that I was falling in love with you, that I wanted you and only—"

"Please don't lie to me, Nicholas—you who value honesty so highly." She wrenched her hand from his hold and faced him proudly. "Has not Lady Montaigne told you of our meeting at the Mendleshams' ball when she did me the honor to compliment me on the heart-shaped pin you purchased for me at *her* suggestion?" She laughed raggedly at the expression of utter consternation on his face. "What did you buy for *her* that day you went shopping together?—the twin to my brooch? Well, she may have mine with my compliments. I never want to see it or you again."

Before he could recover the use of his suspended faculties, Kate had slipped around him and was dashing out of the library after flinging wide the door. Uncaring who saw her flight, she headed for the stairs. The tears she had repressed so far were running down her cheeks and blurring her vision. She was conscious of her husband's voice calling after her, and she put on a burst of speed as she reached the staircase. Suddenly a gray and white object streaked past her—Ulysses, with less than his customary dignity, was heading upstairs too. A loud hiss drew her glance upwards to where another mass of fur accompanied by a menacing growl was moving rapidly toward her.

"*Hamlet, no!*" she cried, frightened for the safety of her pet.

Ulysses rapidly altered his course and started to descend with Hamlet in hot pursuit. Kate was aware of a confusing mass of paws and teeth as well as voices, her own and that of Nicholas, before a sudden impact jarred her off her feet. She grabbed for the railing, but it was falling away from her—or she was falling. The next sensation was pain, sharp and overwhelming in her head—then nothing.

Kate's head ached abominably and her eyelids felt weighted, but she was aware of voices, all sorts of

245

voices, calling her name. She tried desperately to answer, but the pain in her head needed all her attention, and now the voices were drifting away—or she was drifting away.

The pain was bearable now and her eyelids were functioning again. How strange! Everything was in darkness. She peered about her, taking care not to move her head which still ached considerably. She was in her own bed, though she did not remember going to bed at all. She had been dashing up the main staircase when the animals started fighting; she must have fallen. Her eyes closed again and she concentrated on her actions of the morning. She and Nicholas had quarreled and she had run away. How foolish of her to try to escape. Nicholas must know she wouldn't have been so upset had she not loved him desperately. She opened her eyes again and shifted her gaze toward a lighter area to her right. A candelabrum stood upon the table near the bed and seated next to it with his elbows on the table was her husband. He was seated facing her bed but his head was in his hands and she was able to observe him unnoticed for a moment. At the sight of that familiar dark head a wave of longing washed over her. He had said he loved her—if only it were true.

Just then Nicholas raised his head and Kate drew in her breath sharply. Never before had she seen a look of such intense anguish on any face! Either she had made some sound or he could see in the dark because he rose from his chair and advanced toward the bed. His strained expression changed to one of incredulous joy as he perceived her eyes upon him. Of its own volition her hand extended toward his.

"Kate, thank God you're awake!" He sank to his knees beside her and bowed his head over her hand. After a long moment when he simply clung to her

246

hand with both of his, she brought her other hand hesitantly across her body and touched his hair lightly.

"Nicholas, what is it? What is wrong?"

"I thought I'd lost you," he whispered, a trace of recent suffering still clouding the eyes he raised to hers. "It's been so long."

"What time is it?"

"Almost ten. You've been unconscious for better than eleven hours. Tell me, is your vision blurred? The doctor warned us you might have trouble focusing at first." His grip on her hand had tightened involuntarily, but Kate found she enjoyed the pain of the contact.

"I can see fine," she answered gently, "but my head aches and I should like a drink of water."

He reached for a glass on the table beside the bed. "Don't try to sit up, darling. The doctor says you must stay relatively flat for a time." Kate relished a few sips from the glass he held to her lips, but it was a relief to sink back the few inches to her pillow again. She closed her eyes briefly.

"Are you all right?"

The anxiety in his voice brought her eyes wide open. She managed a tremulous smile and both were silent for a time, looking rather searchingly into the other's face. Her husband's drawn expression worried Kate and she spoke quickly.

"I'm sorry, Nicholas. I did not mean what I said about never wanting to see you again."

"I'm glad of that, dearest, because you'll be seeing me for the rest of our lives. Perhaps it is not chivalrous to continue our discussion when you cannot very well strike back or run away, but I must tell you one thing before I call Mrs. Ekstrom to bring you one of the doctor's powders for your head." The small smile that had flickered at mention of running away faded to an intent, earnest look. "I love you and only you, and I

247

have never been unfaithful since our marriage—this, I swear. You have to believe this, Katie," he added with great urgency, and the look on his face told Kate more than the most cogent argument could. It was absolutely vital to him that she accept his assurance.

The smile that illuminated her pale face was the most beautiful that Nicholas had ever seen. He leaned over the bed and kissed her very gently, loving the way her lips clung to his. After a moment, though, she moved her head restlessly and a shadow appeared in her eyes.

"What is it, sweetheart? Tell me, please; let's have no more secrets."

"Nicholas," she hesitated, then plunged, "how could you let that woman assist you in selecting a gift for me?" Tears that were ninety percent weakness spilled from under her lids. He wiped them away with his fingers and kissed each eye.

"Do not cry, please, darling. I wish I could explain how Cécile found out about that pin, but I cannot. The only contact I had with her before she made that claim was an accidental encounter on the street, and this was before I purchased the pin. I had planned to see her just once more to break off our *affaire*. Since you overheard that revealing conversation, you will understand that I felt I owed her an explanation, but before I got up nerve enough to do so, I had given you the pin and you had met Cécile. After that I was too concerned with what was happening to us to give her a thought. The only person who saw the pin before you, except the jeweler of course, was Robin, and I cannot imagine him blabbing to Cécile. He is barely on nodding terms with her so far as I am aware. It's a pretty thin story I know, but dammit, Katie, no man would let his mistress choose a gift for his wife; it's insane!" The viscount pushed his fingers through his hair and regarded his wife with patent sincerity.

Her lips twitched slightly but she agreed solemnly, "It did not seem quite the thing to do." She brought the hand holding hers up to her cheek and cuddled it lovingly. "I'm so glad you love me, Nicholas, because despite a firm resolve to do otherwise, I began loving you almost from the beginning. I . . . I did not think there was much chance we could have a successful marriage, though, so I tried to avoid you whenever possible."

"You certainly led me a merry dance." He grinned boyishly, then became serious again. "It was a difficult situation to say the least. I was furious that my father could coerce me into taking a wife of his choosing, so I was not at all interested in trying to make it a good marriage until after I met you, Kate. Oh, I'm not trying to claim it was a case of love at first sight—at that time I didn't even believe in love, for myself, I mean. But from the moment I first clapped eyes on you, I liked what I saw; and, I must admit, your attitude intrigued me more than if you'd been willing to be pleased with what fate had dealt you."

"That was precisely what I was afraid of," Kate retorted with spirit, "and what I attempted to prevent."

Nicholas laughed and kissed the side of her mouth swiftly. "You get high marks for determination, darling, but if you want to discourage a man, you should not be born with such a kissable mouth." He pushed himself resolutely to his feet. "I should not be keeping you talking. You need those headache powders and a lot of rest. Could you drink some soup, do you suppose?"

"Yes, thank you, I am famished," declared Kate, who did not possess the proper instincts to derive any profit from the status of "interesting invalid."

249

Nicholas smiled at her in a way that made her toes curl with delight, and went out of the room in search of the housekeeper.

Kate regarded the closed door with a contented expression while the image of that last smile of her husband's remained in her mind, but after a time her gaze sobered and became thoughtful. Nicholas had admitted that he had planned to see Lady Montaigne once to end their *affaire*, but he had not done so up to that awful night when the woman had arranged to be presented to her. It was as clear as crystal now that his mistress had planned that meeting for the express purpose of driving a wedge between her former lover and his wife when he had not immediately resumed his visits to her. And her tactics had almost succeeded in wrecking the marriage because the initially unwilling bride and groom had not had time enough to become secure in their love for one another. Had not Nicholas been so determined to arrive at an understanding with his wife, once he had struggled through the first rage and hurt of their estrangement, the coldness between them might easily have become permanent. Kate acknowledged with a little shiver that she had been too hurt and too proud to make any overtures toward her husband. She could never be grateful enough for his persistence in believing that what had been growing between them was too valuable to surrender without a supreme effort to retrieve it. And she loved him ten times more for making that effort!

It had not escaped her notice, of course, that he had made no mention of whether or not he had actually seen Lady Montaigne at some time during that bitter period of believing that his wife had been unfaithful. Being a woman, she longed to know if such a meeting had taken place—or several meetings, but Kate, too, had learned something from this unhappy interval. It would be the height of folly to allow her jealousy of Lady Montaigne to propel her into playing the unsympathetic role of the suspicious wife. Through some happy miracle Nicholas loved *her*, not Lady Montaigne, despite the latter's provocative beauty, and he had sworn that he had not been unfaithful. She must accept this and go on from this moment to create the kind of marriage they both desired.

Kate had never felt more at peace with herself or more sure of her course in her life, and it was Nicholas who inspired this newly gained confidence. She settled back comfortably into her pillows just as the door opened.

"How are you feeling now, darling?"

"Gorgeously happy," replied Kate, smiling radiantly at her companion in joy, the husband of her choice.

Love—the way you want it!

Candlelight Romances

		TITLE NO.	
☐ **A MAN OF HER CHOOSING** by Nina Pykare $1.50		#554	(15133-3)
☐ **PASSING FANCY** by Mary Linn Roby $1.50		#555	(16770-1)
☐ **THE DEMON COUNT** by Anne Stuart $1.25		#557	(11906-5)
☐ **WHERE SHADOWS LINGER** by Janis Susan May $1.25		#556	(19777-5)
☐ **OMEN FOR LOVE** by Esther Boyd $1.25		#552	(16108-8)
☐ **MAYBE TOMORROW** by Marie Pershing $1.25		#553	(14909-6)
☐ **LOVE IN DISGUISE** by Nina Pykare $1.50		#548	(15229-1)
☐ **THE RUNAWAY HEIRESS** by Lillian Cheatham $1.50		#549	(18083-X)
☐ **HOME TO THE HIGHLANDS** by Jessica Eliot $1.25		#550	(13104-9)
☐ **DARK LEGACY** by Candace Connell $1.25		#551	(11771-2)
☐ **LEGACY OF THE HEART** by Lorena McCourtney $1.25		#546	(15645-9)
☐ **THE SLEEPING HEIRESS** by Phyllis Taylor Pianka $1.50		#543	(17551-8)
☐ **DAISY** by Jennie Tremaine $1.50		#542	(11683-X)
☐ **RING THE BELL SOFTLY** by Margaret James $1.25		#545	(17626-3)
☐ **GUARDIAN OF INNOCENCE** by Judy Boynton $1.25		#544	(11862-X)
☐ **THE LONG ENCHANTMENT** by Helen Nuelle $1.25		#540	(15407-3)
☐ **SECRET LONGINGS** by Nancy Kennedy $1.25		#541	(17609-3)

At your local bookstore or use this handy coupon for ordering:

Dell	**DELL BOOKS** **P.O. BOX 1000, PINEBROOK, N.J. 07058**

Please send me the books I have checked above. I am enclosing $_____
(please add 75¢ per copy to cover postage and handling). Send check or money
order—no cash or C.O.D.'s. Please allow up to 8 weeks for shipment.

Mr/Mrs/Miss_____

Address_____

City_____ State/Zip_____

INTRODUCING...

The Romance Magazine For The 1980's

Each exciting issue contains a full-length romance novel — the kind of first-love story we all dream about...

PLUS

other wonderful features such as a travelogue to the world's most romantic spots, advice about your romantic problems, a quiz to find the ideal mate for you and much, much more.

ROMANTIQUE: A complete novel of romance, plus a whole world of romantic features.

ROMANTIQUE: Wherever magazines are sold. Or write Romantique Magazine, Dept. C-1, 41 East 42nd Street, New York, N.Y. 10017

INTERNATIONALLY DISTRIBUTED BY DELL DISTRIBUTING, INC.